# THAT MAN
# IS MINE

***Also by Faith Baldwin in
Thorndike Large Print***

Beauty
Give Love the Air
He Married a Doctor
The Heart Has Wings
The Lonely Man
No Private Heaven
"Something Special"
And New Stars Burn
Enchanted Oasis
For Richer For Poorer
Make-Believe

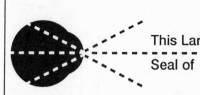

This Large Print Book carries the
Seal of Approval of N.A.V.H.

# THAT MAN

# IS MINE

*Faith Baldwin*

**Thorndike Press • Thorndike, Maine**

*4379*

**Library of Congress Cataloging in Publication Data:**

Baldwin, Faith, 1893-
    That man is mine / Faith Baldwin.
        p.  cm.
    ISBN 1-56054-270-5 (alk. paper : lg. print)
    1. Large type books. I. Title.
[PS3505.U97T47        1992]                91-38968
813'.52—dc20                              CIP

Thorndike Press Large Print edition published in 1992
by arrangement with Henry Holt and Company.

Large Print edition available in the British Commonwealth
by arrangement with Harold Ober Associates.

Cover design by James B. Murray.

**The tree indicium is a trademark of Thorndike Press.**

This book is printed on acid-free, high opacity paper. ∞

*To*

*The Rodgers Book Store in Brooklyn*
*The English Bookshop in Manhattan*
*and*
*The Argus Bookshop in Chicago*

*I dedicate this story of a most unlikely*
*bookshop, in gratitude for the kindness*
*and assistance each has given me —*
*their beholden customer.*

# Chapter I

On the fourteenth day of February, little Miss Loring was walking rapidly through a side street in the East Fifties in the City of New York. The wind was sharp but the snow had ceased and lay feather-light and not too trodden or grimy as yet, beneath her small, galoshed feet. Her dark red hair curled beneath a pert fur toque and the furred collar of her coat, to which was pinned a rose no redder than her lips, was drawn close about her throat. She walked with speed because it was cold and with animation and pleasure because she was twenty years old, in excellent health, and almost — but not quite — fancy free. It was the not-quite part of it which made everything so entrancing — a blue sky, swept clear of the sullen gray clouds of earlier morning, a yellow sun; in short, taking it by and large, it was a very fine day.

Little Miss Loring's arms were burdened with parcels, for she had been shopping. She was a careful shopper, a bargain hunter, in the nicest possible way, careful or not, given to whims and impulses. She had just bought herself a new hat, which she couldn't afford. She would have to borrow against her allowance. She trusted that her father would be in an amiable mood and would not remind her, as he had on similar occasions, that there was a depression. Little Miss Loring did not feel in the least depressed. In fact, she felt perfectly splendid.

So thinking, she tripped a little faster, and then quite literally. She slid, she dropped her parcels, she waved her arms frantically and eventually sat down hard on that treacherous coating of snow which had cloaked a bit of hard and gleaming ice, and thus precipitated herself into the life of a grave, rather handsome young man who wore horn-rimmed spectacles and a brown smock.

For Miss Loring, by dint of earnest twisting and turning in order to regain her balance, was slowly sliding down the temporarily inhospitable steps which led to a basement bookshop, over which a sign swung to assure all and sundry that this was "Ted Morrison's Bookshop . . . Old and Rare Books — First Editions . . . Prints . . ."

"Ouch!" exclaimed Miss Loring.

Her little fur toque was on one ear, she had a really dreadful pain in her ankle and a curious sensation in her stomach. "Ouch!" she mourned again, and slid, this time involuntarily, to the last step. There she essayed to stand. An engrossed passer-by hurried

8

down after her with the dropped parcels and placed a timid, solicitous arm about her waist. "Shall I call an ambulance?" he asked eagerly, for he was a gray little man to whom nothing ever happened and it had long been his wish to be a star witness in a murder case — failing that, a good accident might do.

"Do you know any good-looking interns?" countered Miss Loring, a little shakily. She brushed at the snow and she straightened her hat. She took the parcels in her arms again and started up the steps. Not far. "Ouch!" cried Miss Loring for the third time, and sat right down again.

"Perhaps I'd better — ?" said her good Samaritan, with a gleam of hope in the mildest eyes in the world.

"Do go 'way," Miss Loring commanded, a little peevishly. She wished her ankle didn't hurt so much. She hadn't far to go, merely a few stately blocks, but there wasn't a cent of money in her purse for a taxi. Mother would be out, Father would be out, and it was a question whether Frieda, the cheerful maid of all work, had fifty cents to her name, what with the brothers and sisters and cousins in the homeland whom she supported.

The mild gentleman stood on one foot. Miss Loring looked at him. Her eyelashes were preposterous. He remembered that later. She stated, "I have a book, I believe. I was just going in here, anyway."

By this time quite a few people had collected to watch with interest the spectacle of a pretty girl sitting on a basement step on the fourteenth day of February, talking, apparently, to herself. For no one noticed the Star Witness. That was his lifelong blessing and his curse. Presently he stole away to the street. Miss Loring never even saw him go, yet she wasn't an unkind girl by nature.

At this moment the shop door opened and the owner, attracted by the slight commotion beyond and above his door, appeared. He wore the brown smock with grace, and the horn-rimmed glasses with an air. He had an arrogant nose and a sensitive mouth. His eyes were very blue. His voice, when amiable, was pleasant. Just now he barked. He barked, crossly. He inquired:

"Come, come, what's all this? What are you doing here?"

Miss Loring giggled. She was a perfectly hopeless girl. It was her parents' fault. They were nice people but they spoiled her. For some reason or other they set great store by Miss Loring.

"May I be your Valentine?" she said absurdly.

Even at that moment he was quite aware

that her eyes might very well be green. Or were they gray? He flushed, deeply. He had quarreled, three days ago, with the girl he had loved for six months. She was a poetess. She had heart and soul and genius. Only, within the last week she had sold her first poem to a magazine of standing, with shiny pages, and since then she hadn't, somehow, held with his ideas. She had sold herself to Mammon!

"Get up," ordered Mr. Morrison. "Clear off," he added to the crowd.

Miss Loring made a face at him. She sat perfectly still. She said sadly, "I thought all booksellers were gentle, unworldly soft-hearted people. You are perfectly impossible. How much do you charge an hour for your steps? I can't get up. I'd like to. I've never fancied pneumonia. I can't spell it. But you see, Mr. Ted Morrison, Rare Books and First Editions, I've sprained my ankle, or sumpin'."

Her eyes, which were neither gray nor green, filled suddenly, for like most people who start making out cases for themselves, she was abruptly overcome with self-pity.

"Gosh!" cried Mr. Morrison, forgetting he was an Intellect. "I'm awfully sorry!" And so saying, he picked Miss Loring up in his arms and somehow managing the door, carried her proudly and competently over the threshold of the shop. The crowd said, "Well, I never!"

Someone laughed. The Star Witness peered wistfully through bifocals. Presently the street was as it had been. People hurried by and never even glanced at the basement shop with its swinging sign. No one wanted books that morning.

Mr. Morrison was breathing a little heavily. Little Miss Loring was not as little as she looked. She had small, firmly fleshed bones. She was curved in the right places. She had made it no easier for him. She had been a dead weight in his arms, her hatbox had bumped his chin, other parcels had scratched him and as he set her down the silly little mink tails on the fur-banded toque tickled his ear.

It was a nice shop, if small. It invited. It appealed. There was, in the small back room, to which he had conveyed her, a wood fire burning, and a large armchair. Two large armchairs. A cat sat on the hearth and washed its silly face with an industrious paw.

"This," remarked little Miss Loring, "is very nice. . . . If you're not too busy?"

She extended her galoshed right foot. Mr. Morrison looked at her severely. She knew quite well he was not too busy. There wasn't a soul in the place. There hadn't been for several days unless you counted the addled female who rushed in yesterday to buy belated valentines. He had let his assistant go. He was

12

alone, in the shop — except for Miss Loring — and alone in the world, as well.

"It may have swollen," she said reproachfully.

Scarlet, he knelt to remove the galosh. It was a pert affair, snug-fitting and trim. Off it came and beneath it he saw a pretty foot, a charming ankle. He frowned at the little shoe. The heel was ridiculous. No wonder she had turned her ankle!

"It is swollen," diagnosed Miss Loring sorrowfully, "a little."

"And no wonder!" almost shouted Mr. Morrison in his embarrassment. "The heels you wear!"

"What's wrong with them?" she asked mildly. "They're walking shoes, aren't they?"

Mr. Morrison snorted. "Walking shoes! Have you ever considered what you are doing to your metatarsals?"

"No," replied Miss Loring meekly. "I can't say I've ever given them a thought. Should I? By the way, what are they?" she asked, as an anxious afterthought.

He flung the foot away, suddenly, realizing that he had been holding it for some time. Miss Loring winced but someone laughed. Probably it was the cat, a very feminine creature.

"Consider —" said Mr. Morrison portentously, still on his knees.

"Not," cried Miss Loring, "the lilies of the field?"

He gave her a look of sheer disgust. She thought, How blue his eyes are. This is really a nice creature . . . if one took the trouble to shake him out of — well, say the smock.

"I was going to say," he continued with dignity, "the peasant women of Europe. The feet which have known no shoes."

"And no water," murmured the cat, or possibly Miss Loring.

"Except on Sundays," he continued, ignoring her. "The beautiful, free carriage."

Miss Loring yawned. "Flat," she said distinctly, "very flat." She sat up, perfectly straight. "Ease my shoe on, please. Yes . . . carefully. That's all right. I haven't broken anything. I can wiggle my toes. Now, if you'll help me up I'll try to walk. Always walk on a wrenched ankle," she advised absently.

In another moment Mr. Morrison found himself conducting this unexpected noncustomer on a tour of the two rooms. At intervals she ejaculated, "It hurts!" and at other intervals she exclaimed, "How nice!" Eventually she limped her supported way back to the chair and sat down and beamed upon Mr. Morrison genially.

"And now," said Miss Loring in a clear

14

voice, "I would like to open a charge account."

Mr. Morrison's jaw dropped. He hadn't had a new account for months. In fact, a number of his old accounts had been closed recently. It was nip and tuck, or perhaps touch and go, with the bookshop. He said feebly, "But —"

"Yes," said Miss Loring, "I have come to the conclusion I do not read enough. I'd better begin at the beginning. Classics," she explained solemnly. "Then there's the rental library for my lighter moments, which are apt to occur on any off Tuesday. Besides, I'd like to borrow fifty cents. And if I've an account it makes it a lot easier. Put it on the cuff, you know," she said benevolently.

"Are you serious?" he demanded.

"Rarely," admitted Miss Loring. "You are, though. Too much, too often. We'll have to see to that," she threatened vaguely.

Mr. Morrison, his lips somewhat compressed, made his way to a desk and returned again with a pad and pencil. He found his new charge customer singing to the cat, which had in the interim perched upon her knee. Mr. Morrison exclaimed, "But Keturie does not like women! She never goes to them."

"I'm not a woman," said Miss Loring gently, "I'm practically inhuman. Sometimes

I think I'm just a good idea someone once had . . . and at other times I'm not so sure. Keturie and I are sisters under the skin. Don't," she admonished sharply, "stand there goggling at me. Snap into it. This is business. Remember other customers are waiting."

Startled, Mr. Morrison cast a look over his shoulder into the farther room. It was empty except for bookshelves and books and little tables of cards and of gifts which no one ever bought. He glared at Miss Loring, who sat there demurely scratching the head of Keturie. Keturie purred.

"Well," said Mr. Morrison, not at all as one speaks to a potential charge customer, "I suppose I'll have to have your name and address."

"No," said Miss Loring, "you don't have to. It isn't a must. It isn't compulsory. You can, if you prefer, address the bills to Irritating Female with Wrenched Ankle, care of General Delivery."

Mr. Morrison said, and smiled:

"Forgive me. But, look," he went on, engagingly, "I've had a rotten morning — everything's gone wrong. And somehow when you slid down my steps and began laughing at me . . ."

"I'm not really," she said gently. "Only I *am* an irritating female. I haven't a thought in my head. I'm a sort of Mayfly. I like being that way. But seriously . . . to business."

"Name?" asked Morrison briskly.

"Valentine Loring," she answered, and added the address. He didn't even hear the address. He said, gaping, *"Valentine?"*

"For my sins," she sighed. "And today's my birthday. That's why; I mean, parents are so sentimental, aren't they? But sort of sweet."

"I never knew mine," he said shortly.

"I'm sorry." Definitely, her eyes weren't green. They were gray, gray as early dusk, on a darkish day, quiet and tender. "You've missed a lot."

"Oh, I don't know," said Mr. Morrison with an effort at bravado, "sometimes I believe that children would be better off given to the state to bring up."

Little Miss Loring looked at him. "Better? Better taken care of perhaps, in a sensible brush-your-teeth-and-take-your-cod-liver-oil way. But happier? I wonder. No spoiling, no softness, no mistakes, no warmth. The state has a very cold sound to me."

He said, "You wouldn't understand things like that."

Her eyes were green, they sparkled. She agreed, "No, I suppose not. I'm pretty childish, really."

"Well-to-do parents," he diagnosed, "finishing school, Europe, debut."

"It would have been fun," she said, "it was meant to happen. It didn't, as a matter of fact. By the way, I do wish you'd take my address."

He took it. And now Valentine rose to her feet. She said, "You think me all paper lace frills, don't you? Name and all. It's Val for short, if you'd rather."

She limped a very little. Affectation, he thought, she's no more sprained her ankle than I have!

On the way to the door, she stopped by a bookcase. "Is that a new murder mystery," she demanded eagerly, "and is it any good?"

"It's considered one of the best of its kind," he replied grudgingly.

"I must have it," she told him. "My father adores mysteries. He sits up half the night and jumps if anyone speaks to him. I'll take it to him with many happy returns of my birthday. Oh, and could you get me a taxi . . . and lend me fifty cents — on the cuff?"

Ted Morrison took the book from the shelf. It had a bright, confused jacket, dripping blood, daggers, clawlike hands and large magnetic eyes. He handled it with marked distaste.

"You don't like mysteries," decided his customer.

He shook his head. A well-shaped head, plenty of hair, in color a dark brown. "I'm afraid not. As an escape, of course, they are to be recommended to — well, a certain type of person."

"You don't believe in escapes?" asked Val, and took the book from his hand.

"Of course not," he told her stoutly. "Life's to be faced . . . one mustn't turn away from it — even in the pages of a book."

"I see." She mourned for him, somehow, with eyes that were gray again. Then she laughed, suddenly. "What a lot of books you must sell! You do need an assistant. One who approves of escapes."

"I had one," said Ted, "but I couldn't afford him any more."

"Would I do?" she asked, the practiced fingers of one hand doing devastating things to the curls beneath the toque. "For nothing? Just for the experience? I'd like to work."

"You!" Now he laughed at her. "What do you know about books?"

"You don't know anything about them, either," she countered, "not this type of book, anyway. And they're awfully in demand."

Ted Morrison fished in his pockets and gave her the fifty cents. "I'll call a taxi," he said, and smiled at her, a bit patronizingly.

He went out, smocked, bareheaded, into

the clear, frosty air. Val ruffled the pages of her purchase and spoke softly to Keturie, who came to sit and stare, with round and fascinated eyes, at her feet. Val's ankle still hurt, a little. But she'd had a good time. She'd tell them about it at dinner, Mother and Father and Bill. . . . She found herself making a long face. She'd borrow her father's glasses. "Consider," she would say, "the peasant women —"

Ted found her making the face on his return. He asked, anxiously, forgetting that he had suspected her of malingering, "Does your ankle really hurt so much? Here, I'll help you up the steps and to the cab."

For a young man with a strong mind he had a strong arm. Unusual. Val, her parcels gathered to her, the book topping them perilously, went up the steps and to the taxi. She leaned from the window of the cab as the door shut. She cried clearly, "Think it over . . . I really meant it, you know. I'd love to slave in your shop. It needs me. And your cat likes me, very much."

The cab drove off. Ted, returning to the shop, found it empty. Keturie played on the floor. She chased her tail. Presently when he was sitting at his desk in the alcove between the two rooms she came leaping toward him, for all the world like a Spanish dancer, for she was a black cat and between her sharp white teeth she carried the stem of a red rose.

Ted bent down and retrieved it. Affronted, Keturie retired to a corner and dreamed, closed her yellow eyes, which were, at night, so green. She dreamed, a pointed ear twitching, of jungles and of bigger game than bookstore mice.

There was a glass of water on Ted's desk. He put the rose in it and looked at it a moment. Valentine! What a name for a girl. He'd read English novels in which Valentines figured. But they were always men. Still sillier. He opened a ledger and frowned at it.

How much longer could he hold out? People didn't want, could not afford fine books any longer. A year ago when he had opened this place, against the advice of all his friends, he had had such high hopes. It wouldn't be just a bookshop. It would be a meeting place of congenial people, of people with gravity and intellect. A meeting place, too, of the serious collectors. He'd slaved for that opening. At twenty-one he had come into the possession of the small legacy left him by his parents. He had hoarded, he had lived frugally. He'd missed a great many things youngsters of his age thought essential. They weren't essential, of course, the parties, the cars, the visiting around, the surface way of living. He hadn't been able to go to college but he'd worked, after high school, and he'd taken his degree nights. . . . There had been hundreds like him, serious, and intent on wringing the last drop from the education offered them, working by day, studying by night, taking long years to complete their courses.

Then, employment in a book section of a department store, learning the ropes. Then Masters' big, well-patronized shop. Then his own little place in the Village, and now this.

He was twenty-eight, and he believed he had failed. It wasn't his fault. The cards were stacked against him, he told the indifferent red rose, its petals perking up a little in the life-giving water, its fragrance very marked; what chance had you, in a world like this . . . a world where greed had ruled so long? But it wouldn't — not always — your day was coming, the day of others like you.

The shop was quiet. Lunchtime. He'd brought a sandwich with him, a bottle of milk. He spread them out on the desk. Valentine Loring. A dime novel name. A girl, not from a dime novel, but from the pages of some expensive, trivial fashion magazine. A rich girl, very likely amusing herself with the thought of working, and robbing some girl who needed the money to live at the same time.

But she'd said she'd work without money.

For a few minutes he imagined her there

in the shop in a jade-green smock, with her dark red, ruffled hair and her altering eyes and her quick voice uttering absurdities. He smiled, a little.

But that was, of course, stupid. He'd never see her again. He'd send her the bill on the first of the month. It would be two dollars for the detective story and fifty cents "cash advanced." Perhaps she would pay it. Perhaps not. Write it off to profit and loss. It was mostly loss, anyway.

He found himself thinking of the picture she had presented when she sat on the steps. He heard her ask, "May I be your Valentine?"

Her birthday. He rose from the desk and the half-eaten sandwich and went rummaging along his shelves. He'd show her he wasn't as stuffy as she'd doubtless thought him. He'd give her a birthday present. And administer a rebuke at the same time. He'd improve her mind in spite of herself — providing she had a mind. Better begin with the easier things at first, words she might understand. . . .

He stood, irresolute, a copy of *Woman and Labor* in his hand. After a while he laid it aside, and picked up another book. Here was beauty. This she could understand, perhaps — provided she had a soul.

That evening on his way home he went out of his beaten path to leave a small wrapped parcel at the Loring home. It was a house, a brownstone house, in the lower Sixties, and not an apartment. Lights at the windows glowed behind the curtains. An elderly servant came to open the door. Of course, he had known it all along.

He had a glimpse of the hall and the room beyond and of people, and he heard laughter. He had an impulse to snatch back the package. Trivial laughter. There were roses on the hall table, heavy and red, dozens of them, massed in a great deep bowl.

"For Miss Valentine?" asked the manservant. "And whom shall I say?"

But Ted was gone, plunging down the long steps. The night was dark, with distant stars, and very cold. He turned up his coat collar and walked toward the subway wondering what on earth had possessed him to leave, with his card, the specially bound, tooled, small edition of Edna St. Vincent Millay to which he was so attached, and which, as it was expensive, he had not been able to sell.

# Chapter II

"Really, Marcia," announced Mr. Loring in no uncertain terms, "I don't think Val should do such things."

The front door had just closed behind Mr. Ted Morrison. Val, in the absurdest frock imaginable, all ruffles and furbelows and quaint nonsense, was turning the small tooled leather book over and over in her hands and saying, "That was pretty sweet of him. Poor darling, he takes himself so seriously."

Her mother, who was rather like her, in a more complete edition, smiled. She argued softly, "But, Harry, it's her birthday."

Mr. Loring was a chemist. He was a fine chemist. He reduced everything to formula. Everything, that is, except Marcia, his wife, and Valentine, his daughter. The only formula for them was in a nursery rhyme and contained, in varying quantities, sugar and spice. Mr. Loring shrugged his shoulders and looked toward the only other man in the room for assistance.

"What do you think of her, Bill?" he asked. "Barging down steps, turning her ankle, and the heads of bookish young men?"

Bill Rogers grinned. He was a tall young man with wide shoulders, and his grin was almost as wide. He was very fair and his hair was practically always rumpled. His eyes were clear gray, they did not change their color even when he regarded Valentine Loring, with whom he had been in love ever since the days when she slapped his face in Central Park for stealing her hoop.

"She turns all heads," he said ruefully, "and then turns them back again, quicker than lightning. You can hear 'em snap. Talk about osteopaths!"

"Oh, were we?" asked Val with interest, and laid the book aside. The servant appeared with cocktails. Val had hers, which was a light one. "Not that I object to liquor," she would explain gravely on those occasions when explanations seemed necessary, "but, after all, I don't need it yet. I'm frivolous and giddy enough without it. Seems silly to add synthetic gaiety, subtract what common sense I'd have left and get as your total sum a bad headache and an insatiable curiosity about what-happened-last-night."

"Hurry," said Marcia Loring practically, "and let's have dinner. I do so detest missing half the first act, trailing in over people's feet and making myself as obnoxious as I feel the latecomers are when I am early."

26

After dinner Val had a moment alone with Bill Rogers. She said, and displayed a slender wrist, "I haven't thanked you for it properly, Bill. It was sweet of you . . . I shouldn't take it, of course."

On the wrist a slim gold bangle, with little charms depending from it . . . a gadget which spelled "I Love You" in black letters on white enamel, when you twirled it quickly, a pussy-cat with emerald eyes, a pearl heart.

"Why not?" asked Bill.

"Oh, I don't know. 'Flowers and books,' " she recited glibly, " 'are the only gifts that a young girl —' "

She was laughing at him as usual. But this time he was able to disconcert her. "— unless she is engaged," he finished for her.

"But, Bill, we aren't engaged."

"And whose fault is that? I've asked you forty times."

"Thirty-seven, to be accurate." Her dark red curls were massed high on her small head. Her face, which was the face of laughter sobered, was grave and kind. "Dear Bill," she said.

But he knew it all by heart. "I do like you, Bill, I love you, I think. But I'm not in love with you. At least I don't believe I am. I don't know that I want to be. I know you so awfully well. I don't think one should slip into loving

27

so easily. It should come like — like a thunderclap, something splendid and exciting and unexpected, from one minute to the next. Shouldn't it? Bill, are you sure you love me — that way? Why, we've known each other since I was three and you were ten! It's just because you're used to me . . . yes, it is. And I don't want to be married, Bill, not yet, I'm having such a grand time. I'd make a perfectly futile wife . . . you've said yourself I have the mind of a grasshopper!"

The elder Lorings came downstairs. Bill's car was outside. They would step into it presently and go to the theater and afterwards to supper. That was Bill's party, that part of it. But the birthday dinner had to be at home. Val had insisted on that. A real cake, with real candles, and just the four of them.

After the play, at the night club to which he took them, they danced. Mr. Loring and Val, Mrs. Loring and Bill. Later, "No, let's not dance just yet," suggested Val, at the table with Bill, "let's watch a moment. Look at Mother and Father — sweet together, aren't they?"

"You're sweet," Bill told her.

"Don't," said Val, "or I will dance with you and step all over your toes. Look here, I'm tired of doing nothing. I'm going to get a job."

Bill shook with laughter. "What can you do?" he inquired. "You can't type, you can't take dictation — I ought to know — you'd hate the stage, you —"

"Spare me," she interrupted, her pointed chin in her cupped hands, her elbows on the table. "I know all that. I was just thinking — a specialized job perhaps? I can add and subtract, I can make change . . . I think I can sell things. I can at least provide atmosphere. So I want Ted Morrison to take me into his shop."

"But I thought," said Bill, in frowning astonishment, "that he couldn't afford an assistant — didn't you tell us?"

"I know. He can't. He's as poor as Mr. and Mrs. Church Mouse's only son, I suppose," said Val, "which is why he needs me. I'd make him look prosperous. 'Ha,' they'll say, 'if he can afford to hire this redheaded woman who has obviously no qualifications for any position whatever,' which if you don't believe it write to Mr. William L. Rogers. . . ."

"What's the 'L' for?"

"Pro Bono Publicum," responded Val absently. "I wish you wouldn't interrupt. 'Yes, if he can afford to hire her, he must be doing very well indeed.' And more customers will come in because an aura of success is a nice thing to hang in your shop windows. I know someone said that before I did and differently."

"More briefly."

"Well, anyway, it's true. Even if I had qualifications I wouldn't have any right to use 'em. We aren't exactly rolling but we have enough to get along on. I have that little income Grandmother left me. It dresses me, and keeps me in mischief. Of course, Father's guardian of it till I'm twenty-five — shows you what Granny thought of my common sense, doesn't it? — and I can't touch the principal. But I couldn't take a paying job. We aren't rich enough . . . I mean, if we were very, very rich, with gold-plated bathtubs, and seventeen yachts, all in different colors, shops would create a job for me — jobs no one else could fill — because I would draw the curious crowds. And we aren't poor enough either! So — the best thing for me is a volunteer job. I'm no good at welfare work. I go all soft and sloppy at the wrong moment and all hard and skeptical at an even wronger one. I tried it last year. Remember? I made so many mistakes of judgment that they threw me out. Nicely, of course. But the fact remains."

Bill said, "I've been offering you a job for a long time."

"I haven't any qualifications for that either,"

she admitted, "and that makes thirty-eight. Or does earlier this evening count? Thirty-nine then."

The Lorings came back to their table. "Your father," said Marcia Loring complacently to her daughter, "still knows how to dance — with me. It is very gratifying."

She looked from her daughter to their host. She and her husband were very fond of Bill Rogers. They hoped . . . but what was the use of hoping where Valentine was concerned? The child was a continual source of excitement to her parents. Not anxiety, for she gave them nothing approximating the usual parental-filial "trouble." But excitement. There wasn't a dull moment living with her. They had found it so for twenty years and Bill, or whoever would marry her some day, would find it so in his turn.

"I'm going to ask that bookshop young man," announced Val, "for a good nonpaying job. I'm going to ask him some sunny Tuesday after he's had a good luncheon. Or maybe sooner. I can dust and I can charm. Books first, customers second. Or the other way round. It doesn't matter."

"Val," asked her father, "you're not by any chance serious?"

"You should know her better," remarked Bill.

Val said, "Well, anyway, I'm thinking of it. Here comes the food. I'm starved. I do love these glass bells over things. They look twice as eatable. I could sit for hours glaring through glass at recumbent chicken on triangles of toast with mushrooms necklaced around its folded paws. . . ."

"Chickens," said her father, "haven't paws." He smiled, however, as the waiter removed the glass coverings. "It does look good," he said.

"You'll pay for it tomorrow," his wife reminded him.

"Yes, I know I shall," he informed her, "but that's tomorrow."

On the following day Mr. Loring had a slight pain in his interior but said nothing about it. Valentine hadn't an ache or a kink. She woke early, filled with pleasant and mischief-making plans. She put on her robe and slippers and, while the water was running in her tub, she sat herself down at a small desk and wrote a note to Mr. Ted Morrison. And then, after breakfast, at an unreasonably early hour, she delivered it, in person.

Mr. Morrison, who had spent the night wondering how many plentifully adjectived kinds of idiot he had made of himself on the evening before, came to his shop shortly before half past nine and prepared to open it.

On the steps of that shop sat Miss Loring, in her mink-banded toque and, presumably, her right mind. She said brightly, "I seem to make a habit of it. Really you should get to work earlier. I came to bring you a note of thanks and an invitation."

The thanks were for the book, the invitation was for dinner at a not too distant date. She followed him down the steps and stood by while he inserted his key, frowning at her. He did not wear the glasses this morning or the smock. She suspected that they were props, for store use only. He looked nice in a dark blue, double-breasted suit. He said, "I never expected to see you again."

"Oh, you'll see me," she told him casually, "often. I've taken a fancy to your shop and your cat. By the way, tell me her name again?"

"Keturie," he said shortly and stood aside to let her enter.

"Nice," said Val comfortably, "did you think it up all yourself?"

"Why, yes —"

"Then there's hope for you. What becomes of her when you are away, nights and over Sunday?"

"She roams," replied Ted darkly, "and hunts in the backyard." He walked through the shop and showed her the door leading to steps into the yard. "The people upstairs feed her when I'm not here."

"She isn't very fat," complained Val.

"She shouldn't be. She's here to catch mice. Feed her too well and she'd grow lazy and wouldn't do her job."

"I see," murmured Val. "Do you feel that way about people too? Better to be lean and hungry like 'Cassius' . . . or was it someone else?"

He looked astonished. She said demurely, "I read a book — once."

Now the blinds were up and there was sun in the shop. Dust danced along the rays. "Where's your duster?" asked Val abruptly.

Too amazed to protest, he gave it to her. She employed it with excellent effect, moving as rapidly, he thought, bewildered, as the vibration which is a hummingbird's flight. As suddenly as she had demanded it, she returned the duster to him.

"Just a sample," she said gravely. "And now, we'll expect you to dinner on Friday. At seven. Fancy dress not essential. A simple sports costume, shorts and visor —"

He was still gaping when the door closed and she was gone. He thought, She's a pest. He felt himself adopted and he didn't like it especially. He wouldn't go to dinner on Friday. That was out of the question. He would write her a dignified little note. "Dear

Miss Loring," he would write, "I regret that a previous engagement . . ."

At eleven his telephone rang. He went to it with a feeling of uncertainty. If she telephoned? No, of course not, perhaps it was an order. He spoke into the instrument with conviction. "Morrison Bookshop, Ted Morrison speaking."

It was the girl with whom he had been in love for six months, a long time ago, a week ago. She was telling him in her high, fluttering voice, which soon was to be heard from the platform of practically every important woman's club in the city, that she had had another poem accepted and couldn't they celebrate by having dinner together Friday night?

When Ted hung up he felt as though he were in some sort of bad dream during which he said and did things which were exactly opposed to the things he had intended to say and do. He had told Flora that he had a previous engagement; and he had congratulated her with genuine warmth upon her second success. He put his hand to his forehead. "What's come over me?" he demanded of himself, in that sterling phrase. Keturie, prowling around under tables, came to rub herself against his ankles. Her back was arched like a Chinese bridge. She had a knowing look.

On Friday evening, at seven o'clock, in the newly pressed blue serge suit and with brightly shined footgear, Ted presented himself at the Loring house. The quiet servant admitted him and Valentine slid down the banister at the same time. At least that was her guest's impression. Perhaps she merely ran down the stairs. At all events, first she was at the top and then at the bottom and there was a flash of green which was her gown and then something bright and dazzling which was her smile.

"I knew you'd come," she said.

He'd written her, stiffly, that he'd come, so this remark seemed superfluous. Still, he felt a little uneasy, as if she had been able to read across space and hours his changing mind which at least ten times a day had warned him . . . don't go . . . send an excuse . . . grippe . . . scarlet fever . . . a trip to Europe.

He followed Val into the pleasant big living room and was there presented to her parents. Grudgingly he thought them attractive people. People who were attractive and secure irritated him. He was at all times preoccupied passionately and seriously with the thought of the many people who were unattractive, possibly, because they were not secure.

Mr. and Mrs. Loring accepted him without

36

question. The fact that he had met their daughter in a slightly unusual way didn't appear to matter to them. He admitted to himself later that the table conversation was solid enough: judiciously conventional perhaps, but not as light as he had expected, except when Val led it. Mr. Loring introduced current national and international politics and situations; listened to the younger man's opinions with grave courtesy. Mrs. Loring spoke of books and it was quite evident that she had read them. The meal was simple, well cooked and well served. Afterwards he was offered an excellent cigar and an even better liqueur.

Later, after a proper interval, Mr. and Mrs. Loring went upstairs to the second-floor sitting room and left Ted alone with Val. She sat in a deep chair and issued orders to a Welsh terrier who lay on the hearthrug, his eyes fixed on her. He was a very special dog, she told her guest, a Christmas present. His name was Sound and Fury, so they called him Saxophone for short.

She said, refusing the cigarette Ted offered: "No, I don't smoke. It handicaps me. It takes my mind off my work, hunting for brands, lighting matches. You like us better than you thought, don't you?"

He was astonished into honesty. "Yes, I do."

"Good. I believed you would. We are really nice people. We do not have our names in society or gossip items, but we are what is known as backbone with background."

Now she was laughing at him, of course. He said stiffly:

"Of course, you are nice. But I'm not accustomed —"

"To nice people? Yet Sax took to you right away," she said.

"I didn't mean that. I mean — oh, everything has been so different with me, you wouldn't understand."

"I would. Tell me about yourself."

He told her, he didn't know why, but once he had started he couldn't stop. She didn't interrupt him as other girls had interrupted him with comments on the sociological aspects of his story. She merely sat and listened and the bangle tinkled on her wrist as she put out her hand now and then to quell the rising restlessness of Sax, who came to sit at her feet and regard her with an unfaltering devotion.

It was perhaps a commonplace story. Ted's mother had died at his birth; his father, less than a year afterwards, in a railway accident. There had been some life insurance, the principal of which would come to him at twenty-one. Meantime there had been small monthly payments which were not sufficient for a private school and college education, but which paid for his clothes and his board with various distant relatives who managed to care for him, in a haphazard manner. He hadn't really lived with any of them . . . he'd visited mostly, in Jersey, and in the city, as it had suited their convenience. Then, night school and work, and more work, and finally the legacy intact, which he touched as little as possible until he was ready to open the shop. He lived, he told her, in a room in the Village section where most of his friends were.

She said, when he had finished:

"I'm sorry."

"What's there to be sorry about?" he asked, alarmed, for he dreaded sentiment. "I did very well, learned my way about, was on my own earlier than most boys. If I'd grown up with people of my own, if I'd been sheltered, spoiled with money, I wouldn't have made anything of myself, I wouldn't have known what it's all about."

She said, "You think that of me, don't you?"

He looked about the room. It was a quiet room, a safe room. "I suppose you cry when you see bread lines and perhaps look in your purse for an extra quarter. You couldn't be expected to do anything else."

"Poor-little-rich-girl theme," she said, with sudden animation. "You make me tired! My father worked for all this, worked hard. He's brilliant, he's one of the best in his line. He headed a really big firm. There isn't a chemist worth his salt in the country who doesn't know and respect Harry Loring. But at the beginning of the depression . . ." She shrugged and went on. "We have enough to get along. Father has a position, it pays enough to feed us and keep up the taxes on the house. We'd like to sell it, we can't, it's impossible now. We'd like to move into an apartment. We can't do that either. The money my grandmother left went in the crash too. Father's a better chemist than businessman. All but the little she left me, that's in trust. But even if it hadn't all happened, what difference would it make? My father has brains and ability. He worked to get some place; he used his talent. He's entitled to anything his ability can bring him . . . for he earns it. I don't think much of your socialism or whatever it is if it denies a man the right to make the most of his learning and knowledge and opportunity. That seems pretty silly to me."

She was pretty when angry. He observed that against his will. Sax observed it too perhaps, for he growled and stood beside her, his head against her hand, ready to defend

40

her against all comers.

Ted said:

"I'm sorry if I annoyed you. I couldn't, in ten minutes, tell you what I feel, explain my convictions. We're arguing at cross purposes, I think."

"Cross," she repeated reflectively, "is exactly the word. Suppose I do know how you feel? In lots of ways, I think you're right; in other ways, I think you're terribly wrong. But that makes it all the more interesting."

"Makes what all the more interesting?"

"Us. But if you feel the way you do, why a bookstore? You probably think people who write and are successful at it are a lot of parasites, most of them. And the people who come to buy, as well. If the workers are closest to you, why don't you work too? — with your hands, I mean," she demanded.

That was an entirely childish question, he told her. He wasn't a worker with his hands. He couldn't further any cause by doing something badly. The only thing he knew well was how to run a bookshop. So he ran it.

"And you expect to make your living at it, don't you . . . and perhaps a profit?"

He did, he replied. Not that he had.

"Well, there," she said triumphantly. "That has a slightly capitalistic sound, hasn't it? Especially the profit?"

41

He wanted to shake her. She was muddled as well as redheaded.

She asked, "You've been an employer too, haven't you?"

Ted Morrison laughed at that. She was so serious, trying hard to convict him out of his own mouth. He said, "Well, in a small way and for a short time."

"Look here," said Val, "I like you. I think you're demented but I like you. Your shop's all right, your cat is a darling. I must introduce her to Sax sometime, at a reasonable distance. Let me come and work for you. For nothing. For a year —"

He cried, "But that's absurd. Voluntary workers are a nuisance. They can't keep hours, they take too much time for lunch, they go away in the summer."

"We don't. Dad can't now, so we won't leave him. He has a two weeks' vacation; sometimes we take a short trip somewhere. I'm entitled to two weeks," she said, smiling. "Well, if you won't make it a year, how about six months? If I haven't doubled your profits by then, you can fire me."

"As they are nonexistent, it shouldn't be hard."

"No, I mean it. I like books. I want something to do. I haven't any right to draw a salary. I'm supported. I'm all right. I'm not afraid where the next meal's coming from. How about it?"

He felt himself weakening. Dinner had been good, and ample. He hadn't had one as good for — how long? He couldn't remember. He was better acquainted with restaurant cooking, and not good restaurants at that; he hadn't dined in a home since his boyhood and that had been quite different, anyway. The cigar, the liqueur . . . the cocktail before dinner. He had turned soft or something. He found himself snapping his fingers at Sax, who responded with caution. And he also found himself saying feebly:

"All right . . . but it won't work. At the end of a week, you'll find that out."

She said cheerfully, "Leave that to me. I promise you I'll quit if I don't like it. But I will like it. So will you."

"Your parents," he began.

"Leave them to me too," she begged him, "they'll be amenable. They won't like the idea any better than you do. In fact I've broached it to them already, but they'll give in. They'll have to. After all, they're probably as tired of having me around the house thumb-twiddling as I am to be here. So that's that. I'll be at work on Monday morning. Nine sharp."

"Half past."

"Nine. Give me a key — you've an extra key, haven't you? — and I'll open up for you. Dust and everything. You've a cleaning woman, I suppose?"

He told her that he had, for a few hours, once a week.

"That's all right then. Nine o'clock on Monday. I get an hour for lunch. I quit at five. Is it a bargain?"

"It is," he agreed, laughing, more entertained than he had been in years and yet experiencing grave misgivings.

"All right." Val sat up in the big chair, came to her feet and crossed the room to the radio. "Dance?" she asked casually, turning the dials.

"Well, no," he said, "I don't care much about —"

"Nonsense," she said, "I'll teach you. I've a little radio of my own, it was a Christmas present too. It's almost as noisy as Sax but doesn't wag its tail or lick my hand. Suppose I bring it along to the shop? There'll be times between customers when we might like to know how to make a potato salad or where the next political campaign is going or perhaps Keturie likes to dance too. Stand up. Put your arms about me. I won't bite you. There . . . let's go!"

# Chapter III

Monday morning was very unpleasant. It was a gray morning and rain fell, at times despondently and at times with a vicious, bad-tempered quality which resulted in sleet. Ted Morrison, slipping and sliding and inwardly cursing every step of his way from the subway to the shop, was convinced that this indeed was blue Monday. Black and blue. He had not slept well for several nights and he felt as if he had been severely beaten. He had seen Flora on Saturday evening, rather late, at an alfresco party which he had attended, and she had reproached him lyrically for his desertion of her. To which he had responded sullenly that, after all, he couldn't be expected to travel her present path with her, a path which appeared to wind far into a rosy distance dotted with literary teas and platform appearances.

"Oh, of course," said Flora, "like all failures, you believe that success puts anyone beyond the pale!"

She was extremely angry, sitting there on her hostess's broken-down divan, and wearing the straight, loose-sleeved type of gown she affected. Someone was playing a piano fairly well and being hailed as a genius. He was saying, over the clattering keys, "You understand, in the orchestration the taxi horns come in here and the steam drills in here and the rattle of the lunch pails a little further on, after the noon whistle blows? It is a Skyscraper Suite, from the proletarian angle."

Considerable liquor was being consumed, of a most indifferent variety, and Ted Morrison, scarlet with sudden rage, was forced to listen involuntarily while his hostess explained, about three feet away, why she didn't believe in marriage as an institution.

Flora shook her head at him. She had fair hair, cut like that of a medieval page, or as she fancied a medieval page's would have been cut. It belled about her heart-shaped face, which was fragile and a little haggard and would one day be beautiful when she ate more and smoked less. She cried:

"Well, don't sit there glowering at me!"

Ted said, with an effort:

"I'm not glowering. I — you didn't believe I was a failure — a few months ago."

"Well, aren't you?" she asked. "You haven't done half the things you've sworn you'd do." She laughed, thinking of their plans, the bookshop "salon," the kindred souls, the encouragement of new and vital talent, of real self-expression. "And just because I sell two poems and have an opportunity to sell some more . . . just because I see some light ahead after working so hard for so long, you turn stuffy on me!"

"It's not I that's stuffy," he informed her. "A couple more sales and you'll forget the rest of us ever existed . . . you'll get out of here —"

"And as fast as possible," she agreed quickly. "I'm fed up with it. As soon as I find a publisher for my book, I'm going to take a flat somewhere where I can work in quiet and know that the rent's paid ahead. I'm tired of living from hand to mouth. It's terribly destructive to the creative spirit. I want some peace of mind, and security."

He said bitterly, "Six months ago you were assuring me that the atmosphere of struggle, disappointment and stark reality was the only possible one for an artist."

"Six months ago," decided Flora Carr, "I was a fool!"

That included him, he supposed. He left the party a little later, the smoky "studio," the laughter, the arguments, the high-raised voices, and went back to his room. His last glimpse of Flora discovered her sitting on the piano — she had really lovely legs, slim and beautifully made — talking with great animation to a strange young man who had just wandered in and whose claim on her attention proved to be the fact that he "knew an editor."

Saturday had been bad; Sunday was worse. Half a dozen people climbed Ted's Bank Street stairs, which were decidedly unsteady, and insisted on smoking his cigarettes and drinking his little store of liquor until far into the night. They had come to talk about Russia and about Russia they were going to talk if it killed them — and him.

By Monday morning Ted was not himself. He had quarreled definitely with Flora Carr, and although he told himself repeatedly that she wasn't worth his love and his admiration — brilliant perhaps, but unstable and too easily swayed by the first rewards of her talent — he couldn't quite convince himself that he no longer cared for her. Then there was this business of Valentine Loring. Why he had ever permitted his better judgment to be seduced into an arrangement as absurd as the one she had proposed, he couldn't imagine. He'd go to the shop, as usual, and he would tell her — provided she was there — that it had all been a joke, and that he hadn't really meant it. He would shoo her out, gently but firmly. He didn't want her around. She would only unsettle him. She hadn't a brain in her head, and the entire experiment was doomed to failure from the first.

He approached the store therefore in no gay mood and half fell down his own steps. The shop was already open. The window dressing had been tampered with, there was now a goodly scattering of bright-backed novels — the lighter sort, those he usually kept on the back shelves — in the foreground and there was also a deep blue urn-shaped vase filled with branches of bright red berries. Grudgingly he admitted that it looked gay, if not dignified.

Val, in a green smock, greeted him without dignity.

"Hie, boss!"

"Good morning," said Mr. Morrison coolly and rushed past her to the back room where he proceeded to rid himself of his dripping hat and his overcoat. Staring after him, a finger on her lips, Val reflected aloud to Keturie, who rolled at her feet in an excess of affection, "Cheery lad, so glad to see me, so delighted at the result of my toil — me who have worked my fingers to the bone! Oh, well, that's life," she ended philosophically, and went over to a gift and card table to arrange it to her better satisfaction; "they're all alike, the brutes."

Ted marched in from the back room. He had put on the smock and the glasses. Neither improved him, yet he looked impressive enough and really quite sweet, thought Val, grinning at him. His mind was made up, she saw that too. She thought, Much good that will do him! and waited sedately.

"Look here, Miss Loring —"

"Val, to you. Only my very best friends are permitted to call me by my surname," she said.

"Val, then," he said, desperately determined not to smile. But it was impossible . . . after all, she looked comic and very pretty in the green smock, with her curls ruffled and her expression a perfect example of what the docile employee should wear.

"That's better," she approved.

"Val, you don't really mean this . . . that is . . . are you sure your people approve?" he began falteringly, all his grave and reasoning phrases fleeing and uncapturable.

"No, not especially," she replied promptly; "they think I'm too frivolous."

"Ah," said Ted with satisfaction. At least Mr. and Mrs. Loring were on the side of the angels.

"And that you're too — how shall I put it? — unfrivolous," she went on serenely. "Father said, 'For heaven's sake, Val, you'll die of malnutrition in a week!' "

"Oh," said Ted, with a long face. He felt ridiculously wounded. So they hadn't liked him, amiable as they had been toward him. It had been all façade, the air of friendliness, of interest in himself as a human being. He might have known it!

Val's face changed too. She said sharply, "Don't look like that. They liked you a lot. You should have heard the things they said, nice things. But, you see, they believe I'm a little mad and —"

"Don't try to explain," he said stiffly, "and I must say I agree with your parents. Your — your especial form of insanity must be contagious, I had a touch of it myself Friday night. So, you see, you can't work here. It's impossible. We'd never get along."

"Am I fired?" she inquired mournfully.

Craven, he looked away from her. Keturie rose and stalked off to the corner. Her arched back had a look of menace and reproach. Even the cat had turned against him. "Please understand," he urged feebly.

But now Val was smiling again. She said briskly, "I understand perfectly — and I'm not fired. You can't fire me, you haven't hired me yet. I'm staying. A week. Two weeks. Give me a trial. Look here, play fair. I've got to prove to my father and mother — and to you, and, yes," she said, thinking of Bill's infuriating laughter only yesterday, "to someone else that I'm good for something. Please?"

"Someone else?" he repeated. Oh, a man, of course. Not that he cared or ever would. He agreed sternly.

"All right, stay. I warn you, if you do stay you'll have to —"

"Oh, I'll mind, all right," she interrupted with a misleading effect of meekness. "I won't infringe on the voluntary worker part. I'll pretend that you're paying me fifty a week and that I have to earn it. There's the phone."

She rushed to it, before he could move a muscle. She seized the instrument and cooed into it. "Morrison Bookshop," she reported.

Ted, rooted to the spot, listened with apprehension. So did Keturie, one black ear twitching.

"No, Mr. Morrison's assistant speaking. Yes . . . yes . . . I see . . . very well."

She replaced the instrument quietly.

"Well?" inquired her chief impatiently.

"I don't know," sighed Valentine. "Not very, I think. It wasn't an order. It wasn't even a customer. It was, I think, a girl friend. She said she didn't want to talk to you. I'd told her you were here too. She said she might call you later, and then she hung up on me. Very unemilypost," added Val sorrowfully.

Flora! Flora calling up to say she was sorry for Saturday night! What would she think? Ted took a step toward the telephone and then a step back. Let her think it, serve her right. Let her believe he had grown affluent and could afford an assistant, a dozen assistants.

Or, let her think he couldn't afford it but that some girl, less brilliant perhaps but more discerning, was working for him — for love.

Val marched herself over to the bookshelves, a duster in her hand. She took the books down, she clapped their covers together, she flicked them with the feathers, and smiled a little to herself. Ted, walking about aimlessly, halted before the display window.

"You don't like it?" she diagnosed anxiously. "I thought maybe you wouldn't. But look here . . . most of the people who read books aren't awfully high-brow. Anyone — just the average sort — passing by wouldn't have given that window another glance. All very dull, you know, books on what-are-we-coming-to and have-you-had-your-morning-psychology? You have to attract everyone. Bookshops should be like gregarious people, open-minded, openhearted, with plenty of room for all sorts of friendships and acquaintances. So I put in a book on diet, and three detectives and a couple of romances and some travel books. Now it offers a more varied fare, doesn't it? Something for everyone. And don't you admire the bittersweet?"

"Is that what you call it?" he asked, looking at the orange-red berries on their stripped stalks, colorful and autumnal in the deep blue vase.

"That's what it's called," she agreed. "I brought the vase along . . . I hope you don't mind."

He found that he didn't. "No, of course not. It was sweet of you. I —"

"Look," said Val wildly, "a customer, or I'll eat my hat and it isn't even paid for and they'll have to operate. Here, get away from there and let me decorate the window!"

She pushed him aside. Startled, he watched her lean there at the window, needlessly rearranging the books. Ted followed discreetly and looked out. Beyond the steps, at street level, a middle-aged gentleman had halted and was looking in. He remained to look, for a long time. Now at the books and now at Val, her curls bobbing, her small hands fussing about the display. The middle-aged gentleman hesitated no more but came, if gingerly, at least with determination, down the steps. He opened the door and popped in, rather like Santa Claus without the beard. He said, smiling, "I see you've a new Van Dine."

"Oh, yes," answered Val and smiled at him in return. "I adore him, don't you? And if you like mysteries. . . ."

She began naming them over to him, one by one. She darted away, she returned with her arms full. She plumped the books down, she opened a page here and there. "This one

54

has four murders," she confided in a whisper, "and is simply too creepy for words. Good solution too, doesn't stretch the credulity."

The gentleman had meant to buy one book. He bought three. He paid for them and pranced out again, with a neat little parcel under his arm and a whistle on his lips. Looks as if it might be a morning after all, he reflected. He liked stories replete with slayings. He was a banker who had involuntarily retired, and sitting in club windows was not the fun it once might have been. Nice shop, charming little girl. He made a mental note of the address and walked on toward Fifth Avenue.

"There!" cried Val. "Three books. What's your profit on them?"

Stammering a little, Ted told her. She said, her head on one side, "That being the case, we'll have to do even better. But that's not bad for a beginner — and a beginning."

Ted broke in desperately.

"It's fine, of course, very gratifying and all that, but I have made it a rule never to force books on my customers. I hate that commercial attitude . . . like a waiter trying to make up your mind for you. I've always wanted the shop to have a noncommercial attitude. I don't know if you'll understand — but I want people to feel that they can come in here and look about unmolested and go out, if they like, without buying, and without the feeling that they've been coerced into something."

"You think I coerced that nice old man?" inquired Val indignantly.

"He wasn't very old," Ted reminded her, "and well, yes, I think you did." He added reluctantly, for he was not really an unkind person, "And it is impossible to persuade women that to use their sex appeal in business is most unethical."

Val's face did not change although he examined it with more anxiety than he cared to admit. She asked slowly, "You think I used my sex appeal?"

"Well, yes," he admitted again, relieved that she was taking his criticism in the spirit in which he had offered it, "showing yourself at the window like that and —"

Val laughed. She laughed until her sides ached. She held her sides, she rocked. She said feebly, "Oh, dear!" She added weakly, "Oh, my good gosh!" She wiped her streaming eyes and looked at him. He stood his ground, flushed, annoyed, but determined. She said, "Oh, my poor Ted. Of course I coerced him, but he doesn't know it; and of course I used my sex appeal, if that's what you call it. I understand the Greeks and the Romans and even the Scythians had a phrase for it. This one's outmoded, by the way . . . I call it vitamin M. Naturally I did. How on earth do you expect to sell anything?" She began to laugh again. Then she sobered. "I will not bring ill repute upon your fair fame, dear boss. But as Keturie knows mice . . . so do I know men. Our first customer went away happy. He'll come back again. There's the phone. Shall I answer?"

"No," said Ted hastily, "thanks — I'll go."

It was Flora again. She said, "So, it's you," rather snippily. She added, "Since when have you had to have an assistant?"

"This morning."

"You didn't tell me about it."

"It was arranged only on Friday."

"I saw you Saturday!"

"Well, really, Flora, you didn't give me much time to —"

"Oh, I see. I'm so glad the shop is doing so well."

"I'll explain when I see you," said Ted.

"Never mind," said Flora. "I can tell by her voice that she's young. Is she pretty?"

"Hideous!" shouted Ted.

Val grinned and bent to stroke Keturie. "Either he's an awful liar," she said aloud, "or else I've been misled all these years." Keturie purred knowingly. "Meow," commented Keturie, closing one wicked eye.

Ted hung up the receiver. He said briefly:

"I've some office work to do, but before I start, suppose you let me explain something of the stock to you. Not everyone who comes in will want detective books."

He explained. Val listened. She trotted after him, obedient, and he was forced to confess to himself, intelligent. At least, she seemed intelligent. They were interrupted by another customer. A woman this time. Val prodded him. "Do your stuff," she insisted.

But the woman, who was thin and meager and rather rattlebrained, didn't seem to know just what she wanted. Ted followed her about, suggesting book after book: "for an invalid friend who is sailing for Rome . . . they say the climate will be just what she needs . . . I don't really approve of her going . . . I had a friend who went last year . . . Do you approve of Mussolini, Mr. Morrison? You are Mr. Morrison, aren't you? No, I don't think she'd care for a love story . . . she hasn't had a very happy life."

He was dripping with perspiration at the end of ten minutes. Vaguely, still talking, the customer moved toward the door. But somehow Val was there, a book in her hand.

"I just thought," she said, with a deprecatory gesture, "that if your friend is going to Rome for the first time. . . . This book is quite new . . . it deals with Roman society. Of course," she added, "it's rather sophisticated . . . but we've sold a good many to people planning to travel in Italy."

"Oh?" said the lady doubtfully, and hesitated.

When she left she took with her the book dealing with Roman society, a novel of the Irish hunting country, and two bon voyage cards.

"Ouf!" said Val, and sat down in a chair which she had placed rather skillfully that morning and which would invite, she hoped, the unwary.

Ted said, "How you could sell her that! She'll —"

"She'll read it first," said Val complacently, "and be rather shocked. I've read it. . . ."

"And were you?" asked Ted, who had *not* read it.

"No. But that's another story. And then she'll give it to her friend, who will love it."

She added, "You ought to read more, really."

He was outraged. "I do read. Worth-while things. If you think I want to ruin my eyesight and fritter away my time —"

"I love them," she said suddenly.

"What?"

"Fritters. Corn. Clam. Haven't had any in

a dog's age. What were you saying?"

"It doesn't matter," said Ted, resigned.

"I remember," she said, "so don't cudgel the great mind. Personally I think you ought to know what's in the package you sell. That will be my job. Now here's an arrangement. You do the first and rare editions and the prints and the heavy things. Leave me the fiction, both the selling and the rental. I think it will work. I'll take 'em home at night and spin through them or during off moments in the store; how about it?"

"I haven't sold five books in six days, much less in two hours," said Ted glumly.

"This," said Val, "is only a starter." She looked at her wrist watch. "When do you go out to lunch?" she asked.

"I brought mine with me," he told her.

"I see . . . in that envelope?"

It wasn't an envelope, he said. A package. Sandwich, small bottle of milk.

Val said, "No wonder you're thin. It's twelve. I'll run home, and be back at one sharp."

She went into the back room. The smock came off. She emerged in a rusty brown wool frock, with large, schoolgirl buttons on it. She pulled on a beret which she took from the pocket of her coat. She said, "Don't look so hopeful. I'm really coming back."

The door closed behind her. The bitter-sweet nodded in the blue vase and the day was grayer than before. Ted, at the window, could see her going up the steps, her unhooked galoshes flapping about her slim ankles, her tweed coat collar turned up against the rain. She paused on the sidewalk to glance back and down and wave, and then walked away. She had a valiant look, he thought without volition, gay, courageous. Scatterbrained, of course . . . but. . . .

He regarded the clock on his desk, when he returned to munch his rather tasteless sandwich. An hour can be a long time. But he said to himself savagely, I can get a lot done in an hour, without having to worry about her. He thought further, She'll interfere with my work, she'll upset all my habits.

Still, she'd sold five books.

# Chapter IV

They sold more in the days to follow. Business picked up at the bookshop and there were days when it was even brisk. Val announced at the end of the second week, "We simply must advertise."

"We haven't the money," Ted reminded her instantly, not even resenting her use of the plural . . .which had a possessive sound no matter what it might be called in the grammars.

"That doesn't matter. We will have to risk it. A little ad, the sort that will entice people. I don't suppose they'll buy but they'll lend an air. After all, if people pass by and look in and see a lot of other people — it's human nature, you know, to want to join the mob. I'll write the ad."

So they advertised, in one weekly paper devoted to the doings of the literary world and in the Sunday book supplements of dailies. And people did come . . . to look around . . . to browse. "I hate that word," said Val, who had avoided it in her advertisements; "it sounds like a lot of rabbits and I don't like rabbits much . . . or lettuce."

One of their best customers was Bill Rogers.

There were days when Bill drove Val to the shop and called for her again. Ted disapproved of Bill yet he did not dislike him. Of course, the man was besotted about Val, it was perfectly evident, and it would be sensible of her to take him as, apparently, she had had plenty of opportunity. She wasn't serious about working. She was just amusing herself, getting a "kick" out of it, in her own words. And Bill Rogers was eminently suited to her. He had money, he was idle, he was frivolous. A better match couldn't be made in heaven or out of it. Ted asked one day in the early spring:

"What in heaven's name does Rogers do with his time?"

"Didn't you know?" asked Val in astonishment. "He's writing a book."

"I don't believe it!" said Ted flatly.

"You wouldn't. It isn't your kind of book anyway, so don't look as if your private world had come to an end. It isn't even my kind of book. It's all about game fishing. It will be privately printed with marvelous illustrations and sell at twenty-five dollars a copy, if it sells at all."

"How absurd," said Ted, "and how utterly futile. Twenty-five dollars." He choked with indignation. "What does he do when he isn't fishing?" he wanted to know.

"Oh, he big-game hunts and he has a sailing

yacht — not a very big one, but complete enough — he goes off on scientific expeditions sometimes. . . ."

"Pseudoscientific," corrected Ted. But now the name came back to him, Rogers, William Rogers . . . that was the fellow who'd brought the fish back to the Aquarium that time . . . what were they? He never could remember the names of fish, he didn't like fish anyway. . . . Oh, of course, he might have known.

"Where'd he get his money?" he inquired.

"Ted, don't be so stuffy, please. He didn't grind it from the faces of the poor. His grandfather and his father made it by honest and conventional means and they left it to him. He still has a good deal of it because it was in trust or something and mostly in government bonds. A manager looks after the estate."

Ted said, "He doesn't look like a parasite. He seems a good fellow, in a way."

"I won't have you patronize him," she cried. "Bill's all right. He does more darned good —"

"Ten dollars to an organized charity, I suppose?"

Val stamped her foot. "You're being very disagreeable," she said, "I won't listen to you."

"Why don't you marry him," asked Ted,

"if you're so crazy about him . . . and approve of his millions?"

"Perhaps I shall," she agreed, her eyes bright and very green, "but whether I do or whether I don't, it certainly isn't any of your business!"

And she went to lunch fifteen minutes early and got back fifteen minutes late.

When she returned Ted was stalking about the shop. He remarked, "You're late," unnecessarily, and she said, her anger evaporated, after an hour and a half, and a rather pleasing sensation warming her heart instead, which wasn't altogether the result of the luncheon at the Plaza with Bill, "I know I am, I'm sorry."

"I'm going out," he said, "I've an engagement."

"Ted! Why didn't you tell me?"

"It doesn't matter . . . I only made it." He stopped, unwilling to admit that he'd thought of it after her departure.

"Flora," surmised Val. "Well, there's money in the petty cash."

She hadn't been there a week before Flora had come in for the first time. They'd had quite a talk, the two of them, with Ted standing around, one-legged, like a crane, and uneasy.

There had been subsequent visits.

"No," said Ted, "it isn't Flora."

After he'd gone she sat down in the back room and pondered. She loved the bookshop. She liked Ted. Despite his efforts to make her dislike him, she liked him very much. Perhaps she was falling in love with him. She didn't know. Bill had taxed her with it, at lunch. "You're falling in love with this bird, Val, because he's a grouch and because you're sorry for him, he has you sold on this life's-one-vast-injustice stuff."

"He has not. I think he's goofy!"

"I don't mean that he has you sold on his ideas. Merely on himself. You'd like to take him out of that Village dump he calls home and put him up in a suite with valets and cars and chauffeurs. You'd want him to have everything he's missed and you want to protect him from the world as he himself sees it. In short, you're sorry for him and you feel rather maternal toward him and that's pretty dangerous . . . for. . . ."

"For whom?" asked Val coldly.

"For you. And for him; and for me," said Bill, with a wry smile, "because, damn it, I don't seem able to stop loving you — and here I am hanging around as I've hung around for too many years to mention and getting nowhere. See here, Val, there's some talk of my taking the boat and a couple of good eggs and going off to the South Seas and such un-likely places in the late summer. Marry me, and come along."

"Forty-six," enumerated Val, "and you didn't think that all up by yourself?"

"I certainly did. And Mom thinks it's a darned good notion, too."

"She would," said Val, laughing. She loved Bill Rogers' mother, a small, black-haired woman who was going on sixty and looked about forty, with a quick wit, plenty of spirit and an inexhaustible fund of unsentimental tenderness where her son was concerned. "If I ever do marry you," she confessed, "it will be because by no other means could I obtain such a mother-in-law."

"Come on, Val, kill a couple of stones with one bird. Make up your mind. Marry me and we'll go off in the boat for several months. And when you get back, there's the mother-in-law, all ready and made to order."

"You forget I have a job," she told him.

"I wish I could forget it," he said.

She was alone in the shop most of the after-noon, for Ted came in late, and without an apology. It had been, as it happened, a busy afternoon. There had been customers, cash customers, and three more names had been added to the rental library records. Two peo-ple had telephoned that they wanted books sent to ships, and had given her carte blanche. "Oh, say, twenty dollars' worth," one man had said magnificently. And Val was feeling herself the prototype of all Successful Businesswomen when Ted returned.

He heard her report without much enthusiasm. He'd had a bad time of it. His luncheon engagement had been manufactured out of clear air and he'd spent an hour in a very dull restaurant quite alone. After which he had gone to the public library. But he didn't tell Val that.

She said, "Ted, please don't be cross. I didn't want to quarrel with you . . . I didn't mean to — and I'm sure you didn't mean to quarrel with me. Only, you see, I've known Bill most of my life and I like him so much. He's really awfully fine. He hasn't millions or anything like that . . . you do exaggerate so dreadfully. It just happens that he has enough money so he doesn't have to work, in your sense, and has leisure to do the things he wants to do. Maybe they aren't very important. But they are important to him. He lives simply and — Oh, Ted, do be sensible. You like him, you know you do! And you like his mother. How could anyone help it? You said yourself, the time she came in and opened her account, that you'd never met a more delightful and intelligent woman."

Ted looked at her and grinned. "Sure. I admit it all. I'm just a natural-born crab, I suppose." It was a handsome apology, for him.

"Look," she said, "I've been here since February. It's April now. Can't you admit something else? Admit that it's worked? That I've helped a little? I know you don't approve of my system, but that doesn't matter. I — I've worked hard, Ted, honestly I have."

He sat down, there in the back room, beside her. He said, after a moment, "Of course you have. I've just been pretty small about it. It irritated me to see you walk in here and succeed where I had failed. We're out of the red. Not much. But still, out. How long it will keep up, I don't know but — Of course, summer's dull as ditchwater anyway."

"We'll have a mailing library," she suggested, "people would like that . . . the rental people. We'll send 'em so many books a week, those who sign up for it. Not as many people leave town in the summer as used to, and there are always people who come to New York for their vacations. We'll manage somehow. There's the phone. . . . Come to dinner tonight and talk it over."

Ted had dined at the Lorings' more than once since that first time. Val's father and mother insisted upon it. "Let's hear how our rattlebrain's doing in the big business world," they urged him. "Come on, Ted, tell all."

It was fun, being taken into a family like that. Yet he wasn't quite sure that they did it for his sake, so he held back a little, he couldn't help it. He told Val, "I can't come as often as you ask me, Val. I've no way to return it, you know."

"Must you be stupid?" she demanded. "You can take me out now and then. Rob the petty cash. Table d'hôte, sixty-five cents, all the red wine you can drink and I don't like. It'll be swell."

So he did, now and then. And along about the middle of April Val went to her first Village party. Flora blew in, chic in her curious clothes, which were of better cut and more impressive material since she was being paid for her lectures. For Flora had sprung rather suddenly into prominence. Several magazines were inquiring for her poetry.

The party was given for Flora, which was probably why Flora was late. She'd issued the invitations herself, coming to the shop to tell Val, "Jimmy Morris is giving me a divine party next Saturday night — do have Ted bring you."

Val was a little uncertain. After all, such a roundabout way. After Flora had gone, "borrowing" a book, as she usually did, "Oh, I simply must read this. I'll take it along, Ted, and return it in a day or so," she asked Ted, "Should I go, really? This Jimmy . . . will he think I'm a gate crasher?"

Ted was somewhat irritated. Flora was behaving strangely about Val. He had expected, when she came into the shop for the first time and saw how pretty his "assistant" was, that she'd be — well, at least annoyed. For Val was pretty, you couldn't deny that, not if you had eyes in your head. But curiously enough Flora had seemed amused. Still, it wasn't long after that that she'd written the poem about wayward lads and brighter eyes which had appeared in the book section of a Sunday paper and had ended on the if-you've-broken-my-heart-I'll-never-tell note.

He replied:

"Of course you won't gate-crash! What an idiotic expression. You will be going with me, won't you?"

"Oh, shall I, Ted?" she asked with such Cinderella docility that he looked at her sharply. But her face was as demure as Keturie's when Keturie slept, curled up like a moth ball, the picture of feline innocence.

"Naturally," he responded, further annoyed, "and Jimmy isn't a man. She's a woman, Jimmy Morris. An artist. Very clever. We're not formal, you know, in the Village. We don't issue engraved invitations."

"I didn't know," she said meekly. "I thought the Village was a State of Mind anyway and that it — had rules and regulations, too, if somewhat Utopian and in reverse."

"What are you driving at?" he demanded crossly.

"Nothing. What'll I wear?"

"Anything. For heaven's sake, don't dress up too much," he warned her in alarm.

"I won't," she said.

Yet she selected her frock with care. It was a black dress with a lamé jacket. She'd bought the material, she'd found a dressmaker. It fitted her almost too well. She looked sleek in it and not too demure. In fact, she looked more sophisticated than Ted had ever seen her and he was somewhat uneasy to find her so. The riotous dark curls had been brushed back severely from her forehead. From the top of her head, however, they cascaded to the nape of her neck in a most unmannerly fashion and one was drawn forward behind each ear to curl there, at the lobe. And the brushing back wouldn't last long. For Val's curls were really permanent and had a way of escaping brush, lotion, discipline.

"Will I do?" she asked.

"You look pretty splendid," he said gloomily, conscious of his much worn and brushed serge. But when you're paying a heavy rent and have to keep up your stock you can't go in for dinner jackets.

"I didn't mean to. It's only an afternoon dress, cocktail or something, dinner at home, or picnic in the backyard," she assured him. She put on her fur coat which had seen service for a number of years and cocked a tiny black turban over one eye. "Let's go," she suggested.

Mrs. Loring surveyed her child. "You look sweet," she said, "have a good time. Don't keep her out too late, Ted, but if you do, how do you like your breakfast eggs?"

Mr. Loring grunted from behind a newspaper. But when the door had closed behind the two he dropped the paper and his air of indifference. "Look here, this Village business . . ."

"Don't you upset yourself," advised his wife, "it doesn't mean anything. Just a lot of youngsters. It doesn't matter much what they go in for, does it, art or tennis, football or internationalism. Most of them will recover."

"I know. But I meant Ted Morrison and Val. If it's serious. . . . I tell you I don't like it, Marcia."

"Then don't tell her," his wife said practically, "if it's the last thing you never do! It would be fatal. Ted's a nice boy. He's good for her, in a way, and she's good for him.

As to its being serious, well, if it is we haven't much to say about it, have we? And it isn't . . . I don't think it is," she concluded doubtfully.

On the steps in the sweet cool April night: "I'll get a taxi," offered Ted.

"We'll take a subway," decided Val firmly. "Don't be a nut."

"In those clothes?" He indicated her grandeur.

"In these clothes. They've been worn in subways before this. Come on, let's get going, I do so hate to miss anything."

Jimmy Morris lived in something called a penthouse. It was on top of a more or less decrepit building but there were two floors and a rooftop. Jimmy herself, a middle-aged woman, with rusty hair and a rusty voice, welcomed Val absently and kindly.

"Is this your new girl, Ted? She's lovely . . . I'd like to paint her . . . I suspect she is more intelligent than she looks. No, Flora isn't here yet. . . . For heaven's sake, Whistler, will you leave me alone?"

This last was shrieked. Val looked about, alarmed, and discovered a pop-eyed Peke pawing at his mistress's trailing skirts.

Jimmy had taken off her smock for the occasion. She was done up regardless in a green frock which had seen better days; she was an untidy woman with a small private income, an authentic passion for art, and a small, mouselike talent which would have expressed itself neatly in another generation in painting China. But she went in for murals. She had a heart which was still on the gold standard, but she never remembered anything or anyone very long.

The room in which the party was taking place was crowded. Some of the guests were oldish and some were extremely young. Some were good-looking and others were not. The motley collection of garments gave the affair the effect of a costume ball. Val looked at a couple of girls in tweeds and decided that she was overdressed. She looked at a woman in a backless evening frock and decided that she should have worn her white. It was that kind of party. There were no tails and no dinner coats. The men didn't go in for that, apparently. During the course of the evening, she counted three pullovers, two velvet smoking jackets and one with Byronic collar, complete with flowing tie.

"Mercy!" she said to herself, inadequately.

But she had a grand time. She always had a grand time. She didn't much mind the questions some of them asked her. She said to herself, Poor dears, they don't know any better, they try so hard to be startling. She didn't even mind the man who planted himself in front of her and Ted and said sonorously, "But you're dressed all wrong, sweetheart. You should wear jerkin and hose and run through the Forest of Arden, your cap in your hand and the sun on your lovely curls. . . . Rosalind, 'from the east to western Ind, no jewel is like Rosalind. . . .' "

He departed. "Good grief!" said Val mildly.

"He used to be a Shakespearean actor," explained Ted.

That explained also the rather long hair, the sunken eyes. Val said, "Well, he's nice, but I don't expect he was a very good actor."

"No," said Ted, "I don't expect so either." He looked at her and they laughed. He was proud of her suddenly, proud to be seen with her here, the prettiest girl in the room, the nicest. He said seriously, "Don't think badly of them, Val, they do mean awfully well. This isn't my crowd, not really. Mine's a little different . . . more — well, more stable, working for something. Sometime you must come to a meeting with me. We've a man speaking next month who will wring your heart. He's an Austrian . . . a social democrat, of course."

When Flora came in it was late. By that time Val had forgotten her and certainly Jimmy had. Jimmy looked at her blankly and Flora asked, "Don't you remember me,

Jimmy? You're giving the party for me."

"Why, of course," said Jimmy, her lined face clearing. "So I am." Then she spoke a little tartly, "If I'd forgotten," she said, "it was because we were getting on all right without you."

There were quarts and quarts of a fairly harmless and very acid red wine. There were thick delicatessen sandwiches. There was a lot of laughter. Someone played a guitar and someone recited and along about one o'clock Flora stood up and folded her hands in front of her and spoke three or four poems. Val's eyes stung with sudden tears. She whispered afterwards, "But they are lovely, Ted, they really are."

They were exquisite. Not great perhaps, but heart-haunting. Val thought, watching Flora afterwards, watching her shake her head till the fair hair belled out in the way she had, watching her preen herself, It isn't fair, it's a really big talent, too big for her, somehow.

Yet she didn't know Flora well, she reminded herself, she mustn't misjudge her. Perhaps she wasn't shallow and vain and silly, after all.

Still, she did take Ted off in a corner, for a long time, and with a malicious remark and a more malicious look, "After all, you have him every day, all day, darling."

It was a little later, and just about two, when the young man, who, so far as Val was concerned, was nameless, dropped to his knees before the divan on which she sat and told her that if she would marry him in Greenwich, he'd make her "terribly happy — for a week — two weeks — after that it doesn't matter . . . most people aren't happy as long."

She was struggling in his sudden and really upsetting embrace while the people about them laughed and commented, casually enough, when Ted looked around, removed Flora's hands from his shoulders and made his way to the divan. He ordered, "Here, cut that out!" in a very businesslike manner and gave the importunate gentleman a slight, but satisfactory push. The wooer sprawled and Val laughed and presently she found herself out in the clean air with her hat on the back of her head and her coat over her arm and Ted beside her.

"He didn't mean it," he was explaining kindly.

"I'm afraid he didn't," she agreed instantly, "and I really can take care of myself. Here, hold my coat." She shrugged herself into it, poked her hat forward over her eyes. "It was fun," she said, "until you dragged me away."

"I'd had enough," he said briefly.

He hailed a taxi. This time Val didn't expostulate. Monday she'd sell a dozen books. She was tired and her eyes smarted from the smoke and she hadn't much liked the look of Flora draped over Ted's shoulder.

They drove uptown in silence. When they reached her door and the cab halted, Ted sat perfectly still. Val nudged him impatiently.

"We're home," she said. "Or are you asleep by any chance?"

"No, I'm not asleep," he said, "or else it's a dream . . . maybe it's a nightmare, I don't know."

He took her very abruptly into his arms and kissed her three times, hard. He said, when he had released her, and she sat back too astonished for speech, "I don't care what you think of me."

"I'm not angry," she answered carefully.

"I don't care about that, either. Get out," said Ted rudely, "it's long past your bedtime."

Val got out, quite alone. She went up the steps, quite alone. She put her key in the door and heard Ted shout, apparently to the driver of the taxi, "I don't care *where* you drive me but do something about it, will you?"

Thoughtfully Val went tiptoeing up the stairs and removed her finery and brushed her teeth and washed her face and said her prayers. She said these according to her own way, which wasn't a formula at all, but a short conversation carried on somewhere in the depths of her mind and heart. And then she went to bed. She thought, I liked his kissing me. But Bill's kissed me, and I liked that, too. But Ted needs me and Bill doesn't . . . I wonder?

She fell asleep still wondering. And when she woke it was Sunday noon and Bill was waiting for her with the car and they drove out into the faintly green Westchester hills for lunch.

On Monday morning Val went to the shop. She wasn't feeling as happy as she usually felt Monday mornings. Bill had been very serious, for him. Once she'd said to him, "I couldn't marry you, Bill, you're no more serious than I am, we'd make such a frivolous couple." But yesterday he hadn't been frivolous. This Ted business worried him more than he'd admitted. He admitted it now. "I can't stand by and watch you slipping away from me like this."

And in the end they'd come home, and hadn't talked much on the way, and he hadn't stayed for Sunday supper as he usually did. She was so fond of him, she couldn't bear to hurt him but there was Ted . . . and she couldn't make up her mind about Ted. Or her heart, either. She told Bill that, clasping and unclasping her hands. And he'd listened, rather white, and said gently, "All right, Val, it's your day, you know. It's up to you. I won't bother you any more."

So on Monday she walked into the shop. If Ted said . . . If Ted asked her . . .

He was there ahead of her, waiting for her. He looked as if he hadn't slept. He looked nervous, jumpy. And before she had time to take off her hat he spoke in an unnecessarily loud voice, as if he couldn't believe his own ears, but was trying to convince them, as well as her:

"Look here, Val, I'm sorry about the other night. I don't know what got into me. Only, if you're going to stay on here and work, you've got to get this straight. You mustn't expect me to make love to you because of what happened. I don't intend to. Love and business don't mix."

# Chapter V

The sound of his own voice in Ted's ears making this unspeakable statement terrified him. But he had to make it. This couldn't go on any longer. Magnanimously he admitted that it had been his fault — not all of it, but the other night, in any event. And you couldn't mix business and sex. Oh, he knew people did. He had not only read about it, but he had seen it with his two eyes and without glasses. But he couldn't afford to — it was out of the question. Besides, he wasn't in love with Val, he was in love with Flora. No, damn it, he wasn't in love with Flora, but he had been, and you didn't fall in and out of love like that . . . not and remain a sane, reasoning human being.

Val made a little sound. It wasn't exactly a gasp, and it wasn't exactly a miniature wail, a whispered scream. It was the sound Keturie might have made had you smacked her face. Ted disciplined his eyes and fixed them upon his assistant and for a moment knew a genuine and breath-taking fear. He had never seen a face so white, and certainly he had never seen eyes so blazing and unnatural a green.

He said quickly:

"I haven't been very tactful about this — but you understand?"

"Oh, I understand, all right," said Val evenly. "And you need not bother to explain further. As a matter of fact —" her chin went up and her color came back, "as a matter of fact I came along this morning prepared to say something of the kind myself." She essayed a laugh, achieved it, and was so pleased with the synthetic result . . . "you'd never know it from the genuine," that she did it again, marveling at her ease. I must do it with mirrors, she thought, astonished at and proud of her feminine duplicity. "So let's forget it — or," she amended at his faint look of alarm, "in order that we won't forget it, how about a contract?"

"A contract?" echoed Ted feebly.

Still hatted, still lightly furred, Val marched herself without further speech back to his desk and seized a sheet of paper. She sat herself down and scratched busily with a pen sacred to the small, meticulous penmanship of Mr. Morrison himself. Completely bewildered, he nevertheless permitted himself a fleeting sigh of discouragement. Val wrote a stern, black hand and pressed down hard on the nib. The pen would never be the same again. Neither would he, he reflected, after reading the savagely blotted manuscript which she presently handed him.

It was full of curious to-wits and to-whom-evers and had a cockeyed resemblance to something, if not legal, nevertheless imposing. It was quite clear, once the verbiage was disposed of and it was to the point.

We, Valentine Loring, hereinafter to be known as party of the first part, and Ted Morrison, hereinafter to be known as party of the second part, do depose and solemnly swear that while our business relations in the Morrison Bookshop do continue we shall not indulge in any of the softer sentiments and their concomitants sometimes known as making love, the penalty for the slightest lapse being the immediate severance of our relationship.

There was a good deal more to it. Val had specified, her underlip caught between even white teeth, and her pen racing to keep abreast of her flying and curious thoughts. Ted, holding the paper in his hand, was amazed at the fertility of the female imagination. She had put them all in, the things about which he would never have permitted himself to dream. Men were different. Something absurd and urgent and probably sheerly biological overcame you and you grabbed the girl and kissed her heartily, but certainly you didn't sit down beforehand and draw up a diagram. In this document Val had neatly itemized all the things which must not happen, from the holding of hands to the kissing of lips. It was, he told himself, cold-blooded and slightly indecent. Why heaven had made women so practical was something he couldn't understand, but that they were practical he understood for the first time in his life.

"There," said Val, and laughed at him, "sign it, Casanova."

"Sign it?" he repeated. "But, Val, of all the ridiculous . . . just because you're mad," he concluded with a flash of insight, but most indiscreetly.

"Mad!" She snorted delicately. "Mad? I'm delighted. You make me tired," she went on, rising to stand before him, one foot tapping the floor. "You — you stuffed shirt, whatever made you think that I wanted you to make love to me? I suppose you came to the shop this morning thinking I'd be sitting on the steps waiting for the touch of your vanished hand or some such nauseating personal attention. Of all the male arrogance. Poor li'l gal, sez you to yourself, how she loves me!"

Now *he* was mad. He was very mad. And Val perceived it with a sudden glow of pleasure. He took her by the shoulders and he shook her. "You can't talk that way to me." This was a purely hypothetical statement or something as she had talked that way and would again if only he would let her go and her teeth would stop chattering. "You can't talk that way to me," he reiterated firmly, "you didn't mind Saturday night. You *liked* it!"

He released her suddenly, so suddenly that she slid back against the utilitarian desk for support. He released her because he had discovered that he was so urgently angry with her that in another moment he would kiss her. And there lay the contract upon the floor, its insulting terms staring up at him in black and white.

"Of course I liked it," agreed Val, on a note of what seemed to him pure, almost idiotic pleasure, "it was swell. It was part of the party. But the party is over, and since you feel as you do — which is the way I feel too," she added hastily, "I suggest that we do our partying elsewhere and with other people. Pick up that contract," she ordered crossly.

Stupefied, he did so. Val thrust the pen into his hand. "There. At the desk. Sign it!"

Immeasurably annoyed, he signed, and Val, recapturing the pen, completed with her triumphant signature, heavily underlined, its utter ruin. She then looked about her. "We need a witness," she said, "two witnesses, for good measure."

Half a minute later she had darted out of

86

the room and returned with a Swedish gentleman who was doing some odd jobs on the floor above. He was as willing as Barkis, but Val's Swedish was not in form this morning. She tried him in German, desperately, *"Bitte, wollen sie —?"* She stopped. Would it be *haben die Gute* or *die Gute haben?* Heaven alone knew. Finally she thrust the pen at him and with her finger on the line which, even if not dotted, would serve, "Name. Write," she said loudly and slowly.

The Swede hesitated. Perhaps he wanted to consult his lawyer. This might mean prison. On the other hand, it might mean money in the bank. But Val stood before him and made remarkable gestures. Baffled, he signed, slowly and with Spencerian flourish, and fled. The contract lacked a second witness, however. Keturie would serve. Val seized her, and inked her little paw. There. On the bottom of the contract, the cat's-paw, perfect.

Keturie retired to a corner and thoughtfully licked off the ink. It made her feel sick and she regarded Val with dislike for the rest of the day.

Val contemplated the completed work complacently.

"There," she said. "We should have two copies, of course. . . . I'll make another and initial it. This one goes in the safe."

"I suppose you think you're very funny?" inquired Ted stiffly.

She smiled at him radiantly. She wanted to weep, to fling herself into the nearest and most sympathetic arms, which were certainly not those of her chief, and to humiliate herself with reproaches. But these things she could not do. She gave Ted the paper. So far she had not been entrusted with the combination of the safe. She stood over him while he fumbled at the dials and the door swung open. There wasn't much in the safe, she thought, with a catch at her heart. It was the complete Mother Hubbard's cupboard. But now there was something in it. The door shut again and Ted rose from his knees.

"I hope you're satisfied," he told her balefully. "Of all the asinine procedures!" He was very much wounded in the region of his male pride. Such a wound is not only painful at the moment of infliction but is open to infection. He had been square with this irritating atom of femininity and lo! she had hoisted him on his own petard, whatever that meant. He wasn't sure.

Val said, "Thank you," demurely.

The owner of the shop sat glumly at his desk regarding the plight of his pen, which now scratched and spluttered when he put it to paper. Val sat down. She said:

"Now let's talk seriously."

Lord, what had she been doing? He dropped the pen, more in sorrow than in anger, and swiveled about to face her. He hadn't assumed his glasses at the moment and his eyes were very blue and very young, she thought, steeling her heart.

"As I pointed out to you some time ago," said Val, "you can't fire me, because you haven't hired me. And now that we have that scrap of paper in the safe," she added with simple malice, "you can't make it so disagreeable for me that I will leave of my own accord." She regarded his rising color with the utmost satisfaction and continued suavely, "So, evidently I am here to stay. But I'd like to put it on a business basis, please. No, don't interrupt me. I know you can't afford to pay me a salary. But I'd like to buy a share in the shop."

"You what?" cried Ted, glowering with astonishment.

"I have a bond," confided Val serenely. "It is a very nice bond. It was once worth five thousand dollars and it's worth nearly that now. There are no strings to it. I don't even have to wait till I'm twenty-one. There isn't a soul in the world who can stop me from marching myself to the bank and delving in a deposit box and taking it out, seals and all, and selling it." She added, "And what with one thing and another, having been in the shop for a couple of months, I can safely conclude that if I do sell it and give you the money, it would entitle me to a third of the profits, if any."

He said slowly:

"I don't know if you're joking or not, Val. I rather imagine that you are. I suppose you dislike me that much."

"Why should I?" she asked coolly.

His instinct informed him why she should, but another and more cautious warned him not to reveal this to her. He went on, "You know, joking aside, that five thousand dollars or any part of five thousand would be a life-saver. There are accounts I have to meet, and a note . . . oh, a thousand things. But —"

"No buts," forbade Val briskly. "I like the shop. I think we could do something with it. You're too precious, Ted. You run this place as if it were an *objet d'art* instead of a solid business proposition. I'll take a little extra time at lunch and go to the bank. And you'll get hold of your lawyer, if you have one, and first thing you know I'll be a silent partner."

A misnomer, he thought, with a fleeting grin. Val looked at him sharply. She wished she had been gifted with mind reading. He said, after a moment, "All right. On the condition that your parents approve. Suppose I come up to the house tonight, and talk it over with them." They'll never consent, he told himself reassuringly.

"Not tonight," said Val swiftly, "Bill's coming."

He wasn't, but he would if she told him to. Besides, she had to have time to browbeat her parents into something bordering on acquiescence.

A customer came in, providentially enough. He was one of Ted's very own, a mild and amiable elderly man who enjoyed browsing. Val, watching his snaillike progress, said to herself, If once I get the thing in my hands, I've a notion I'll put up a sign: No Browsing Allowed. Disgusting term. Why not graze? The truth of the matter is that browsers don't pay because browsers don't buy.

She went about her dusting, her alert eye on the stock. The small shelf containing the mysteries was depleted. She recalled that *Three Murders Last Midnight* had sold well and rented still better. She would call up the jobber and reorder. She cast an oblique glance at Ted, still conversing with the browser. The door opened, a gust of April wind, so clear and fine in texture that one felt it had a color and that the color which a rain pool reflects when the sky is clear, blew through the shop

91

and caused the browser to look at Ted un-happily. He had a weak throat. The door slammed back and another customer came in. This was a lady clad in doublet and hose. On second sight, she was not, but so slim her skirt, so attractive the legs she made haste to display, so belted the jacket with its collar of — one knew at once — sable, and so medieval the haircut, that she gave the troubadour impression.

It was Flora. Having discarded plush curtaining for something which might easily have been Hattie Carnegie, she had come to the bookshop to torment its owner.

Ted spoke to her, paling a little. This fine creature, this successful woman — but, after all, did a few lectures and a few poems constitute Russian sable? — had once been his only love. She said, in that quick light voice of hers, in which the words fluttered like the beating of bright wings, "I'll wait, Ted . . . don't let me interrupt you. . . . Oh, there's Val."

Girlishly she ran across the space between her and Valentine. And devotedly they embraced. They knew each other so slightly, and yet so well, they disliked each other so cautiously that Christian names and embraces followed as naturally as night follows day, or income taxes the ides of March.

"My dear," crooned Flora, and drew Val toward the back room, "you left far too soon the other night. The party had just started."

"I'm a working woman," Val reminded her, smiling.

"On Sunday?"

"On Sunday I work at being a lady of leisure," said Val, and smiled again.

They looked at each other for a long moment. Flora dropped her voice when next she spoke, "Don't tell me Ted's making a go of this at last," she uttered disapprovingly.

"Rather," Val told her, going extremely British. "Things have picked up amazingly. . . ." She halted. She did not complete her sentence "since I came." But she knew that Flora understood it. Instead she said, "But how marvelous you are looking!"

Flora shrugged. She explained, with a disillusioned inflection, "It's part of the act, of course. I signed a lecture contract yesterday."

She had become completely commercial. It was an error to believe that her work would suffer. Flora had a genuine and lovely gift. Because she was now enabled to eat, that gift would not desert her. Poetry can thrive on caviar, borscht, lake trout stewed in white wine, and breast of guinea hen with avocados, as well as upon dry crusts and Chianti. To be truthful, Flora was still writing and writing as well as any woman poet in the United States. She had never looked better nor had she been in more excellent health. She now had an agent and a lecture manager and on the previous Tuesday a gentleman influential in the arts had announced upon the radio that this new talent which had sprung into being in the dour streets of Manhattan, "this incredibly pretty" creature would in five years find herself represented in all the college text books in America and possibly England as well.

Val asked suddenly:

"Look — want to do Ted a favor?"

"Dear Ted," said Flora, smiling, "of course I do."

"When's your book coming out?"

Flora told her. Val calculated and nodded. "Then of course you'll be awfully in demand, autographing copies and so forth. But can't you for friendship's sake give the shop a first chance? We'll give you a tea," said Val, thinking rapidly, "and advertise it well, and send out special invitations. Do, Flora," said Val appealingly, "it would mean so much to the shop."

The browser departed. Ted came into the back room. Flora said brightly, "I hope you sold a lot of books."

"Old skinflint," began Ted gloomily, and was about to relate that the browser only browsed and did his buying in the secondhand shops, when Val broke in quickly, "Oh, he's one of our best customers, Flora, a collector . . . pays fabulous sums. Look here, Ted, Flora's consented to let us give a tea for her on the day of publication —"

Flora interrupted. She couldn't do that. Her publishers were giving a cocktail party at the Savoy-Plaza, she added deprecatingly. "Then," said Val, "on the next day . . . or as soon as possible."

Presently Flora departed, a little perturbed to discover herself outside the shop without having borrowed a book. But her spirits rose as she walked briskly toward the Avenue. Things were breaking nicely for her. It was fun finding herself a celebrity. A very dominant woman who dictated the reading hours of three-quarters of Park Avenue was introducing her at a book luncheon presently and she was assured that after the affair she would find herself with dozens of invitations to prowl and roar in the lion cages installed in various penthouses. Flora was perfectly happy. Or was she? In the clear amber of her innocent vanity the proverbial fly postured, static, his wings folded. Of course Ted was an idealistic fool, and could not understand or justify success. There were hundreds of men more attractive . . . and yet. . . .

Flora walked along. Somewhere in the coiled reaches of her little brain a stanza formed . . . classic in its simplicity, measured in cadence . . . cruel and feline. She had never liked red hair. Could she not say so, metrically?

Months later the poem appeared. It occupied a whole page of smooth paper in a magazine which was both costly and civilized. And Valentine, reading it, permitted herself to wonder, Doesn't she know she's rewriting "St. Louis Blues"?

But that came later. Back in the bookshop Ted scowled at his almost, and never silent, partner.

"What's the big idea?" he permitted himself to ask.

"Ted, you mean Flora? Why not? She's an enormous success. She'll be a bigger one. You'll see. If we give her the tea . . . everyone will come, all we ask and others besides. We'll get new accounts. It will give us prestige."

"She's spoiled," he said gloomily. "She isn't at all as she used to be."

"Why not?" asked Val.

"Oh, I don't know." It was hard to put it into words, but he tried. "When I first met her she was all eyes and collar bones . . . half starved, believing in herself. We used to sit

96

up till dawn, talking . . . about things which mattered . . . they mattered to her then . . . integrity of purpose, the clear demand of beauty —"

Val said gently:

"Just because she's beginning to have some of the easy rewards — and certainly she deserves them, Ted — it doesn't mean that she's forgotten all that."

She thought, but even three poems in a national magazine and forthcoming lecture trips and an advance against royalties can't run to Russian sables . . . or can they?

Ted was looking away from her. He said, "She was — lovely. Gallant. That's what she was, gallant and frail and informed with genius."

She thought, He's still in love with her. Doubt shook her. She thought of those arguments over integrity which lasted until dawn.

It wasn't any of her business. Whatever the relationship had been between an unsuccessful bookshop owner and a poet whose voice had not then been heard, it was over now. Or was it?

Val went home that evening through the blue April dusk, with the uninquiring stars looking down upon the perpendicular city, her head bent against the wind. She would have a difficult time persuading her family that she was in earnest about the bond. But until she persuaded them Ted would have none of it. An honest young man, she informed herself, smiling not too happily.

She thought, When I came in the shop this morning and he spoke to me as he did, why didn't I drop down dead at his feet, of humiliation? I ought to despise him. I *do* despise him. I could see him boiled in oil, drawn and quartered, hanged and on the rack, and thrown to the lions for good measure, without a moment's grief or regret. Then why, she asked herself, trudging presently up her own front doorsteps, then why am I doing this . . . buying my way into an uncertain venture?

She'd show him. She'd show him that a woman could enter upon a business partnership with a man and without sentiment. She'd make him a success despite himself. Whether he liked it or not. And eventually he would have to acknowledge her help.

She put her key in the lock and went to the upstairs sitting room to acquaint Marcia Loring of the events of the day. Val could make a day at the bookstore seem gay and exciting. Marcia listened. "Nice," was all she had to say. "By the way, Bill rang you up, he's coming around tonight, on the off chance you might be free."

"Why didn't he call me at the shop?"

"He just called now, honey."

"All right," said Val. "I think I'll make him take me to a movie. There's that Garbo picture I missed . . . I'd like to see that. I adore to see Garbo. When I leave the theater I sort of slink out, with veiled eyes and a wide mobile mouth. I feel mysterious and tragic and lonely, a perfect *femme fatale*. It's good for me."

Her mother laughed. "You're a chameleon. Tomorrow night I suppose you'll go see Gracie Allen and when you come home you won't make sense."

"Tomorrow night," said Val, taking her literally, "Ted's coming to talk business."

"Business?" Marcia lifted a groomed eyebrow.

"I know you don't take me seriously," said Val. She went over to her mother's chair and sat beside it on a hassock and leaned her arms on her mother's knees and looked up at her. At the moment, although she bore no physical resemblance to Raphael's round, bodiless cherubs, she had a look of devotion and simplicity. "I want to sell my bond and buy an interest in the shop," she explained.

Marcia was taken completely by surprise. There had been another occasion on which Val had wanted to sell her bond. That had been when things were going very badly for the Lorings. Her father had dissuaded her, but only after a stormy scene, ending with tears, which, as Val shed them seldom, were so hard to resist.

"But that bond," began her mother gently.

"I know. For my marriage. When I marry. I've heard it all before." She laughed suddenly. "But, look, suppose I marry a rich man, I mean really rich? The bond would be a fleabite. It's not doing me any good now, sitting smugly in a safety deposit box waiting for the scissors to snip through the coupons. I want to have fun with it. The shop's all right, Mother. If it weren't for worrying over the immediate niggling little things, it would be more than all right. It's worth the risk. I want to stay on there, I like the work. But voluntary work doesn't mean a thing, and Ted can't afford to pay me. If I buy an interest, I'll have some voice in the running of the place. I've a dozen ideas, and one of them *must* be good!"

Her mother said, after a moment:

"It's your own money, but with times so uncertain . . . your father will object strongly." She hesitated and then determined to speak her mind and that, expurgated, of her husband. "Are you sure you aren't becoming pretty fond of Ted Morrison, Valentine? I mean, isn't that what actuates you?"

Val's small face was suffused with healthy

blood. She sat up very straight. Little Miss Muffet, waiting for the spider. She said slowly, "No, I'm not fond of him. I like him well enough. He makes me tired, though, he's so impractical. We don't agree very well, on a lot of things. Please don't worry about Ted and me, Mother, it's a purely business arrangement."

Mrs. Loring was almost convinced. "Well, you'll have to talk it over with your father. Run along now and get ready for dinner, and there's a smudge on your nose."

# Chapter VI

Valentine, descending to dinner — how, she wondered, could people live in one-floor apartments when half the fun of meals was in coming downstairs to them? — caught a glimpse of her father's face in the hall mirror. He was not, she decided instantly, in an amenable mood. She did not need her mother's quirked eyebrow and warning gesture to inform her that the head of the house would not be open to any revolutionary suggestion whatever until he had been soothed by warm food and the light conversation of his adoring womenfolk.

After dinner, when the parental brow had relaxed, Bill arrived. He entered as usual in his casual fashion, amiable and unperturbed and perfectly willing to go forth to a neighboring motion-picture house and view Miss Garbo at her most adorably tragic. He said, as he and Valentine drove over, "But there's just one condition — you may weep all you want to — I know you wouldn't have your money's worth if you didn't . . . and speaking of money's worth, do you remember the time we went to the show where the lovely Christian martyr was flung to the lions and you kept your eyes shut for three-quarters of the time?"

"Will you please get back to the point? Talk about women digressing! Of course I remember. I kept poking you and asking 'has she been et?' "

"Et isn't the word for what they did to her," said Bill reminiscently, "but to return to our lamb chops — *if* you cry, remember that I afford you a shoulder to cry upon and also if you wish to hold my hand, you may."

The Garbo picture was sad. Valentine wept. She knew perfectly well that this pleasant emotion of grief was purely vicarious and that she was weeping for herself and not for the lonely and appealing Greta. It was, however, a most marvelous release and she cried until the tip of her nose was quite red and her eyelids faintly pink as well as weary. The clasp of Bill's strong and familiar hand was extremely consoling. She'd been smacked once today and to be comforted now seemed entirely in order.

When the lights went up again she powdered her nose and sniffled, with a catch in her breath, "I've had a perfectly gorgeous time." The strange man on the other side of her, an insensitive brute, laughed heartily and Bill rewarded him with a murderous glare which nevertheless managed to inform him

103

that he knew just how he felt and weren't women simple and idiotic and rather sweet?

"Let's go and eat," suggested Bill when they left the theater. "I believe you need a restorative."

Val agreed with him and presently they faced one another across a small glass-topped table. In front of Val was a large, whipped cream decorated chocolate soda and a sandwich of Swiss cheese on rye! A more horrible combination had never occurred to her escort, who shuddered slightly and drank, not without grimaces, a long, exceedingly sour lemonade. Val, toying thoughtfully with her brace of straws, was conscious of an inner glow of gratitude that she need not watch her weight. She said so complacently. And then she added:

"At that I may lose some eventually, I'm going into business."

"You?" asked Bill. "I thought you were in business." His tone, which was tolerant and paternal, infuriated her. She looked at him with some hostility and replied, with dignity:

"I mean really business. I'm going to buy into Ted's shop. I'm going to sell my bond."

The lemonade glass rocketed alarmingly with the sweeping gesture of Bill's hand. He righted it. "Have you gone completely nuts?"

"Bill, don't take that attitude. I've almost won Mother over, and I'll have to tackle Dad tomorrow night. Ted isn't convinced yet, either. I mean he won't let me do a thing until Mother and Father have consented."

Bill didn't believe that, not quite. His mind registered the fact that Morrison was probably smarter than he had thought him. For it was certainly on the cards that he would jump at the chance. Bill was singularly upset. After all, he had offered Val a partnership time and time again, with no string attached, and no money down.

He said:

"My dear infant, I understand of course that you'd like a share in the shop as long as you are devoting your time to it. But you must realize how precarious such an investment is, at the best, and especially nowadays. I must say I shan't think very highly of Morrison if he permits you to risk your money."

"I want to risk it," said Val stubbornly.

Bill pushed the unfinished drink aside. The lemonade was indeed very sour. So were the grapes. He stated, after a minute, "You do care a lot about him, after all."

"Who, me?" asked Val wildly ungrammatical. "About Ted Morrison? You're goofy," she added with conviction. "Why, I wouldn't look at him twice if he were the last man on earth."

"Oh, yes, you would!" murmured Bill.

"Well, perhaps," she conceded with a fleeting smile, "but anyway, not now. He isn't the last man on earth as it happens. No. But he's got a good property in that shop, Bill, and it isn't being handled right. He could make money. I don't mean a fortune. But cash money, enough to live decently. And he won't. He's just dumb," she concluded inadequately.

Bill didn't think so. Any man who had Val working for him gratis, and offering to stake her one and only available bond in his present and his future, wasn't dumb. He was very bright. In fact, he was probably the brightest citizen of Manhattan Island.

He confessed after a minute:

"I hate to think of it. Look here — wouldn't you let me — ?" He thought, astonished, Well, am I that much of a damned fool?

Val was interrupting quickly:

"No, I wouldn't. That's sweet of you, Bill, but I couldn't, of course . . . and Ted wouldn't permit you to."

"Why not?" asked Bill. "My word's as good as your bond in this case, isn't it?" He was proud of that. It was rather neat.

"He doesn't approve of you," said Val.

"Of me?" Bill looked amazed. "Of me . . . than whom no more upright young man ever paid for a death-dealing soda and a

106

lethal sandwich?"

"You needn't sell yourself to me," she announced gaily, "I've been sold for a long time."

"C.O.D.," he told her. "But seriously, what's wrong with me . . . at least so far as Morrison is concerned?"

"Well, you're a parasite or something," she explained gravely, "you are an idler, you live on inherited income, you cumber the earth, or is it cucumber? I've never been very clear on that score."

Bill grunted. His pleasant face became less pleasant. He said, violently for him, "That sort of talk makes me sick. The voice of disappointment. If someone dropped a few hundred thousand in your young friend's lap tomorrow, he would sing a different tune. Do, re, mi — emphasis on the do."

"I don't believe it," said Val.

She didn't. She despised Ted Morrison, of course; if he dropped dead a week from Wednesday she wouldn't care, and so far as that went, if her own personal emotions were consulted, if she never saw him again it would be at least forty years too soon. But, she reminded herself, she could still be fair. She had to be fair, and she didn't believe that Ted's convictions had arisen from his circumstances. She couldn't and didn't see eye to eye with him but she believed in his integrity and she said so, a trifle hotly.

"Well," Bill replied, rising and clutching the check, "he may be all you say, all for one and one for all, a canvasback in every pot and an equal split of all rewards, no matter who has worked for them . . . but I doubt it. Still, we'll never know."

He reflected that even were he a man so rich that he could afford an experiment in human nature — he toyed with the idea of having Mr. Morrison legally informed that an uncle in New Zealand had died and left him half a million pounds sterling — even were he in such a position his magnanimity could not go quite so far in order to prove to Valentine Loring that the Colonel himself as well as Judy O'Grady's old man were brothers under the skin.

Yet when he delivered her at the house and lingered with her for a moment in the hall, he stood looking down at her, wondering why in heaven's name he continued this hopeless and irritating pursuit, she tilted her face and he kissed her without further thought, unless an amazed gratitude be thought. Then she pulled herself away.

"That didn't mean anything," she warned him in a panic.

"Val, if I didn't know you so well, there

are a lot of names I could call you."

"I have heard 'em all," she said. Her dark red hair was tumbled and her eyes were bright. She was a little thing, a man could pick her up in his arms and run away with her. She would scratch and kick and even bite — but —

"You ought to be ashamed of yourself." He was trying hard to be stern and wounded and disapproving, but he found himself laughing.

"I know," she admitted, it appeared penitently, but you couldn't tell, with Val. "And I shall be tomorrow morning at a quarter past eight. But just now . . . well," she said defiantly, "I *wanted* to be kissed."

He kissed her again, over her protests. When he released her she had color in her cheeks, bright and brave. She said, "You're so darned old-fashioned. I suppose you'll send the announcement to the papers tomorrow."

She thought, I don't go around kissing people and he knows it. He knows about himself . . . not often . . . and he doesn't know about Ted — once. And he knows that I'm not cheap —

Bill held out his hand so suddenly that she was startled into putting her own in it. He shook it gravely and briskly and impersonally. He said, "Thanks for a delightful evening, Miss Loring. I'll be seein' you," and took himself off. Val stood in the hall and pondered. She flung her hat, which was dreadfully askew in any case, upon the floor. She ran her fingers through her hair. She thought, Bill's a grand person . . . he's still unexpected after all these years. I suppose he'd stay unexpected even if I married him.

She trudged up the stairs, leaving her hat where it was. She thought, her hand on the polished banister, But I don't want to marry him!

On the following evening Ted came to the Loring house. He had seen very little of Val all day. Business had taken him out of the shop and when he returned to it he found her entertaining three customers and a member of the Salvation Army. Moreover Keturie was not very well and demanded skilled attention between clients. Val was very self-reproachful. It must have been the ink, she mourned. She coaxed the reluctant cat with a saucer of warm and doctored milk. A little electric grill had been her idea and contribution to the shop. "If you must bring in sandwiches, you might as well toast them," she'd said.

Keturie, like all cats, infinitely preferred to suffer in complete solitude but she was a courteous creature and bore her cross of petting and crooning with a certain weak amiability which was very endearing.

Ted had little opportunity to talk privately with his assistant. A young man wandered in with a portfolio of woodcuts under his arm and wondered whether they might be shown in the shop and sold on commission. They were remarkably good woodcuts as Ted could see and he spent over an hour in the back room with the artist, discussing ways and means. However, at closing time, he spoke to Val directly.

"Have you thought it over?"

"What?"

He stuttered a little. What a woman. He said, after a moment, "I mean what you said yesterday — your proposition."

"There is something about that word," she mused, "which much mislikes me."

"Val, please be serious."

"Oh." She came back from remote vistas, purely out of politeness, as it were. "You mean about buying an interest in the shop. Of course I haven't thought it over. Once I make up my mind I never have to think things over," she explained magnificently.

She must have been a handful as a child, he reflected. He reflected further that a course of leather slipper in the parental hand in some improvised woodshed might have done her incalculable good at an earlier period of her life.

"Have you spoken to your parents?" he asked her as gently as one speaks to an idiot child.

"Mother thinks it's a marvelous idea," reported Val mendaciously. "I haven't said anything to Father yet. You'll be along this evening? Half past eightish."

"All right," agreed Ted gloomily. He felt utterly sunk. He envied the vanished aristocracy which had gone with such publicized glee to the guillotine. As a matter of fact he didn't believe they had. They'd been sunk too.

Val went on home. Ted stayed in the shop. There were evenings when it remained open until six or later. This was such an evening. No one came so he sat down to consider his position.

Here, as he saw it, was that position. He had never wanted Valentine Loring in his life or in his shop. She had slid, literally, into both. She had taken possession of him. She was one of those deceptive females from whom it behooved a man to keep away. She had great physical charm and a mentality which she managed too successfully to conceal when it entertained her to do so. She was, in fact, a little like Keturie.

He had permitted himself much against his will to allow her to amuse herself with the shop. In all justice he had to admit that she had done well. She sold a lot of books, for that particular shop. It had never occurred to him that the bookshop business might be a little better off for a judicious touch of sex appeal. It occurred to him now and he resented it bitterly.

He hadn't for a moment believed that the arrangement would last. She would play at shopkeeping and book-selling and then she would get fed up and be off about her other activities. He thought of Bill Rogers as an activity, and then realized not for the first time that it was quite possible for Val to combine her business and her love life. He didn't like that idea much either.

However, she showed no intention of leaving. On the contrary, she now wanted to buy an interest in a venture peculiarly his own.

He was in a tough spot. Not very many evenings ago he had taken this ridiculous girl to a party and had not handled her with the care such dynamite well deserved. He had made love to her, because, to be frank, he had wanted to make love to her and could not recall ever having wanted anything more. And so far as Val was concerned, unless he was utterly blind and totally misguided where women were concerned, she had taken his love-making . . . and liked it.

He had spent a pretty unhappy few hours

after he'd left her. Such a situation, in all fairness to them both, couldn't continue. He could not have about him in his shop a woman who would expect kisses between customers, who would stoop over him at the desk and rumple his hair, causing miscalculations on the ledgers and other misfortunes.

Nor did he want to be stirred continuously by the presence of a girl who had what it takes . . . it would be a slur on his intelligence and self-discipline. Women, mused Ted profoundly, as greater and lesser men have mused before him, should be the playthings of a lighter hour. Or, had he read that somewhere?

He did not wish to become serious over any woman. He wasn't serious when it came to Val. Since the Flora episode he abjured gravity in the sex relation. And as it was obvious, despite Val's natural charms, that only gravity was acceptable, there seemed no middle course.

He had been unnecessarily brutal about Saturday night. There had been no need of such frank and earnest speech. Val had once told him she disliked frank and earnest speech: "Such nice boys, but one rarely encounters them socially," she had said. No, he had been a fool, and had told himself so a dozen times since the fatal words had escaped his aghast lips. All he had needed to do was to carry the thing off lightly, with a word, laughter, a careless joke.

But he liked Val, although she exasperated him; he had felt he owed her more than that. That had been his mistake.

And now, by way of coals of fire, she came offering her ewe lamb, her bond.

If he refused it she would leave the shop; if she left the shop it would reflect upon him. How or why he didn't know but he maintained that conviction.

Moreover, financially speaking, he was not in a position to refuse. If he accepted there would be enough to relieve the pressure of immediate urgencies and to carry him over the summer. He was certain that once he was relieved of worry he could make a success of the shop. Otherwise, it must close, it must spell failure in large red letters and he could go back to a job in someone else's shop — provided such a job materialized, which he doubted.

Val, purely as a business partner, was an asset and not a liability. That, he admitted now, and freely. It stung, the admission, but he made it.

He thought, walking over to the Lorings', well, it will be taken out of my hands, I suppose. Her people will never consider it, and that's that. He felt immeasurably relieved as any man does when the outcome of an issue is beyond his machinations.

He took with him the ledgers. He took with him his lease and the careful statement of his running expenses. He took with him the names of his active and inactive accounts. In short, he took everything but the electric grill and the contract which he and Val had signed.

Meantime Val had not been idle. Not at all. Lavish the bath salts in her tub and fresh and charming the selected dinner frock. Also before dinner she had gone downstairs and cast a reflective eye over the contents of her father's very modest wine cellar. It was contained on two shelves of a closet. There was left from a gift of other years a bottle of excellent burgundy and this Val took from the shelf and put on the sideboard to attain room temperature, having learned that the main dish of the evening was to be roast beef.

There were other bottles on the shelf. A year or so ago, during the exciting days of prohibition, Val had met at the home of friends who collected unusual guests a retired bartender who vowed that not until repeal would he desecrate his art. But he had taught Val a thing or two. Most good cooks are not hearty eaters; and most good bartenders do not drink. Val was intelligent and interested, in consequence of which, thanks to her friends' demoted guest, she could wield a mean shaker.

She did so now.

She presented the finished masterpiece to her father and mother. She carried the tray without a tremor and on it, with the shaker and the glasses, was a small plate of intricate appetizers. "Well," inquired her father, who was tired but felt a small gleam of interest in life returning to his eye, "well, what's all this about?"

Marcia Loring smiled slightly and looked with admiration at her child, one woman's tribute to another.

"It's a birthday," explained Val, pouring.

"Whose?" asked Mr. Loring with a sinking feeling. Surely he hadn't forgotten . . . but no, Val's birthday was in February and Marcia's in June . . . and his own, to the sorrow of his childhood, fell on Christmas Eve.

"Lots of people," said Val, "one born every minute. Try this. I think it's called 'Heaven's Gate.' "

Mr. Loring tried it. He tried it slowly and smiled beatifically, nibbled a square of delectable toast and tried again.

Marcia nodded over her own. It was strictly a man's cocktail but even women, whose palates are notoriously uneducated, could appreciate it. Val poured herself a third of a glass and sampled. She smiled.

Mr. Loring passed his glass. "I don't know what you're up to, but I'm game. Gimme another."

Dinner was plain and dinner was good. The burgundy gave it the right touch of sober festivity, drew it together like a basting thread. Mr. Loring, drinking with caution, remarked, "But I thought I had only one bottle."

"You haven't even one bottle now, darling," said his child.

"But I was saving this for —"

"No, you weren't," she contradicted. "What guest should be more honored than ourselves? Who stretches a better leg under this groaning board?"

It was altogether a pleasant evening for Mr. Loring until, back in the living room with a small brandy and a good cigar and Val curled up on the arm of his chair, his daughter announced that she was going to buy part of a bookshop.

They were still at it when Ted rang the doorbell. Val said, "There he is now . . . you'll have to back me up. You see, he doesn't really want me to buy it. He needs the money but he thinks I'm a congenital moron or something and he is certain that once I — and my money are in — it will be a complete loss."

Mr. Loring, stimulated and relaxed at one and the same time, warmed and fed, had been hard put to it to offer sufficiently cogent reasons why Val shouldn't buy the bookshop or a dozen bookshops if her five thousand ran to that, which in his ignorance of the purveying of the fine arts he thought it might well do. Also the congenital moron remark irritated him. By the time Ted had offered his greetings and made his opening gambit and exhibited his ledgers, Mr. Loring, faintly aware that all this was delusion and against his will, was ready to do battle for Val's sake. If she wanted the damned bookshop, let her have it.

Moreover, his wife had murmured something casual while Val was employing the cocktail shaker. Nothing to which you could pin her down, women were like that, but something which left the distinct impression that this bookshop employment wouldn't be a life job and that, after all, Bill Rogers might safely look forward to the ultimate reward of his long and patient waiting.

Now Mr. Loring scanned the ledgers and listened to the pros and cons. Ted was conscientious. He offered more cons than pros. Val sat in a corner, more demure than a mouse under the throne of royalty, and watched. Mrs. Loring knitted because she knew if she didn't she would box someone's ears — she wasn't sure whose.

"Well," decided Mr. Loring weightily, "it all seems perfectly shipshape to me, and if Valentine is willing to risk her money in this venture, Ted, I for one see no reason why she shouldn't. In fact," he added, paternally fatuous, "with Val assuming more responsibility I don't see why it should be such a risk after all."

Ted could have murdered him.

Val spoke from her corner: "That's that. I don't know much about the legal part of it, Ted, but if you'll see your lawyer . . ."

Her father nodded. The girl had her wits about her, and all her buttons on. He was proud of her. He was also sleepy. Mrs. Loring dropped a stitch and said something femininely vicious about it under her breath. Ted closed his ledgers. "I'll attend to it," he promised, with the gravest misgivings.

And now Val advanced upon him with her small hand outstretched. She placed it in his none too ready hand. She shook that hand briefly. She said, "O.K., partner," and there was a wicked glint in her eye. Both eyes.

Ted reflected that any man so unfortunate as to marry this deceptively childish and secretly managing woman would also see a lawyer . . . and that right quickly, once he

120

discovered what had happened to him.

Emotions seized him. He had lost something very valuable to him, his independence. He had been eighteen different piebald kinds of a damned fool to let the shop go: let the world disintegrate, starve on a park bench, but preserve your independence.

He had delivered himself into the hands of his enemy. He disliked her very much at the moment. He would always dislike her, he thought. Well, that was one good thing about it. This deal into which he had permitted himself to be coerced had at least removed from him the danger of any personal interest in his new partner. He essayed to speak, to voice his gratitude and his hope of a long and successful association in the tones of grave irony, but to his horror he succeeded only in emitting sounds couched in the shrill falsetto of strangulation.

Val regarded him with concern. "Do give him a brandy," she urged with solicitous malice, "he's overcome with rapture."

# Chapter VII

"My aunt's ill," announced Ted one sunny morning in June. He looked faintly perturbed. Val, at the desk, going over some accounts and mentally composing tactful but urgent letters to delinquents, regarded him with mild astonishment. "You must get those glasses straightened," she remarked, "they're completely haywire. You don't need them of course, but if you wear 'em crooked like that you soon will. I didn't know you had an aunt."

"Well, she isn't exactly. She's a second cousin or something of my mother's. Old maid. I stayed with her for a time, while I was living around," he explained vaguely; "anyway, I've got to go see her."

"Where does she live?" inquired his silent partner.

"Outside of Boston. She used to live in Jersey but she moved back."

"Back?"

"Yes, back," he responded querulously, "she was born there."

"I understand perfectly," said Val, a trifle miffed. She was chewing, he observed with irritation, the end of a pen. It was now her pen, however. "You make everything so delightfully clear. Run along. Money in petty cash for traveling expenses. Remember that summer's drawing on and don't stay at the Ritz or whatever it is. Tourists Welcomed would be better."

She stopped and observed his face closely. "Why, Ted," she added, "I believe you were fond of her!"

"Oh," said Ted grudgingly, "I liked her, all right. I haven't laid eyes on her for ten years. I've written her now and then. She was decent to me . . . and kids are easily bought with cookies and a nickel now and then."

Val thought swiftly, He really did like her. Poor forlorn youngster, bet she was the only one of his tribe who made anything of him.

"Does she live alone?" she asked gently.

"There's an ancient companion, a sort of general houseworker, I believe. It was she who wrote," he explained.

He looked about the shop. There was sunlight in it, and certainly the small but attractive line of "unusual" gifts which Val had insisted upon their adding didn't detract from its appearance. Ted had fought this addition long and lustily. First thing one knew his bookshop would be a drugstore, he had said acidly when, after his capitulation, Val unpacked various boxes containing sachets of fresh lavender. "Too, too ducky," Ted had remarked, snorting. But he had had to eat his words, if not the lavender, for not one but many of their casual customers, stopping to look at a book or buy a greeting card, had carried away an "unusual" gift in triumph.

As a partner, Val wasn't half bad. She was pretty chirpy, of course, and this business of going over the books with her every month hadn't proved to be nearly so routine an affair as Ted had expected. Her judicious advertisements had brought them some business; while the recent tea for Flora had been a great success. It had also been a source of grave discomfort to Ted. But Val had managed it nicely. She had corralled half a dozen spectacularly pretty girls of her acquaintance and had arranged with a caterer to serve, borrowing the janitor's kitchen as a base. The janitor and his wife were infatuated. They ran their heels off for her. She begged and borrowed and stole chairs of some approximate comfort and tables which did not teeter. Flora, looking her best in a straight black velvet frock, high collared and belted in metal, wearing a pancake beret, artist's variety, in matching black velvet, had drunk tea, and signed books and even made a little speech which was accepted with almost uproarious applause by an otherwise decorous audience. Val had rounded up a couple of critics and a bookish person or two. The tea had been noted in the papers and Flora's publishers had sent out proper publicity. The net result was that although their expenditure in order to do the poetess honor had startled Mr. Morrison no end, the shop was now on the map and the baker's dozen of new accounts which that day had added looked healthy.

Next autumn Val planned a series of book-shop teas, with speakers. "I can get a woman in to help me, or Mrs. Swenson will do. It won't cost much, Ted . . . tea and some biscuits and some lemons."

"What if they take cream?"

"That will be just too bad. Anyway, we'll do it. We'll get the place talked about. That's the only way to do business. See that people talk about you. It doesn't matter much what they say."

Ted groaned. His ideals lay shattered about his feet. His dream bookshop was a small haven of rich bindings and twilight quietude, with a stained glass and organ effect. In it he would dispense only good literature to kindred souls. Val was transforming this dream into a nightmare, a commercial merry-go-round. He admitted to himself that as he hadn't succeeded she had not upset his applecart literally. She had merely taken a moribund struggling little business and by sheer force of personality set it on its feet. Not that they were out of the woods as yet.

Now he asked:

"Think you can carry on without me for a few days?"

"Of course," said Val brightly, "you'll be surprised."

He was afraid he would be. He corrected her gloomily.

"The word is astonished."

"Thank you, Mr. Webster. I might know," she added spitefully, "that of all people you would never be surprised."

They were always quarreling like this. Over nothing. Val said abruptly:

"I'll get Eva Harkness to help me. She has plenty of money and lots of time. She can be decorative . . . and also useful. She'll adore it. I'll bring lunch in. How long will you be gone?"

He would leave that day, he told her, and stay a day and two nights with his aunt. Back on the third day.

"Go in peace," advised Val. She wondered silently and practically, I wonder if she'll leave him any money? Probably not. She hoped that Ted would not fall heir to any unexpected legacy. If he did, she reflected, it would be just like him to buy back her interest in order to get rid of her. But it isn't for sale, she reminded herself vigorously.

Things had really turned out very well. Despite the reluctance of her family, which included Bill, and of Ted himself, she had inched her way into the business, chiseled her path, so to speak, with the assistance of the bond. So far Ted had no cause for complaint. He had paid the interest on a small note and had paid an even smaller note entirely. His bills were paid. The shop was itself again. With any luck they could squeeze through the summer, decided Val. She had signed twenty-six people, mostly vacationing schoolteachers and housewives, for a weekly fiction parcel post service. She had put on sale the used lending library books which had been read to tatters and had realized something from them. Now that summer was upon them they could have a couple of narrow tables of books at the foot of the steps outdoors. That attracted people. Sometimes they came in to buy.

The windows were full of gay volumes for summer reading and of some quite charming water colors which Val had taken on commission, and a gay parade of idiotic shell animals which she had discovered a woman making in the back of a small novelty shop. Val bought all she could manage, put up the price, and marched them across the front windows. Ted had viewed them with dislike.

"What on earth does one do with them?" he had inquired. "Does that matter?" Val had asked him gaily. "They're swell. People will love them — favors, place cards. Look, I bought you this camel and paid cash for it. It looks exactly like you, pet," she said sweetly.

He snatched it from her hand, and she fancied for a moment that he would fling it dramatically against the wall. Keturie waited, her eyes gleaming. This was going to be fun. But Ted put it on the desk. After all, there was something comic and engaging about it, the painted shell head, with its baleful expression, the body and the spindly pipe-stem-cleaner legs. It disappeared from the desk presently and adorned, although Val could not guess this, the dresser in his Village quarters. Now and then he found himself looking anxiously in the mirror. Did he really resemble a camel?

Shortly after his departure Flora came in. She was enjoying visibly and rather attractively the fruits of her success. She and Val had by now cemented a rather unusual friendship. That is to say, they liked each other, in a way, they trusted each other not at all, and each had an authentic admiration for the other's capabilities.

"I'm off," said Flora, and promptly sank into a chair and called for a cigarette. Keturie came and sat at her feet and a moment later sprang up on her knee. Keturie's satin paws were folded beneath her, her ears were upright, she closed her eyes and purred. Val felt a pang of jealousy.

"Where to?" asked Val, giving her guest a cigarette.

"Oh, New England," said Flora largely. "I've four lectures to do . . . the end of the season. My dear, what I've suffered!" She launched into a description of her recent trip through the Middle West, the poor connections, the hotels, the women's clubs. It appeared, finally, that what she had suffered was a good time and plenty of free meals.

"Where's Ted?" she asked, not too idly.

"He's gone to Boston," said Val, "an aunt of his is ill."

"Really? I never imagined Ted with relatives. How entrancing! Perhaps she'll leave him money," Flora said brightly. Val looked at her with intense dislike. How hideous to think that poets could be practical too.

"Perhaps," she admitted, "but not likely."

"No, I suppose not. Still," said Flora, "money would improve him, don't you think? Gild the chip on his shoulder?"

"You used to have one too," said Val, "or so I've heard."

Flora laughed. "You're so amusing, Val, re-

129

ally. Of course I had. When you're hungry and wondering about your next meal, when you know you could have things other people have if only you could get someone to listen to you, naturally you have a chip on your shoulder."

Val grinned suddenly. Really, Flora was sweet, with the bell-shaped haircut and the pointed face which all the interviewers referred to as elfin, whimsical or puckish. And she had a great gift. Val was sober before that. She wondered merely why of all people a great gift had to devolve upon Flora.

"I suppose so," she agreed. "Well, you've built your better mousetrap, Flora, and now you're giving lecture tours."

"That reminds me, where can I find Ted?" asked Flora. "I'll be in Boston tomorrow night."

The address lay there, on the desk. Possibly Flora had seen it, in Ted's handwriting. Val copied it for her, carefully. "There it is," she said, "only I don't believe he'll be staying long. It's outside of the city, Flora."

"Perhaps the old lady has a telephone," said Flora. "Well, we'll see." She put the address in her handbag and crushed out her cigarette. She rose. "By the way, haven't you some books to lend me for the train trip?" she inquired. "My publishers are sending a man with me but, poor dear, he'll want to escape from me sometime."

"He hasn't a chance if you don't want him to," said Val ambiguously. "No, I haven't," she replied firmly. "You always want the newest ones, Flora. You can't have 'em. Yes, you can. Here, sign on the dotted line. Give me a dollar. That's the girl," she said, seizing the money from Flora's almost enchanted hand. "Now," she said triumphantly, "you're a cash customer. You can rent a book. Fifteen cents for three days, or a quarter a week." She mentioned two cents a day for overtime. Flora gasped faintly. "You are," she remarked, "a most mercenary woman!" and presently found herself out on the street with two novels and a five dollar biography on which she was now paying rent as well as the deposit.

Val watched her go. She stood at the window and watched the small feet twinkle up the steps and away. She grinned, jingling coins. "That," said Val to herself, "was a remarkable bit of business."

Flora thought so too. She thought, looking about her for a taxi, wait till I tell Ted!

Ted returned not on the third day, but on the fourth. He had a sheepish look, thought Val, when he finally strolled in, rather late in the afternoon. He greeted her with an elaborate courtesy and asked politely after her welfare. Val reported rapidly, "Rentals falling off, sales above our weekly average owing to European travel and fellow citizens doing the proper bon voyage offering on friendship's altars. Sit down. Tell me about everything."

Everything, reported Ted, was all right. Aunt Bella hadn't been very ill after all. Acute indigestion. The old housekeeper had become unduly worried. He'd had a talk with the doctor, a nice old chap. Poisonous village, though, he added, sentimental as a greeting card, plenty of charm and scads of genteel poverty. Aunt Bella's house was ramshackle in the extreme, and dusty. He wondered that she could live in it. She was pretty hard up, poor old girl. Had depended for years on a tiny income from certain investments and by now most of 'em were not worth the paper they were printed on.

He's given her money, thought Val, and he'll starve himself to send her more. She would have liked to shake him. That was just like Ted Morrison. Talk about not letting your right hand know . . . well, she was his right hand, wasn't she?

"Flora was in," she told him, when the subject of Aunt Bella appeared to be exhausted.

"Yes, I know."

"Oh, you saw her then?"

Ted flushed slightly. "She wired me," he

explained, "you'd given her the address. I — when I found I couldn't be of any real use at Aunt Bella's I went in to Boston."

"So that's why you stayed over!" Val said. "Did you hear her lecture?"

"It was splendid," he praised warmly, "she has the most miraculous manner with an audience." He stopped abruptly aware that his enthusiasm was eliciting no response. "Not that I approve of her commercializing her art," he concluded hastily.

"You make me sick," Val cried at him. "Of course you approve! You think it's just dandy! So do I. Why not? But you feel bound to live up to all those half-baked theories of yours — you can't come out flat-footed on either side . . . you just mugwump along the fence, as it seems most expedient to you!"

They were quarreling again. After ten minutes Ted grinned at her. He asked gently, "Not jealous, are you, by any chance?"

That, she thought furiously, was Flora. Flora must have planted an idea or two in that addlepate of his while they were in Boston. By the way, what had they been doing in Boston together? Flora didn't lecture all day or all night. And he would never have thought of that question all by himself. Flora had said, most likely, "Take care Val doesn't fall in love with you, Ted."

As a matter of fact she had said nothing of the kind. She'd said merely, "I had the devil's own time getting your address out of Val. She's a possessive little thing, isn't she, Ted?"

That had made him angry.

"Jealous," repeated Val savagely. "Why, you . . . !" Words failed her. There was no adequate profanity. She said chokingly, as if she were about ten years old, "Why, you darned old idiot!"

"I didn't really think so," he said. Val was pretty and quite dangerous — in a temper. He got up and walked about the shop. He commented, pulling down one of Val's pet mysteries, "Six copies . . . aren't we overstocked?"

"No, and you know it. Look at 'em. They've been out every day . . . this just happens to be a time when they're all in."

She said, after a minute:

"Look here, I was talking to the family last night about vacations. I'd like mine in July. About the middle. Bill's going away, you know."

Ted hadn't known, or had forgotten. He said, "I'll see. It's all right by me, of course. I hadn't planned on a vacation myself."

"All work and no play —" she warned absently, "you'd better change your mind." She jabbed a pencil at a blotter. "Well, that's that," she ended flatly.

It wasn't her fault, she assured herself, that she opened Flora's letter on the tenth of July. Flora had had a bill for some books she had ordered as gifts so she had sent her check to Ted at his house and her letter to Ted at the shop. Flora did things like that sometimes; we all do. From the very first endearing word Val was quite aware that this was no check. She read the letter to the bitter end, however. She had no excuse for herself.

"You are so stubborn," Flora had written. "I thought after the happy time we spent together in Boston . . . Why haven't you written me since or called me up?"

There was more to it, reproaches, intimately couched. Val, returning it to the envelope and marking it "opened by mistake," thought, I might have known it. She wants Ted to give up the shop. To build a life together, I suppose, a farm somewhere and books and a few friends. On what? Val asked herself. On what, if I dare conjecture.

On the fifteenth Val went off to a quiet place on Long Island with her parents. They found her curiously subdued. Her golf had not suffered, nor her Australian crawl, nor her tennis. On a dance floor she was as fleet of foot as ever. But there was a difference. Mr. and Mrs.

Loring inquired about it of each other, mutely and not so mutely.

Val spent her last week-end at Southampton with Bill and his mother. It was very pleasant. A big rambling home, quiet, efficient service, a household running on oiled wheels. Bill, whose boat had undergone its final overhauling in dry dock on the west coast, was leaving by plane to join it and his amateur crew on the following Monday.

There was something terribly relaxing about the Southampton place and Bill. She could forget that the bookshop ever existed. She could forget a lot of things. On the last night they dined quietly at home and Mrs. Rogers was not inept in making an excuse to leave them alone together. They went out presently and walked on the dunes, those sculptured shapes marching to the music of the seas. The air was cool and fresh after a sultry day and Val raised her small face to the dark and starlit sky with a sigh of relief.

"I wish you were going with me, Val."

"Sometimes I do too. It would be fun."

"Change your mind and come. I'll wait over a day. We can be married, take a plane . . . twenty-four hours will see us there and almost ready to start. It's adventure, Val, real adventure . . . and I do love you so much."

For a moment she was tempted. Blue water,

strange waters and stars in a South Sea sky. Sea monsters and sea beauties, and Bill . . . Then she shook her head.

"I can't, dear."

"Val, how long must you keep me dangling like this? It will be months before I get back . . . a year perhaps."

She said, after a moment, "Bill, I don't know. I'm . . . sometimes I believe I *do* love you."

"Val —"

"No. Please. Look," she said desperately, wanting to be fair, hating to hurt him, "when you get back . . . if you still feel as you do —"

"Could I alter after all these years?"

"You might. If you still do, Bill, and if I — if I find that I can't get along without you . . ."

She permitted his kiss then, and if it gave her no sweet and intolerable ecstasy, it did not affront her. She responded to it, perhaps because she was young and her senses were unblunted, because it was a summer's night, and there was melancholy in it and in the unceasing whisper of the sea.

Mrs. Rogers, walking out on the balcony of her bedroom, saw them come back from the beach, the garden way. She nodded her small alert head. Things would come out right, after all, for Bill. She had wished this for a long time. Because Bill wished it. She was very fond of Valentine Loring, she knew no girl whom she could so sincerely welcome as Bill's wife. Yet she would serve Val's head on a silver charger to her son if that was his desire.

She had a long talk with him that night after Val had gone to bed. She knocked at his door and found him sitting by a window smoking and looking out over the ocean. He smiled at her when she came in. His mother was, he thought, an entirely marvelous person. How much she hated the idea of his expedition only he and she knew; and she never complained. He hadn't been away now for almost three years. It was time, he thought restlessly, that he went away. Only one thing could hold him here; and that was Val. But if he married Val, she would go with him.

He told his mother presently that that was what he hoped to do on his return. "It isn't definite," he said, "but she's partly promised."

His mother shrugged her still shapely shoulders. She could have shaken the girl. What was she about, shilly-shallying, unable to make up her mind?

She thought, If her hand is forced, a very little?

She kissed her son, and said, smiling, "I'm

138

sure that when you come back — Val's very fond of you, Bill."

"Oh, fond!" he said.

"Well, more than that perhaps. This absence may be just what the doctor ordered."

She couldn't, she reflected, announce an engagement which wasn't "definite." Or even one that was, as such an announcement must come from Val's parents. But there were ways. She sat down at her desk, very late that night, and wrote to the society gossip editor on one of the great dailies. She knew the woman rather well, and liked her. If "Madame Gadabout" wished to hint, in her columns . . .

On Monday Bill left for the Coast. Val and his mother went with him to New York. His mother would see him off on the midnight plane. Val had shaken her head. "No, I'd hate it," she said, "I loathe good-byes."

Yet in the afternoon he came in to say goodbye to her parents. He had brought a jeweller's box with him. His mother had given it to him. In it was her own engagement ring, which recently she had had reset. "Val, if you'd wear it . . ."

"No, Bill."

"Will you keep it, then, until I come back? And then, perhaps . . ."

"Perhaps," she said, after a moment. Her heart sank definitely. A year is a long time.

"I'll keep it," she said.

On Tuesday she went to the shop. She found somewhat to her dismay that it had run serenely in her absence. She was a day late but Ted made no comment. She found evidence also that her partner had gone suddenly literary in a personal sense. The ribbon on the shop portable was worn to a frazzle; and in a waste basket which hadn't been emptied overnight there were torn and crumpled pages of white and yellow paper and a dim sheet of carbon.

"Turned poet?" she inquired.

"Who, me?" He had the grace to look abashed. "No, of course not. Tried my hand at some — well, call them sketches. Flora knows an editor —"

So it was Flora's fine Italian hand. Val went about her business of straightening up the shop. It was clean, it had been dusted but it lacked something. It lacked herself, she decided, not without vanity. She answered Ted's courteous questions about her vacation with as much courtesy. She asked, "Wasn't it awful hot in town?"

"Terribly. I got away the two week-ends. Saturday noon to Monday morning."

He did not have to explain to her, as he did, that Flora and a married couple, artist friends of hers, had taken a camp near Carmel.

She already sensed that he had been with Flora these last two summer Sundays. She's converted him, she thought dismally, and welcomed the appearance of a customer with such a display of helpfulness and cordiality that this lone, simple-minded man was stampeded into buying one pocket volume of G. K. Chesterton and two lavender-scented ladies' dress hangers instead of the book on dietetics which he had wandered in to purchase. He wandered out again with his package and left behind him an afternoon paper.

Ted picked it up, glanced through it idly. He skimmed the women's page, the society page. A name leaped at him. He turned the pages, folded it after the neat manner of men and read again. Then he threw the paper on the floor and Keturie ran at once to creep under it spookily and then stand up, completely covered. She adored newspapers.

"So," said Ted, "you got yourself engaged, did you? I suppose it slipped your mind and you forgot to tell me. Congratulations."

# Chapter VIII

Val ran to uncover Keturie. Keturie sulked and went off in a corner to wash her face, the last refuge of a lady. Val rattled the newspaper and eventually found the item.

Madame Gadabout had in addition to her usual social items a "rumor" column. She also possessed a sprightly and eminently readable style. This style fascinated Val, perusing the lines. There was mention of Bill "terribly good-looking, my dears, and, oh, so eligible!" of his "charming and extremely social mother," and of his South Seas expedition and the amateur crew, "all of them young men who are very well known in Gotham society." There was mention as well of Bill's forthcoming book "now in the hands of his publishers . . . by subscription only — a fabulous sum — but worth it to collectors." And then there was the Rumor.

"One hears," reported Madame Gadabout, in her over-the-teacups manner, "that upon Bill's return from parts unknown his engagement will be formally announced to Valentine Loring, daughter of —" etc., etc.

There was even a line about the bookshop. Mrs. Rogers hadn't included this in her discreet hint to her acquaintance, but Madame Gadabout always did things thoroughly.

Val was red, so far as her own personal color scheme went. She did not suspect Bill's mother any more than she suspected Bill. That part of it didn't matter. This wasn't the first time she'd been prodded gently in the column. She hadn't minded. She swallowed hard and stated:

"Good publicity for the shop."

"Oh, quite," agreed Ted icily, "provided that anyone who reads it also has the energy to read a book. Which I doubt. Only, you might have told me."

She said, "There wasn't anything to tell."

"Then it isn't true?" he asked, and tried to keep a certain eagerness from his tone. Not that he cared. Hadn't he advised her to marry Rogers? Elegant match. When she did, he'd buy back the interest in the shop, by hook or crook. It couldn't matter to her if he took his good American time about it. She'd have forgotten by then that the shop existed. He might have known that he'd let himself in for something of the sort when he permitted her to override his judgment and buy in.

"It isn't true?" he repeated as she hesitated, and then the telephone rang.

Ted was the nearer. He reached it in a couple of long strides. He barked into it and Val thought subconsciously, Oh, dear, another good customer blown to fragments. Then his voice changed . . .

"Yes —"

"Of course . . ."

"Yes, marvelous . . . never had a better."

"Tonight? All right . . . seven then. Good-bye."

Flora, of course. Val's chin went up. She said, when he turned from the telephone, "No, it isn't true, Ted. Not exactly."

"What do you mean, not exactly? Either you're engaged or you aren't."

"Well," she asked suddenly, "are you engaged to Flora?"

"Me . . . to Flora?" he asked, astonished into uncertain syntax. "No . . . I mean . . . that is . . ."

"There, you see!" cried Val in triumph. She found herself laughing wildly. "There we both are," she said, "neither flesh nor fish nor good red something or other. Herring? Haggies? What are haggies?" she demanded gravely.

"Val, have you gone crazy?"

She replied, sobering:

"No. Look here, we're partners, and good friends. About Bill . . . I'll be honest with you. I — I told that if — when he came back . . ."

"Oh, I see."

"No, you don't. And what did *you* mean about Flora?"

He said uncomfortably:

"I don't know, Val. You see, Flora doesn't believe in marriage."

Val stared at him open-mouthed. "Doesn't believe in marriage?" she managed to articulate at last. "Of all the phony, moth-eaten . . . ! Do you mean to say that she still falls for that stuff," she demanded incredulously, "that post-war gesture? I don't believe it! Flora's too smart."

Ted shrugged.

"It may be all you think it is . . . all *I* think it is, as a matter of fact. But . . . she's different from us, Val. She has genius. She has to be free."

"Now where have I heard that before?" pondered Val.

"*Ann Veronica?* Or was it earlier than that? As if," she concluded magnificently, "anyone was ever free!"

She thought shrewdly, She doesn't want to marry him, she's going places and he isn't, she wouldn't marry the best man in the world unless he came gold-lined and plutocratic. She wants to have her cake and eat it too, and she knows which side her bread's buttered on, at the same time. Poetry may not always pay, but hers will. But she doesn't want to run a house and a husband on it.

She said aloud:

"The next thing I know you'll be preaching doctrines of free love to me. Doctrines which went out with the jazz age and baby vamps."

He said quietly, because he was growing seriously angry:

"We don't give it any such ridiculous label, Val."

So, she thought. Well, I know where I stand, if I haven't known all along. The telephone rang again. Ted answered it as before. "It's for you," he reported, "I think it's Mrs. Rogers."

He didn't think, he knew; Mrs. Rogers had told him. Val went and held the instrument to her ear, her lips at its black round mouth. Mrs. Rogers said, "Val dear . . . this business in the paper . . . your mother just called me. Bill won't have seen it, of course. I'm so awfully sorry —"

"Why?" asked Val clearly, "It's true, isn't it? Yes, of course, darling. Yes. I'll wire Bill . . . where can I reach him? No, Mother will attend to that. We might as well announce and be done with it."

She put the instrument down gently. Mrs. Rogers had been moved almost to tears . . . "Val, dear, if you knew how my poor boy —"

Why her "poor boy"? thought Val, irritated. She advanced toward Ted, stepping as lightly as Keturie. "I hate half measures," she said gaily, "so Mother will be announcing it tomorrow — my engagement, I mean."

He asked, "Isn't it sudden?"

"You've missed a cue," she told him, "or mixed it. No. It needed just something like this really to make up my mind for me."

Ted said, after a moment:

"I — he's a good egg. Hope you'll be happy."

"I intend to be," she told him, "but Bill will be away a long while, Ted, maybe a year. Isn't it lucky," she asked, and made a most hideous face at him, "that I've something to take up my time?"

"What?" he asked dully.

She waved a comprehensive arm at the shop. "This," she said, "and now that you're rid of me . . ."

"Rid of you? What on earth do you mean? Do you mean," he asked with a faint dawning of something that was neither hope nor horror but a mixture of the two, "that you're quitting?"

"Of course not. But as an engaged young female I should be off your mind. Contract or no contract, confess that you believed I had designs on you," she said and looked him sternly in the eye.

"Don't be silly, Val."

"I will be silly. Look. I'm engaged. You're

— well, sort of engaged. Let's celebrate."

He thought, She's a cute kid. He liked her a lot. He was always fighting with her, but he liked her. She was swell. Flora liked her too, she had said so. Perhaps Val could argue Flora into common sense.

Queer about Flora. There'd been a time not so long ago when he'd thought they were all washed up, that she no longer cared a rap about him and that he, well, in fact, that he was getting over her. But lately it had been different. Flora had been a little jealous of Val. Her interest had obviously revived. There in Boston she had been extraordinarily sweet. She couldn't, when you came right down to it, help her success, and she deserved it. She wasn't an Emily Dickinson, to hide herself away from the world in a closed garden. She was of a more earthy temperament. And it hadn't spoiled her much — all the sudden adulation.

He felt at peace with himself and all the world. He said, looking at Val as if he had never seen her before, "Let's go out to dinner."

"You've a date," she reminded him, laughing, "and I must go home to be wept over by the family."

"That's so," he agreed, disappointed. "See here, how about coming up to Carmel with me and Flora next week-end . . . The Gateses are driving us up, I know they'd be glad to have you."

"I'd love it," said Val insincerely.

Ted whacked her between the shoulder blades with a painful heartiness. "That's the ticket," he said.

They were partners.

Walking home, toward her mother's subdued delight, her father's touchingly sentimental gravity, Val told herself, I was right, just because he no longer considers me a menace, we're suddenly good friends.

On Saturday afternoon she packed a small suitcase and put on her best tweed frock and coat and Bill's diamond. The Gateses, Ted and Flora picked her up at the house. An airmail special-delivery letter had reached her from Bill, and several wires. They fortified her, a lot. After all, she did care for Bill . . . he was real, he mattered very much. And at the end of a year she would have had plenty of time to reconcile herself to marriage.

She rode with Ted in the rumble seat. Flora detested rumble seats. Flora had congratulated her charmingly, had looked with obvious envy at the ring, a very spectacular bit of carbon. "You're very fortunate," Flora said, "I've seen pictures of your best young man. The answer to the maiden's prayer."

She was willing, reflected Val, to trust her with Ted in the rumble seat because she, Val, was spoken for. Ted, too.

They rode mostly in silence. The day was warm and windless and the heavy-foliaged branches of the trees scarcely moved. The Berkshires were a climbing line against the sky. Dusk was golden and the shadows long as they came to a group of camps, half-timbered cottages and log cabins clustered on the side of hills, surrounding a clear blue lake. The Gateses were pleasant people, hard working, not in the least rattlebrained. Mentally and penitently Val rearranged her idea of artists. The camp was delightful. Val, sharing a small and well-appointed bedroom with Flora, thought, I bet she hates having me here.

But if so Flora concealed it very well and said, that night after dinner at the club and a long walk in the woods and a comfortable sitting around with drinks and sandwiches on the porch afterwards:

"I once thought that you were in love with Ted."

"How fantastic!"

Flora, in a sheer nightdress under a white silk robe caught around her, her pointed face grave, had the look of a naughty choirboy.

150

She said, perched on the edge of her cot, "But I did. I thought he was rather interested in you, too."

"He's always rather disliked me," said Val evenly, "I think it's an excellent basis for partnership."

"Partnership?"

"Business partnership." She stopped, regarding Flora's betraying face. So Ted hadn't told her. "I bought a share of the business last spring," she said. "I thought you knew."

"Yes, of course, I knew," said Flora instantly. "I thought it a marvelous idea. In fact, it was I who pointed out the advantages to Ted."

That was, of course, a barefaced lie. Val was enjoying herself. She said gently, "That was sweet of you. There weren't any really. Of course the money tided the shop over, but the advantages were all to me. I wanted something to do, something in which I could have a real part."

"Yes, I understand that," agreed Flora. "It must be hard to feel yourself informed with a creative instinct and with no real outlet," she said generously. "Even building up a business is creative in a way . . just as the woman who keeps house and bears children is creative in her way."

"And how," murmured Val.

"I beg your pardon?" said Flora.

"Not at all. I merely said, how right you are," explained Val. "You do understand. I can't write or paint, act or sing . . . but I can," she added with a slight grin, "run a bookshop. At least I think I can."

"Don't let's talk about bookshops," urged Flora, who was to talk about little else one way or another for the next twenty years, "tell me about Bill."

"Bill."

"Your Bill."

"Oh, my Bill." Val was becoming a trifle confused. She asked, "You don't know him, do you?"

"No, but I'd like to."

I bet you would, thought Val. Aloud she said, "There's nothing much to say — I've known him most of my life."

"My dear, how dull!"

"We don't think so," Val told her.

"And now he's gone off on a South Seas expedition," pursued Flora. "How divine! I wish I'd known sooner. It's something I've always wanted to do."

Val said cruelly, "You couldn't have gone with him, unless you could cook or do something useful. He's got a man to do the drawings, and the rest are seamen. Amateurs, but very good ones. Bill keeps the records and

152

the logs, captains the crew, is general bottle washer as well."

The door was half open. Ted knocked and put his head in simultaneously.

"You girls not in bed yet?"

Flora smiled at him tenderly. She sat cross-legged on the cot. The high neck line, the cowl of the white silk robe were very becoming. She was aware of it. Val in her tailored dark blue pajamas was stretched on the other bed, her red hair tumbled. She was smoking.

"I didn't know you smoked," said Ted, astonished.

"I don't," said Val, "except once in a blue moon. This is it."

Flora invited, "Do come in. I'll make room for you."

She did so. Ted obeyed and planted himself solidly at the foot of the cot. He was fully dressed.

"What have you been up to?" inquired his partner.

"Nothing. Gates and I were talking," said Ted, "Mary's gone to bed."

He looked tired. Gates had been pretty serious. Hammer and tongs. What was the country coming to and what place would art have in the new scheme of things? He didn't know, neither did Ted. They'd become hoarse and weary trying to find out.

153

Flora said, indicating Val:

"Isn't she cunning? Like a cherub." Her tone made the flattery vaguely insulting. Val lay still, turning the diamond on her finger. Ted looked from one to the other. He said suddenly:

"Val, now's your chance to persuade her to follow your example."

Val said lazily, "I wouldn't presume," but Flora's ears were pricked and pointed like a faun's.

"Persuade me to what?"

"Domesticity," said Val, and yawned. She displayed even, white teeth and a small red tongue.

"Oh, my dear," expostulated Flora laughing, "Ted and I settled that long ago. He knows how I feel about things. Marriage is all very well —"

"For the hoi polloi?" asked Val, interrupting. "Well, I don't mind being an h.p., if you can be, in the singular," she said.

Flora was tolerant. "It's different, with you."

"I suppose so." Val considered this a minute. Then she said suddenly, "But I'm on your side, Flora, not on Ted's."

"What?" Ted's jaw dropped and he regarded her in amazement. "You!"

"Yes. Why not? I mean, look here. Flora

isn't like most women. She belongs to herself."
Flora nodded, well satisfied. She had said this
by word of mouth and in print a dozen times.
"She isn't bound by ordinary laws. And as
for you," said Val negligently, "I should think
you'd have too much pride to want to be
known as 'America's Foremost Poetess's Husband.' "

Flora flushed, a little angrily. Ted flushed
too, he'd never thought of that. Val laughed at
them both. She said, "For heaven's sake, Ted,
go to bed, I'm worn out . . . never walked
so much in all my life."

As he departed she called, "Oh, by the way,
when we get back to the shop, there's something we must attend to immediately."

"What?" he asked, turning at the doorway.

"A matter of a contract," she said, "which
isn't necessary now."

He had the last word there. He said, "It
never really was," and vanished. Flora turned
down her blankets. "What contract?" she
asked curiously.

Val was yawning prodigiously. She said,
between yawns, "It wasn't a contract really,
Flora, it was a tabu."

Flora thought that over. Really, being engaged to a society explorer had sent Val
very South Seas indeed. She asked, "What
tabu?" but Val slept, or feigned sleep, and

did not answer her.

Very early on Monday morning Val and Ted and Leslie Gates motored back to town leaving Flora and Mary Gates to sleep the sleep of the justifiably idle. When the shop was reached and opened and the contents thereof set in order for the day Val, who, by now, had been entrusted with the combination of the safe, spun the dials and opened it. The contract was there, just as Ted had put it in. She rose with it in her hands. She said, "This was a very childish business. Let's tear it up."

He didn't want her. He had never wanted her, except fleetingly and regrettably. He was in love with Flora . . . still or again. So much in love with Flora that this pert redheaded, green-eyed atom, standing crisply smocked in front of him, with a silly scrap of paper in her hands, need never trouble him again, would never, in fact, by so much as an accelerated heartbeat, alter his pulses. She was just a nice child and he was in love with another woman. But —

He made a blind motion toward her. Afterwards he told himself that he had merely intended to take the contract from her hand and tear it up. What else could he have intended? he asked himself furiously. But himself was silent.

Val ducked. Val ran. Back to the safe. In

popped the contract and bang shut the door. "Perhaps," she debated, breathing a little hard, "perhaps I was somewhat premature."

"You flatter yourself," growled her partner and went to the telephone and rang up his jobber and inquired furiously why the last order for so-and-so and this-and-that hadn't been filled instantly.

Val smiled faintly and winked at Keturie. Then she caught sight of the diamond on her hand and sobered. What perversity in her delighted in baiting Ted like this, with Bill a continent and more away, loving her, trusting her?

But, she told herself, I was railroaded into this engagement.

She hadn't been. All the king's horses and all the king's men with Madame Gadabout riding the winds of rumor thrown in for good measure couldn't have made her announce her betrothal to Bill Rogers unless she'd wanted to do so. Therefore she had wanted to do so. Why?

She looked at Ted, arguing busily at the telephone, his hair extremely mussed and his blue eyes a little wild. This hopeless antagonism between them, this hostility, why was it more exciting than tenderness, than love, than passion itself?

Val shook her head and went forward into

the shop to greet a dour lady who wished to buy a book of the month, a mystery of the week, and probably the best seller of the day.

# Chapter IX

By autumn Val had settled down to the sober role of an engaged young woman whose fiancé is not at hand to supply her with the suitable excitements, astonishments and rewards of a betrothal. She also presented an exemplary picture of a young businesswoman. Now and then when Bill's ecstatic and reproachful letters reached her — "why couldn't you have made up your mind a little sooner, darling, and come with us? I've been looking forward to this trip for months and now I find myself resenting it and all the adventure and beauty which it brings because you are not here to share it with me, and because it keeps me from you," she sat down to wonder gravely if she was doing him an injustice.

It was not that she did not love him. She did love him. She was perfectly sure of that. But was she in love with him? By all the annals of fiction she assumed that she was not. The sound of his step on the stairs did not cause her heart to perform acrobatics which would electrify Madison Square Garden, and the chance touch of his hand certainly did not freeze — or was it melt? — the blood in her veins. On the other hand, she loved being with him, they were the greatest of comrades, they agreed on almost everything, they were touched by the same things, laughed at the same jokes. And certainly there was nothing about Bill Rogers that repelled her. Her senses were perfectly aware of his physical charm. Yet the romantic books seemed to hold that unless you were actually in love with a man you would regard his embrace as repulsive, affronting all the finer fibers of your nature.

Eyewash! said Val to herself.

She came by slow degrees to the conclusion that this business about the one and only was bunk of the highest order. Granted you were a normal, healthy, moderately intelligent girl you might meet, in the course of a lifetime, or even less, at least a dozen men with whom you could be soberly happy, congenial and physically attuned. Perhaps, she pondered, it wasn't a question of the man with whom you could be happy, perhaps when it came to the romantic love you read about, it was a question of the man without whom you'd be miserable.

She told herself stoutly that, apparently, she wasn't slated for a great love, the kind of love Flora talked about and wrote about, and of which others greater or lesser than Flora had sung and written since man first found an articulate voice and a pen. There must be, she decided, hundreds, thousands like her, who missed somehow, because of some flaw, perhaps in their own natures, this tremendous experience and were content, never knowing that they had missed it. Or were the poets and the fiction writers merely exercising their prerogative of exaggeration?

Dutifully she endured her mother's quiet delight in her engagement and her father's more gloomy prognostications. "You'll make a terrible wife, Val, you don't deserve a good fellow like Bill." But he didn't mean that. He believed, and she knew that he believed, that Bill Rogers was perhaps the luckiest man who had ever drawn breath. Dutifully also she went to see her future mother-in-law. They dined tête-à-tête, they went to occasional concerts and plays, and when the season began Mrs. Rogers gave a small and charming dinner for her, at which Val met, not for the first time, the Rogers clan in its respectable and on the whole charming entirety.

She wrote to Bill: "We drank to you, and to us, solemnly. I drank too. Why should I sit there in solitary state, drinkless? Really, it's pretty awful without you to lighten the burden. All your cousins and aunts embraced me, and I must say your uncles did also, with more enthusiasm. But you should have been there to come in for your share of hand-wringing and backslapping. There is something a trifle out of drawing about a missing fiancé but I must say you provide me with a lot of good excuses, or at least one excellent one not to do the things I don't want to do."

Bill's mother urged, "Now you mustn't shut yourself up like a nun, Val dear, just because Bill isn't here to beau you around. You must go out and have a grand time . . . he'd rather."

Val knew that he'd rather, but she'd rather not. So she refused invitations right and left, postponed the engagement luncheon and the showers and all the concomitants of betrothals until a much later date, and amused herself by spending her spare time in secondhand bookshops and libraries. She was determined to know more about the business on which she had embarked. She spent her lunch hour in the Fourth Avenue sector and often went without lunch at all, or snatched a glass of milk and a sandwich from a drugstore counter instead of going home. She talked to old men, wise and a little musty like the books they sold, and she talked to young men who were more interested in the markdown or the markup than in the contents of the books themselves. She became an avid reader of Mr. Newton and of other gentlemen who spent their lives book collecting, for either personal or commercial purposes. And she rummaged through the dusty counters of broken-backed books on outdoor shelves, hoping someday to make a find . . . hoping someday to pick up for half a dollar some item which Ted would dust off and sell for half a hundred dollars. Not, she told herself doubtfully, that that would be very honest . . . if I really knew what it was worth!

Rare editions, first editions, limited editions were, strictly speaking, Ted's province and in it he was at home. Still Val didn't see why, now that she was a partner in the enterprise, she should be relegated to romance, mysteries and juveniles. She argued Ted into employing an English agent. "Lots of people want English firsts . . . look at that shop which specializes in them. I know you order 'em when people specially want 'em. But that takes forever, and if we already had those which we knew would be in demand . . ."

She had a finger in every pie. Ted regarded her with exasperation. Woman's place was certainly in the home, he decided, not for the first time, and he would be delighted, he assured himself, when Bill Rogers returned from his effete parlor-exploring and married her.

Still, he admitted that he had never done so excellent a Christmas trade as this year. Val selected the cards, there were gayer wrapping papers, seals and ribbons than the shop had ever boasted before, and ordered in recklessly large amounts. Ted groaned, contemplating almost instant ruin; but by Christmas Eve they were completely sold out.

Val had undertaken the decorating of the shop. She had done it charmingly, with a small Christmas tree dripping silver and blue, and with branches of live cedar and pine, and big paper bells and unexpected stars. Ted, who did not approve of Christmas theoretically, "It has become commercialized" was his solemn comment even while wrapping up the last-minute gifts of his customers, had been bidden to the Lorings'. "Don't tell me," said Val vigorously, "that you want to take a pint of milk and a chicken sandwich and sit on the library steps or something. That's too absurd!"

The Lorings celebrated an old-fashioned Christmas. They corralled those unattached cousins and distant relatives who had no place to go but hotels or boarding-houses, and they fed them liberally on turkey and still more turkey at about four in the afternoon. They had asked Mrs. Rogers also, though she was not one of the family; but to Evelyn Rogers Christmas without Bill was not Christmas at all, so she betook herself to Atlantic City in company with an ancient, heavily rich and terribly lonely aunt.

The Loring house was, to Ted's startled vision, holly and greens from basement to attic.

In the living room there was the biggest Christmas tree he had ever seen. And the entire establishment reeked with the Christmas spirit in the shape of sights, sounds, smells . . . odor of pine, of baking, of turkey stuffing, plum pudding and luscious pies, sounds of tissue paper rustling, of laughter, doorbells ringing, a radio tuned to organ music and carols; while upon the dazzled sight Val burst in a bright red dress with no regard whatever for the more subdued red of her hair. "It's the only time I can wear red and get away with it. And I adore red," she explained.

Around her throat was the necklace of polished jade beads, a present which Bill had chosen for her in San Francisco and had sent out to her from there at the proper time. Red and green, for Christmas. She slipped the cool shining beads, heavy and exotic, through her finger one by one and her mother beamed upon her fondly and demanded that Ted admire Bill's taste. Ted, presenting his own neat package . . . of course, a book as his mind didn't run much beyond books, found himself painfully abashed. But Val took the book in her hands and was dutifully exclamatory. He had had Flora's poems specially bound for her, a companion to the edition of Millay which had been his first gift to her. And Flora herself had written in her graceful flowing hand "To

Ted's friend and mine."

"I wish she could have come too," said Val.

For she had asked Flora. "Why not, Mother? You'll like her. And you know you'll get a kick out of meeting her. Besides, she's Ted's girl — in a way."

Mrs. Loring would have welcomed Ted's girl, or any number of Ted's girls even if they were hideous to look upon and of a most uncertain social position. For now that she was assured that Ted's cardiac interest centered in someone other than her own child, she was delighted, and quite took that young man to the family bosom. But Flora had to go elsewhere. "A big party," she explained. "I accepted ages ago . . . of course I'd much rather be with Ted and you, Val, quietly."

Quietly! Ted remembered that, listening to the racket going on about him. Noisemakers, clappers, whistles. His own head was decorated with a red paper concoction suspiciously like a dunce cap and as he pulled a snapper with Val, recoiled from the small sharp shock, he looked over the crowded table with the astonished eyes of one who has never before been made a member of a large, noisy and cheerful family group at Christmastime.

Dinner was simple. Sherry first, and hard biscuits. Then a fruit cup, and then the large impressive turkey, traditional vegetables, pie and pudding. The domestic staff had not been augmented. Mrs. Loring had assisted in all preparations, and if the service was slow, and more or less involved, with Val hopping up to pass seconds on gravy and the like, it was gay in the extreme. A bottle, two bottles of Mr. Loring's small stock had been opened, and even Miss Simpkins, Mrs. Loring's most fiercely spinster cousin, had become un-starched to a degree.

There were presents for Ted on the tree, silly things from the five-and-ten. Ridiculous animals, penwipers, trick spectacles, and a matchbox which exploded in the hand. Val had presented him with ties, an excellent and, he feared, expensive collection. She said, "You need a dash of color, so I've provided it," and in a moment of expansion, he discarded the sober blue-gray article he was wearing and replaced it with a brighter hue, enlivened by a touch of red. The effect wasn't so bad, after all. And after dinner, when replete to the point of coma they were sitting in the living room, he caught a glimpse of himself in the mirror and was somewhat startled. His hair wasn't very well brushed, owing to the giddy manner in which he had worn his cap, his eyes were not hidden behind his professional spectacles and his new tie was under one ear.

There were games and music and some of

the older people slipped quietly upstairs and flung themselves on fresh, cool beds and indulged in naps. And at about eight o'clock Val said, "Put on your bonnet, Ted, we're going walking. I feel like all three of the little pigs."

It was a quiet evening, with a dark, star-splashed sky. There had been snow, and it was still white and shining under the street lamps. In all the windows of the nearby houses there were wreaths, some of them lighted, and the glowing silhouettes of Christmas trees. Val, muffled to the ears in furs, with her fur toque on the back of her head, took a long, deep breath. "Come on," she ordered, "walk fast . . . we've got to get the better of that turkey."

They walked for almost an hour. Cars flashed by, people passed on the street and smiled at Val, a sprig of holly pinned to her coat. Val smiled back. "Merry Christmas," she said, and meant it. Once a woman spoke to them, an old woman, bent, twisted, smelling of poverty. Val popped her hand in her pocket and put a dollar bill into the shaking hand. "God bless you, darling," said the woman in drunken delight.

They walked on and Ted spoke severely to his partner. "You shouldn't do things like that; you don't do any good, you only do harm. These things should be handled through the proper channels. The woman's a professional beggar and a drunkard at that. She'll spend the money in bad liquor."

"Well, let her," said Val defiantly. "Why not? She's old, she's miserable; if her escape is liquor and I can buy it for her, let her have it. How'd you like to be as old as she is, with no one in the world to give a damn about you, and —"

Her voice broke. Ted said, "Why, Val!" He felt curiously stirred. Then he pulled himself together. This Christmas business was affecting his mind. He was becoming sentimental, irrational. Val said, walking rapidly, "I can stand poor people . . . unless they are very old or very young. Then I *can't* stand them."

In the kind of world Ted hoped he would one day live in there would be no poverty, he assured her. He kept on assuring her, at the top of his voice for blocks and blocks. Val listened. She said, after a while, "It sounds pretty dull," and he found his regimented sentences faltering in their steady tread.

"Dull?"

"Yes. Safe and dull. No incentive to recklessness. No crazy ambitions that would force a man to take a chance. No ups and downs. I'd hate it."

She was, he assured her, the most inconsistent woman on the face of the globe. All but weeping over a dirty, down-trodden, drunken old beggar one minute and the next rejecting, repudiating a world in which such a woman would have no place.

Of course, he admitted, she had been reared in an atmosphere of bourgeoise dry rot —

She wasn't listening. They were passing a church. The doors stood open. There was light within, and the radiance of stained glass and candles. She tugged at his hand. "Come on in, let's —"

Ted disapproved of churches. Commercialized, they were, lacking in constructive charity. He did not wholly agree with the Soviet system. He was, he informed himself, wise enough to know that you cannot forbid a people to worship. But churches battened on ignorance, superstition; churches —

He was muttering something of the sort when he found himself inside, his hat in his hand, and his expostulations dying on his lips. He followed Val meekly into a back pew and sat awkwardly beside her while she knelt. It was a service of song for the most part, and sitting there he found himself quietly relaxed and without thought. The music of the organ was like the sound of a sea, the young voices of the boy choir were unearthly sweet, entirely sexless, the disembodied soul of song, rising to the vaulted ceiling.

He never knew what church it was. He never asked. When after a time Val touched him and whispered something, he followed her out like a man dreaming. He said to himself, out once more in the clear cold air, Purely emotional, of course, and tried to believe that this was so. But it wasn't, not entirely.

They went back, in silence, to the Loring house where they discovered that those who had crept away to nap had awakened refreshed and ready to eat again. It was late, Ted found, with amazement. He was also aware that he was actually hungry.

He and Val raided the icebox and larder and set out on the cleared dining room table the remains of the noble bird, a large bowl of cranberry sauce, bread and butter, nuts and raisins. Mrs. Loring made coffee and Mr. Loring produced a bottle of cognac.

"Help yourselves," bade Val, her hands filled with plates and spoons and knives and forks, "every man for himself."

It was after midnight when Ted left. He was alone in the hall with Val for a little while. Standing directly under the mistletoe which decorated the hall light, she gave him her hands. Ted looked up. Was this, he wondered, the kissing bush he had read about in the old English novels? He supposed so, although in this instance the bush had been reduced to a mere spray or two.

"Val . . ."

"Yes, Ted."

"I've had a swell time."

"I'm glad."

He said, after a moment, "I don't remember any Christmas like this one."

It was a pretty inept sentence but it served. She said, taking her hands away, "It's been perfect. I mean, it would have been if Bill had been here, and Flora."

He was instantly estranged. Why did she have to drag them in? He said something, he never knew quite what and she couldn't believe her own ears . . . was it possible he had said *Damn Bill and Flora*? and took her very swiftly in his arms. He said, laughing, excited, angry, "This doesn't count — it's Christmas, and you would stand under the mistletoe!"

He kissed her, very soundly. Not once but twice. She did not struggle, nor did she return his kiss, as she had done once before. As a matter of fact, she was more kissed against than kissing. She stood perfectly still in the circle of his arms, and closed her eyes. When he released her he saw with an instant, unusual compunction that she looked very white and tired.

"Good night," he said gently.

The door closed behind him. Val walked slowly back to the dining room where her mother, her father and a cousin or two were still sitting. Mrs. Loring rose and began to clear away. "Think Ted had a good time?" she asked her daughter.

Val picked up a dish, carried it to the sideboard, and then carried it back again and set it in the exact center of the table. "Of course he did," she replied.

Mrs. Loring looked at her in amazement. "What on earth's the matter with you?" she inquired.

Val flushed suddenly, red staining white. She said, "I dunno. All of a dither, I guess. Too much Christmas."

When the last dish had been stacked and the last guest had departed Val kissed her father and mother and went upstairs to her bedroom. She sat down at her desk, in her Christmas finery and pulled a sheet of paper toward her.

"Bill, darling," she wrote.

She laid the pen aside, very carefully. She put her arms on the desk and laid her head on them. I *won't* cry, she said in a muffled voice.

She wouldn't cry. She couldn't write to Bill. She sat there for a long time until she heard her mother's step on the stairs. Val reached up and turned off her light. Her mother paused outside her door. Val heard the slower, heavier steps of her father. "She's probably fast asleep," her mother said, outside the door.

Val rose after a while, and undressed in the dark. She tiptoed to the bathroom and made as little noise as possible, splashing her face with very cold water. Then she went to bed. Lying there, her arms flung wide, she thought miserably, What's the use of kidding myself like this? I'm in love with Ted, and have been all along . . . hating him is just another part of it; he's in love with Flora, but even if he weren't, I can't let Bill down.

Bill wouldn't want you loving someone else, her own particular still small voice warned her, that would be letting him down, if you like.

I know — but he's so far away, thought Val, and how do I know this is real? How do I know it means anything? And if it does, so what? He'll marry Flora — or won't marry her. It amounts to the same thing. Anyway he'll belong to her. What about me? By the time Bill gets back maybe I'll have got over it and will be sensible again. I'll start being sensible, right now.

And to prove it she cried herself to sleep.

# Chapter X

When next they met in the shop Miss Loring and Mr. Morrison regarded each other with a perfectly unconscious wariness. Each had determined that the mistletoe episode be carried off with a high hand and a gay heart and laid to the Christmas spirit. But once when Val approached the safe on a perfectly sober, demure and legitimate errand, Ted jumped as though someone had stuck him violently with a pin. He watched her twirl the dials, his eyes very round behind his ridiculous glasses. No, she wasn't after the contract!

When a day had passed and two days and then three and nothing had been said, no nonchalant "hope you didn't mind my excursion into sentiment, the other night, St. Nicholas stuff, Santa Claus and all that," which was a speech Ted had rehearsed, when Val by not so much as a lifted eyebrow made it evident that she even recalled such an occasion, nothing could be said. You either had to make your explanations — if any — immediately or not at all.

If there was a slight change in her attitude toward him, Ted did not notice it. She was as sharp with him as usual, she quarreled with him over as many, if not more, trivial subjects and circumstances. But they were, he congratulated himself, good friends. And as it was the first friendship he had ever experienced with an attractive young woman he found himself liking it very much. The business plodded along and did well enough. At least Ted could eat, and be certain of his modest roof. He had insisted when the first of the year came that Val be paid not a salary, but something more nearly approximating a drawing account, against her interest in the business. It wasn't much but it was something . . . it made him feel better, he declared.

In February, a year from their initial and astonishing meeting, they planned a Valentine Day celebration. Ted thought of it all by himself and was overcome with admiration at his own consideration and thoughtfulness. They would go out to dinner and then to a movie he declared magnificently, in commemoration of the slippery beginning of their partnership.

Val asked herself stoutly, Well, why not? As the weeks went by, she was managing to convince herself that her emotional breakdown at Christmas had been just one of those things. It hadn't meant anything. It couldn't mean anything. She simply imagined that Ted Morrison was the sum and substance of her existence. It was like an illness. She would get over it, she had a strong constitution, and Bill was the remedy and the antidote. Having thus decided, she redoubled her attentions to her absent fiancé, on paper. But it took such an infernally long time for a letter to reach wherever he was. He wasn't ever, as it happened, at his base for any considerable length of time. He was cruising about, visiting little-known islands and writing back glowing descriptions of those few which he found as yet unspoiled by the tourist trade. After reading his letters, which reached her such a long time after they were written, Val felt curiously overdressed, and bleached. "What, no flowers in my hair?" she would murmur, regarding herself reproachfully in the most convenient mirror.

But on Valentine's Day Ted did not come to the shop. Nine, ten and eleven struck and he had not yet put in an appearance. Just after eleven he telephoned. He croaked slightly. He announced plaintively, "I've an awful cold."

"So I hear. What are you doing for it . . . taking a brisk walk in a blizzard?"

It wasn't even snowing. But you know how women are. Ted said, "Don't be silly." He sneezed twice. "I'll stay in all day and by tonight I'll feel swell," he told her.

Val said instantly, "I can't get anyone now to tend the shop. But as soon as I close I'll come down and look after you. Of course, we won't go out tonight. We'll postpone the party. Meantime, isn't there someone who can — ?"

"Flora," said Ted sneezing lustily, "Flora's coming in. She phoned early — about something else. She said she'd come down . . . not that I need her."

"Oh," said Val, "that's all right then, you're in good hands." She hung up feeling sad and righteous and ill-treated. She had a new dress for the occasion. She'd made a valentine, all very modernistic hearts and flowers with a funny little verse, unsentimental and merry. She had intended to give it to him tonight. Perhaps it's just as well, she decided philosophically.

She worried about her partner most of the day. There was only one period during which she did not worry about him and that was when, early in the afternoon, she persuaded a charming if inebriated gentleman that she might be someone's valentine but she certainly wasn't his. She was very tactful about it. So he bought six books and a blue pottery vase for which he hadn't the slightest use and staggered cheerfully out into the street again.

At three o'clock the telephone rang. This time it was Flora, in a state of high agitation. She began without preamble:

"He's certainly going to have pneumonia!"

"Well," responded Val, with an unpleasant constriction at her heart, "do something about it. Doctors are usually indicated."

"But he's flying," cried Flora in a species of despair.

Val began to think she had gone completely mad.

"Flying — where?" she asked calmly. Someone was crazy. Whether it was yourself or the other fellow didn't matter. You had to keep calm.

"It's that aunt of his," wailed Flora. "She's dead . . . the housekeeper wired him. He's leaving at once, by plane, to take charge of the arrangements."

"Let me speak to him," commanded Val.

"Ted, Val wants . . . Oh, hell," said Flora unpoetically, "he's gone!"

And indeed it did seem to Val that she heard the faint slam of a door. She could even imagine the clatter of footsteps on a stair, the hoarse hailing of taxis, the hooting of horns, the wild, chilly progress, the whirring of a propeller.

"Tell me about it," she ordered.

Flora cried, "I've told you all I know. I got here, oh, a little after eleven. He was walking around in a dressing gown." Flora sneezed. She added pathetically, "I'm very susceptible to colds. He hadn't had anything to eat," she went on, "so I had something sent in, and got him some aspirin and bicarb and stayed with him. I've been reading to him," she explained carefully. "I had to stay or he would have gone to the shop, which," she concluded dramatically, "would have been suicide."

"What about his flight?" asked Val, perfectly well aware that she was being malicious but knowing Flora would not recognize it for such, at least not immediately.

"Oh, that. If," said Flora, "if she's dead, the aunt I mean, she'll stay dead till tomorrow. I don't see what he had to go for."

Poets are singularly callous. So are women who aren't poets. Val found herself in direct agreement.

"He's the only relative," said Flora. She sneezed again. Then exclaimed, more in sorrow than in anger, "Oh, my God, I do believe I'm coming down with something!" and hung up the receiver.

Val sat back and contemplated the picture of Ted "in a dressing gown" being fed bicarb, aspirined and read to by one of America's most recently recognized geniuses. She did not care for the picture. It was a shade too domestic. Still, she thought resignedly, even poets' love affairs peter out into domesticity. Aren't they always complaining about the metamorphosis in public print?

Yet she liked it no better for her resignation.

She looked in the untidy pigeonholes of the desk and found the Massachusetts address Ted had given her some time ago and telegraphed him there, the usual condolences and the usual can-I-do-anything?

When it was closing time she saw Keturie safely into the basement, locked up and went home and reported. Her mother was pleasantly sympathetic. "The poor boy," she said instantly, "with no one to look after him. He shouldn't have been permitted to make the trip."

"Flora was there."

Mrs. Loring raised her eyebrow. "Flora? Well, I suppose that's all right . . . young people do things differently than they did in my day."

"And high time too," murmured Val absently. Then she seized her mother and kissed her. "You," she said fondly, "are a lamb."

Two days passed and there was no word from Ted. On the second day Mr. Loring, in the course of his business, was forced to make a trip to Detroit. Mrs. Loring went with him. He rarely left home and it was his wife's amiable delusion that he would probably disintegrate into air or a speck of dust without her. In common with most wives she believed firmly that her husband was unable to brush his teeth, order his meals, or otherwise perform the usual functions of an ordinary human being when absent from her side.

On the fourth day, at the shop, Val opened a frantic wire from Ted. It made very little sense the first time she read it:

CAN YOU COME AT ONCE THINGS HERE IN AWFUL MESS DOCTOR SAYS CANNOT LEAVE MAKE IT SNAPPY

He was dead. He was dying. Yet no hand static in rigor mortis or even moderately enfeebled in pulse could have penned this telegram, she reassured herself. Yet all sorts of nightmare pictures moved before her eyes. Ted in the clutches of suddenly appearing ravening relatives. Aunt-whatever-her-name was walking o' nights, or not even decently in her grave, sheriffs and their men riding up on horseback.

She called up Flora. It nearly killed her to do so but she called her up just the same. Perhaps he had sent for Flora also.

But Flora was not at home. Her publishers, a little later, reported that she was in Chicago, autographing books.

Val hung up, sunk her chin in her hand

and pondered. She thought, Mother will have a fit, Father will have two fits.

She didn't care.

At the end of an hour everything had been arranged. She called the young woman whom she had used often in the shop when there was any rush business and bespoke her services for a few days. The young woman was only too delighted. She came down to the shop immediately and took off her coat and rolled up her sleeves, figuratively speaking. Val showed her where everything was, with especial attention to the cash register. She gave her the keys, she enlisted her concern for Keturie. Keturie needed concern. She had passed her kittenhood and it was obvious even to the most unpracticed eye that given another year or so she was bound to become a grandmother.

Then Val went home, telephoned an airport, packed a bag, wired Ted and her innocent parents:

PLEASE DON'T FALL DOWN DEAD BUT I AM GOING TO TED'S AUNT'S HOUSE TO STRAIGHTEN THINGS OUT TED IS VERY ILL STOP SOMEONE HAS TO BE THERE STOP THERE IS A HOUSEKEEPER AND THE CONVENTIONS SHOULD BE SATISFIED HOPE YOU AREN'T BEING TOO GIDDY DON'T WORRY

ABOUT ME OR IF YOU DO TAKE IT IN HO-
MEOPATHIC DOSES LOVE VAL.

She omitted the address, which was clever of her.

She had, she decided, plenty of money. She'd better have more. When you have plenty you always need twice as much. So she cashed a check at a shop where she was well known — the butchershop, in fact — and set out in a taxi.

One regrets to say that flying was not Val's ideal sport. She was very airsick. The most seasoned travelers regarded her with amusement or dismay according to their temperaments. She spoke plaintively to the stewardess. "I'm sorry to be so silly," she gasped. That little lady was briskly consoling. "It gets some people," she admitted. "There. Do you feel better?"

Better, and worse. She was, she confessed to herself, not only airsick but scared to death. However, Boston wasn't so far away. Eventually she had her feet on the ground again, and very comfortable she found it.

She hired a car to take her to the village in which Ted's aunt had lived. There weren't any trains for some time. It was an expensive ride and it took over an hour, but the driver assured her that with anyone else driving it would have been more expensive still and would have consumed perhaps an hour and a half.

Falling out of the car, more moribund than quick, she decided he was right. She paid him, overtipped him and went wanly up the steps.

This village was called Newville. It was a little place, with wide elm-shaded streets. Or maybe the trees were maples. It was dark and Val didn't know or care. The house was hideous. It was green in trim and white of clapboard and should have been the house of one's New England dreams. Perfect Mourning Becomes Electra, or something. It wasn't. It was a little four-square box of a house, two stories, attic and cellar, precise and without an atom of charm. It had a small front yard like a discarded handkerchief. It had no porch. It was entirely nothing at all.

Val rang the bell and it pealed horrifically through the house. There was a pause. She heard someone shouting. A man. That must be Ted, she thought, and her heart lifted for the first time. At least he was still alive. There were hastening footsteps, not Ted's. The door opened. The housekeeper stood there. Her name was Miss Smithers and she was spare and sixty. She wore what was left of her hair in a little bun on top of her head. She wore what were left of her teeth on the outside.

She had chronically red eyes and a sniffle and one had to deduce the kind heart. She sniffled quite a little upon beholding Miss Valentine Loring.

"Are *you* the lady Mr. Morrison's expecting?" she demanded, in a surprising basso.

"I think so," replied Val faintly. Had he expected Flora?

"Come in," replied Miss Smithers. She sniffled some more. "I'm sure I thought you would be older," she announced. "But, come in anyway," she said, "I'm glad you've come."

"Val?" called Ted from the dim reaches of an upper story. He didn't really shout, after all. He barked.

"Coming," she said brightly. Up the stairs she went, straight up, uncompromisingly so. She perceived no gracious, polished balustrade. The stairs rose from a small square hall and kept on rising. They were uncarpeted.

"The doctor's been," announced Miss Smithers, with true New England reticence.

Been? Been *what?* Val wondered, bewildered and tired and very empty, been married, divorced, in prison?

Miss Smithers opened a door. In a bedroom totally devoid of any attraction lay Ted. The bed in which he lay was about the size of Cleopatra's barge. It was walnut and it was carved. Cherubs of a particularly grinning ferocity swarmed over the posts. A dotted swiss doohickey hung to the floor, complete with fringe, and a large canopy overshadowed the occupant. One light burned, unshaded. Ted said gravely:

"They all die in this bed."

"Ted! For heaven's sake!" She imagined that he looked terrible. She knew that he looked terrible. She began casting coat, hat, bags and such to the floor. "Ted!"

"The doctor," began Ted, while Miss Smithers chaperoned vigilantly from the doorway, "says if I'm moved I'll have pneumonia. He says he won't risk it. He says —"

"Ted," interrupted Val, and perched herself upon a singularly hostile chair, "please don't try to talk."

"But I've got to talk," he argued hoarsely. "Why should I bring you all the way down here and *not* talk — or am I supposed to make signs?"

"Well, talk then," she surrendered, "but be as brief as possible and I'll phone the doctor myself."

"He's coming later. He wanted me to have nurses."

"Well, why don't you have them?" asked Val practically.

Ted flushed. Even with the heightened color of fever, one saw he flushed.

"I don't want 'em. Look here, Val, I caught this cold at the funeral."

Val said, "You caught it in New York — go on."

"There's so much to be done," he told her. "You see, she left me almost everything and —"

"Couldn't it have been done later?" asked Val.

"No," said Ted. "I — I thought, if you'd take charge, see the lawyer and all that, perhaps persuade them to let me be moved —"

He was delirious or something. Nothing he said added up. What was wrong with him? Val cast a look over her shoulder. Miss Smithers. He was terrified of Miss Smithers. Perhaps Miss Smithers had expected to inherit all Aunt Bella's worldly goods. Maybe she put poison in Ted's tea.

Val rose. She said, "You shut up and lie still. I'll attend to things. You *would* do something like this!"

She went from the room quietly but with a flounce in her walk. Ted grinned. His head hurt, his chest hurt, he might as well be dead as feel the way he did. Yet he was feeling a little better. Val'd show 'em.

In the hall:

"Is there a room I could have?" asked Val.

Miss Smithers twitched her upper lip. Her

teeth gleamed, in profusion. This, then, was a smile. She said:

"Here — next door to me."

It was one of four bedrooms on the second floor. The guest chamber, in which Ted lay, Aunt Bella's room, now closed, as was only fitting, Miss Smithers' very extraordinary sanctum and the smaller room which was usually used for a sewing room. There was a divan in it with broken springs, an entirely frightening headless dressmaker's dummy, two chairs and a sewing machine. Val entered the room with Miss Smithers behind her. She put down her things. She said, "Thanks, it will do nicely. Is there a bathroom on this floor?"

There was, and Miss Smithers exhibited it. It was a bit leprous, but would serve.

And now Miss Smithers asked, either hopefully or warningly, "You wouldn't care for anything to eat, I suppose?"

"Oh, but I would!" cried Val, ignoring the hope or the warning. "I'm starved." She gave a graphic account of her airplane trip. "Anything, anything at all. And would you give me the doctor's telephone number?"

"There isn't a telephone," Miss Smithers reminded her. "Bella hadn't liked telephones, nasty, noisy things. And the doctor will be around in about half an hour."

Val had some supper, much belated, in the

kitchen. Miss Smithers was thawing. She admitted that Bella had been a good friend but in late years a little trying. However, they had got along very well. Two lone women. She sighed, and set something before Val upon the checked cloth of the kitchen table. It had once been an egg. She made some tea, cut some bread, spooned out some preserves.

Then she sat down and ate three-quarters of it and confided to Val that what with the funeral and all and Ted down sick, she had had a most difficult time.

Val was aware, as everyone is, that New England cooks are sacrosanct, in literature at least. All New England women can cook. But either Miss Smithers was not the rock-ribbed native product she pretended to be or no one who writes, reads or eats had ever met her. For Miss Smithers couldn't cook, not at all. She was the world's most horrible cateress. No wonder Aunt Bella died, thought Val, choking slightly. She had yet to learn that in the relationship of give and take which had existed between Aunt Bella and her companion, Aunt Bella cooked and Miss Smithers sewed, dusted, read aloud, and sang to her own accompaniment, off key.

Poor Ted, thought Val, diligently planning invalid meals.

The doctor arrived, puffing. He was old,

fat, amiable and competent. He liked Val. He said, "Young Morrison's partner, eh? I must say he has good taste." He did not actually pinch her cheek but his glance did. Val warmed toward him but not toward the house. I wonder, she thought, who tends to the furnace?

No, Ted couldn't be moved. Not even to a Boston hospital. Pneumonia? Pooh, of course he didn't have it. He had a badly neglected cold and a touch of flu. He'd be all right presently. The main thing was not to risk a relapse. If he was moved, he, Dr. Evans, would wash his hands of him. He went through the gestures.

"A nurse?" suggested Val.

"He won't hear of one."

"He must," she said firmly.

"Won't. Stubborn young idiot. Nevertheless," added the doctor thoughtfully, "I wonder if he has second sight? Those around here would stop a couple of clocks. Still, I could have sent to Boston."

Val said, "No. What about a practical nurse? Someone to make him comfortable, get up little meals. There's a sort of dressing room with washstands and things opening from his room; it's big enough to put a cot in."

The doctor looked at her with respect. "You persuade him."

191

So Val persuaded him, before the doctor had left. She stood at the foot of the bed, with her hands folded. It was late and she looked very tired. "Ted, if you want me to stay here you'll have to help me all you can. The family will be wild enough as it is . . . but with Miss Smithers and a nurse . . ."

"Hell," said Ted, "have it your own way."

The nurse came in, not more than an hour later. She was round and pleasant and motherly and her name was Mrs. Carson. She took instant and competent charge. Miss Smithers said, sniffling vigorously, "If I'm expected to cook for a regiment!"

Val assured her that she wasn't. Between Mrs. Carson and herself the inmates of this private asylum would certainly manage to be fed. She crawled wearily into the bathroom and out again. She went to her sewing room and placed herself between the sheets Miss Smithers had condescended to put upon the divan. She had never in all of her life slept in so uncomfortable a bed — nor slept better.

Val was in Newville for a week. It was the busiest week she had spent. She wired her parents with a praiseworthy regularity, dwelling upon Ted's miserable state and the fact that both housekeeper and practical nurse constituted a plethora of chaperons. She interviewed Aunt Bella's desiccated lawyer and discovered that while Ted had been left the house, lock, stock and barrel, and that insurance covered expenses, the small amount of cash and securities remaining went to Miss Smithers.

She consulted with Ted at intervals, careful not to tire him, which somewhat maddened that young gentleman who, cosseted and spoiled by Mrs. Carson, had now definitely turned the corner. She placed the house in the hands of real-estate agents, and arranged for a sale of the furniture and personal belongings other than Aunt Bella's clothing and moth-eaten mink cape which she, with Ted's consent, presented to Miss Smithers.

She paid a visit to the cemetery and assured herself that the plot was well tended. Insurance would take care of that, too. There was nothing to do but get Ted home again and leave the place to the tender mercies of the real-estate people. "If," she warned Ted, "you get anything out of it, it will be a miracle. Who on earth would want to buy it?"

Ted said:

"Someone may be ass enough. I don't want the place. Taxes and all . . ."

He was convalescent and peevish. Val, regarding him thoughtfully, wondered again why on earth he had sent for her. There wasn't any business connection with the legacy, the probate of the will and so on which he could not have attended to himself after the slight delay of his illness. She decided that Miss Smithers lay at the bottom of all this. Ted couldn't cope with Miss Smithers. He had known himself intimidated, cranky, uncomfortable and ill; he had sent for Val to rectify all these things.

Val's parents, having returned home and having at last the secret of her whereabouts in their possession, wrote and wired her reproachfully and at length and Val went to the drugstore to telephone them and reassure them. "Of all the crazy things!" her mother wailed. But all Val could say was, "If you could see Miss Smithers, Mother, your mind would be completely at rest. She is a perfect mechanical refrigerator. Not even the tiniest scrap of a moral could go bad in her mere presence."

Yet she and Miss Smithers were becoming friends. In an outbreak of emotion Miss Smithers had even confided to her the great tragedy of her life, her blissful engagement to a Vermont pastor who had distinguished himself with, thought Val, rare fortitude and good common sense, by eloping with the prettiest girl in his choir six weeks before his marriage to Miss Smithers was to have been celebrated.

The real-estate agent, a jaundiced individual, had come and gone. The house was to be sold, as it stood. He thought he had a buyer. Was Mr. Morrison sure that nothing remained in the house, no souvenir of his aunt, which he wished to have?

Ted, sitting up in an armchair with Mrs. Carson bringing frequent eggnogs and feeding him flaxseed and rock candy and lemon juice for his cough, was sure. But Val shook her red head. Let the real-estate agent give her another day before he took inventory, she explained. There were one or two pieces in the attic which she believed Mr. Morrison might like to have.

When the man had gone she explained. There was a ladder-backed chair, and a marvelous lowboy. "If you don't want them," she urged, "let's use them in the shop. We can sell them, Ted. I don't know much about furniture but these look pretty darned good to me, ignorant as I am. And Dr. Evans agrees. I dragged him up there to look at them. And there's a little silver."

Ted was tired. "Well, fix it up any way you want. Set anything aside you think's any good and we'll ship it."

"There's a lot of books," she said, "and magazines. Old *Godey's* . . ."

"Drug on the market — well, maybe not. Look 'em over. Any Currier and Ives?"

"Three or four, bad condition," she said doubtfully. "But I'll go over the things in the attic again."

So she went to the attic, which was not large and which had a higher ceiling than most attics. It had also its full complement of spiders, dust, and slanted sunlight. There was snow dropping from the roof to the sill and a smell of long-deceased mice and bats. The furniture stood piled in forlorn heaps, arms and legs missing, a veterans' hospital. But the lowboy was a delight to the eye even in its present state and the ladder-backed chair would need little restoration.

There was nothing else except one mirror which might or might not be good and a little old washstand — cherry, Val thought.

She sat down on the floor and began pulling the books about and piling the *Godey's* into a little heap. Here were some bound copies of *Frank Leslie's Weekly* and some *Scribner's*. She put those aside also. The backs of the books she clapped together to rid them of accumulated dust . . . half sets, broken backed. Emerson. Dickens. Several little volumes of *The Duchess.* An almost complete Elsie Dinsmore, of a not very ancient issue, therefore worthless; some Laura Jean Libbeys; a dozen novels of the last twenty years.

Ted, half asleep in the room downstairs,

nodded in his chair. Mrs. Carson sat beside him, knitting. Miss Smithers had gone calling to complain to her friends in her martyred way that dear Bella might have left her the house too.

"Ted! Ted!"

Ted jumped as if he had been shot. Mrs. Carson dropped a stitch and said "Dear me!" in agitation. Val was clattering down the stairs. Now she burst into the room. Her hair was wild and full of spiderwebs, her face was smudged with dirt and she was so excited that she could scarcely speak. While Ted stared at her in amazement, she thrust a small, shabby volume into his bewildered hands and stammered:

"Ted . . . look! We're — I mean you're — *rich!*"

# Chapter XI

Mrs. Carson's stitches flew off her needles. Ted, struggling to his feet, casting off encumbering blankets, fighting with pillows, never even glanced at the book which involuntarily he held. He was really very much alarmed. His partner had gone out of her mind. He had always somewhat suspected that perhaps she was a little unbalanced. Now obviously she had tipped over. "My dear Val," he murmured soothingly, "sit down . . . take it easy."

He discovered that his own knees were on the knocking side. He sat down himself, rather abruptly, and waved his free, distracted hand at Mrs. Carson.

"Give her something, can't you?" he asked sharply. "An eggnog . . . a spot of brandy . . ."

But Val was beside him, tugging at him in an exasperating if futile fashion. It was as if Keturie had taken a fit before his startled eyes.

"You nitwit," she was positively shrieking, "you — you goof! Look at it. Open it. Here, handle it with reverence. It's a *Tamerlane*. Can't you see that, or have you lost your sight. . . . *Tamerlane!*"

Ted gasped, swallowed, almost choked. His

eyes went to the volume in his hand. An inconsiderable volume. Title page. "Tamerlane and other Poems. By a Bostonian. Boston, 1827."

"It can't be," he denied incredulously.

"But it is!" Val was babbling. She was at the same time executing a *pas seul.* She flew over to Mrs. Carson, jerked that astonished lady to her feet and while the needles flew in one direction and the baby blanket in another, whirled her around to music unheard by anyone save herself. "We're rich," she chanted. "Rich!"

Mrs. Carson, who suffered from fallen arches and other minor ailments, nevertheless laughed until she almost cried. "There, let be," she said, "let me catch my breath."

Benevolently Val released her. She went back to Ted and sat down on the floor at his feet, clasped her hands about her knees and rocked with excitement . . .

"In the bundle of books in the trunk. It's in very good condition," she said. "Ted, how much is it worth?"

He said slowly:

"I can't believe it. There are only a few copies known to exist."

"Less than ten," interrupted Val briskly. "I looked it up once at the library. A copy is valued at over ten thousand . . ."

"One was sold, not many years ago for twenty-five," said Ted, "and I believe others may have brought more, in better times. I don't know. But look here, don't get your hopes too high. There have been forgeries."

"At least four," agreed Val, in a recitative sort of voice; "one only five years ago in England — so good that only an expert could distinguish it. Very well, bring on your experts, because," she said practically, "your aunt wouldn't go around buying forged copies, would she? Only nuts like collectors would fall for that. She probably didn't buy this at all. Of course she didn't. She used to live in Boston, her people came from here — that book has been sitting around in trunks and attics ever since it was published."

Ted said, "As soon as we get back to New York . . ." His eyes blazed and there was color in his cheeks.

Mrs. Carson looked at him anxiously. She said quickly, "I'm sure I don't know what it's all about, Mr. Morrison, but if you excite yourself so much" — she looked at Val reproachfully — "you'll find yourself running a temperature again and we'll have to put you back to bed."

"I'm all right," said Ted. He looked at Val. He drew a long breath. He asked inadequately, "Ain't this sumpin'?"

Val nodded. There were tears of pure excitement in her eyes. Ted said slowly, "If it hadn't been for you — if I hadn't asked you to come here — that would have gone to the secondhand man with the rest of the junk in the attic."

Val nodded. "I had a hunch . . . it was about furniture though," she admitted. "I didn't expect to find anything like this."

"We'll have an expert see it," said Ted, "and then . . . the highest bidder gets it. We may have to hold it awhile."

He looked around him. "Better not say anything about it to anyone yet." He had the immediate creepy feeling of the person who stumbles upon a treasure. Eyes looked at him from the shadows of the room, the house was surrounded by thieves and murderers. He wouldn't shut his eyes in sleep again until this little, inconsiderable volume was in a safe-deposit vault at his bank, he thought.

"O.K., toots," agreed Val with an infuriating calm.

He leaned down and shook her, to Mrs. Carson's fascinated amazement. He cried:

"Do you realize what this *means?*"

"Of course I do," said Val indignantly, "it means a lot of money."

Her little face sobered. She thought, wriggling away from his clutch, A lot of money.

Flora will change her mind about marriage — maybe. He'll buy back my interest. Oh, hell, thought Val profanely, I wish I hadn't found it.

But she looked again at his rapt face and brilliant eyes and her heart softened.

"We'll get out of here as fast as possible," planned Ted rapidly. "Tomorrow, by plane."

"In the first place," said Val, "the doctor won't let you go tomorrow; in the second, if you go by plane you can jolly well go alone. If you think I'm going to submit myself to that indignity a second time . . . Besides," she added hastily, as he showed signs of beating her down by heavy, masculine, clublike arguments, "besides, suppose something happened? Not that it would matter about us," she concluded magnificently, "but the *Tamerlane.*"

Ted thought that over. It seemed sensible to him. He was no longer his own man. He was custodian of a "rare" item, one of the real literary finds of his generation. He thought suddenly of Edgar Allan Poe, the bleak, beautiful face, dark and somber, marked by doom. He thought of the child who was Poe's wife, and her death; he thought of a man who starved and sweated in the inescapable clutch of his genius. He turned the book again in his hands, with tenderness and a little terror. For someone would, he had no doubt, pay him a price for this volume which would have freed its writer from the incessant worry over money for many long months.

His face was very grave, Val thought; what's he thinking about? She asked him, after a moment; and he told her, stumbling over the words.

She was silent, sitting there on the floor, looking up into his face. And looking down he was aware that her thoughts kept pace with his own.

After a while he said:

"Well, we'll get out of here tomorrow, if we possibly can, and meantime —"

"I'll make the arrangements," Val said instantly. "I'll see the real-estate man again. What's his name? I can never remember it."

"Smith," responded Ted, grinning.

"Oh," said Val, a little dashed. Then she recovered. "Smith. I must write it down," she murmured thoughtfully; she went on, "I'll arrange to have the furniture shipped to the shop. Mother knows a man who's marvelous at restoring things."

Mrs. Carson looked at her watch and went from the room to fetch Ted his eggnog. Ted said, when she had gone:

"You understand that half of whatever we get belongs to you?"

"Don't be silly," Val told him sharply, "it's all yours. Your aunt left it to you. I just stumbled on it, that's all."

"No," he said stubbornly.

"Well, don't get excited," she warned him, "or Mrs. Carson will have my ears. We'll talk about that later. Maybe no one will want to buy it after all," she said, almost hopefully.

Ted came down to dinner that night. The doctor had been in to see him and had reluctantly consented to his leaving on the following day. "But into bed you go as soon as you get back to New York," he demanded; "otherwise I won't be responsible."

Dinner, for which Val marketed and which she and Mrs. Carson put together, was something of a masterpiece. Val had discovered that in addition to the bottle of good brandy which Mrs. Carson used for the eggnogs there was also a bottle of sherry. This she opened with something of an air, and toasted Ted across the table, silently, her eyes dancing. Mrs. Carson, feeling rather in the know, although she still didn't understand what it was all about, was rather pleased to observe the Smithers' eyes darting disapprovingly from patient to partner. But even Miss Smithers unbent under the influence of sirloin steak and excellent, dry sherry.

Besides they were leaving the next day and

until the house was sold or rented Miss Smithers had permission to live on there. The furniture in the curious bedroom she inhabited — like some odd and overfurnished nest — was her own.

Ted, in a moment of expansion, took her aside after dinner and informed her that the rest of the contents of the house would be her own also. After all, the secondhand people would offer only a few dollars for the things and she might as well have them. So Miss Smithers, melted to something approaching archness, was made sole possessor of the cupid bed and the mission chairs and the golden oak. It was an occasion.

On the following day Val and Ted returned to New York by train. The *Tamerlane* went with them. The lowboy, the ladder-backed chair, the cherry washstand and gilt mirror which the doctor had pronounced "pretty fair" would follow with the magazines she had laid aside. The house would one day be sold for the proverbial song. Miss Smithers, until that song was sung, would inhabit it in her singular fashion. The doctor had wished them well and had presented a very small bill, and Mrs. Carson had kissed them both and gone back to her daughter's house to await her next case, to whom she could talk about her last one.

On the train, Val announced:

"You're not going home; you're coming with me."

"What on earth — ?"

"Yes. You aren't fit to be in the shop. You shouldn't be traveling now. You're as white as a sheet. I phoned Mother before we started. She said, of course — so the spare room's ready," she told him in her best imitation of Miss Smithers, "the bed turned down and everything."

"It's an imposition."

"No. Do you think I'd let you out of my sight, with all that money on you?"

"Money?"

"The *Tamerlane*. We'll put it in Father's safe in the library until you can get down to the bank with it."

Ted grunted. He grumbled, "You're very managing — I loathe a bossy woman," and relapsed into silence. As a matter of fact he didn't feel any too chipper. He had been dreading the two flights of stairs and the rather cheerless outlook of his room downtown.

Marcia Loring met the train. She whisked her child and her child's partner into a taxicab and took them home, talking all the way. She had never heard of anything so crazy . . . "running down there by yourself, Val." Ted, she informed that young man, must be out of his mind. And what was this about finding a treasure?

Her heart smote her, looking at Ted's face. He did look miserable, poor boy. She was a woman who adored fussing over invalids and she was a completely frustrated woman, for Val's health had always been practically perfect and the state of Mr. Loring's digestion was such an old story that it had ceased to hold any charm for his wife.

When the house was reached matters took a turn for the brisker. Mr. Loring was at home and after due consideration and exclamatory remarks, the *Tamerlane,* under Ted's eyes, was locked in the safe. Mr. Loring gave him a receipt, despite his protests. "More ship-shape" was his comment. He regarded Val as though his child was a changeling. Yet if there was treasure to find, she would find it, was his inner conviction. He had the healthy respect of the average person for one who runs about nonchalantly picking up odd items upon which curious people — privately Mr. Loring considered book collectors half cracked — set an exorbitant value.

The ceremony having been concluded, Ted was whisked off to bed. "Into bed you go, and there you stay until after breakfast tomorrow morning. We'll have our own doctor in to look you over," said Marcia Loring, firmly rejoicing as the nicest woman will rejoice when she has a member of the male species under her pretty thumb.

Ted hadn't had such a fuss made over him since . . . since when? He couldn't remember. Mrs. Carson had started the spoiling and Mrs. Loring completed it. The bed in the pretty and cheerful guest room was comfortable to a degree, the tray which was brought to him later was a miracle of excellent taste, in every sense of the word. Ted lay back against the pillows and beamed at the world, while Mr. Loring, against his wife's commands, sneaked upstairs to smoke a cigar, astride a chair at the foot of the bed, and to talk over the remarkable luck with which this invalid was endowed.

The Lorings' doctor popped in during the evening and pronounced the young man fit to return to work, after a good night's rest, "provided he doesn't overdo it."

Val saw to that. She had sat up half the night talking to her bemused parents and giving accurate if unflattering imitations of Miss Smithers. In the morning she went early to the shop, having conferred by telephone with her substitute during the evening. The substitute, a pretty girl, met her at the shop before nine and went over the events of the past week with her and gave her a full report which, if not wildly cheering, was at least not too discouraging.

Miss Harkness departed and Val settled down to work. Ted wandered in about eleven o'clock. He hadn't, he confessed, wakened till ten. He'd been horrified.

Val reminded him severely:

"The doctor said you were to take it easy."

"I feel swell," boasted Ted. And indeed he looked himself, if a little on the thin side.

"Have you the book with you?"

He patted his bulging breast pocket.

"On my sacred person."

"Trot yourself down to the bank — take a taxi — you can afford it now — and put it in a safe-deposit box until we can gather up a few experts," said Val, as if experts were sweepings and her hands contained dustpan and broom, "and then," she ordered, "come back here after lunch and get on their tracks."

"What about your lunch?"

"Never mind me," said Val, "after a course of Miss Smithers' and my own cooking a drugstore sandwich, sent in, will look like a feast for Lucullus — whoever he was."

Ted betook himself to the bank. It was a glorious day. The fact that it was overcast and threatening made it none the less glorious. Despite the obvious discrepancy in season, the

flowers bloomed and the birds sang. In his
breast pocket was a little book worth upward
of ten thousand dollars. The money you don't
earn seems enormous somehow. Ten thousand, twenty thousand. The shop was safe;
he was safe; Val's investment, bless her, was
safe.

He found himself thinking tenderly of his
partner in business and discovery. She was —
she was a real person. He had never in all
his life been so glad to see anyone as he had
been to see her — when she walked up the
echoing stairs of his aunt's cottage and into
the dismal bedroom with the ferocious cupids
leaping on the bedposts, grinning at him, ma-
liciously, it seemed, to his disordered mind.

He went to the bank and entered the vaults
and laid the *Tamerlane* in a safe-deposit box.
Then he buttoned up his overcoat and sallied
out to find a taxi and return to the shop. On
the way he stopped at an expensive caterer's
and ordered a magnificent lunch for two,
sandwiches of a melting deliciousness, coffee
in a thermos, little expensive cakes and the
most absurd ice cream in zoological forms,
packed in dry ice. Thus burdened he staggered
back to the cab, and arrived at the bookshop.

There were customers, he was glad to note.
They were new, apparently, because they did

not hail him or stay his progress to the back room. The gate-legged table came out from the wall and the feast was spread. A few moments later Val came back.

"I thought I told you not to — For heaven's sake, what's all this?"

"We're celebrating. I would have brought cocktails," he explained, grinning, "but seeing that it's during working hours . . ."

"Ted, you utter goof!" Val looked at her watch. It was indeed lunchtime. She flew to close and lock the outer door. Anyone who wanted to buy a book could wait. She said, coming back and sitting down opposite him, "You've gone haywire."

"What's a couple of dollars?" he demanded superbly. He toasted her in coffee. "To *Tamerlane* . . . and to you."

For no good reason she found herself flushing. She drank from the paper cup. The coffee was hot. She spilled it. She said "Damn," without much vigor, and mopped up the surplus.

"Now," said Ted, when the lunch was over, "to business."

He betook himself to the telephone while Val cleared the table, put the thermos aside to be returned, and opened up the shop. At the end of an hour Ted had rounded up the three men who were considered the leading experts in their line in New York, if not in the country, and had made an appointment with them to come to the shop on the following evening.

Val said, shaking suddenly with an alarming excitement, "Oh, Ted, if it should be forged!"

"You can't tell," he agreed gloomily, smitten with the same thought. Then he put his arm around her shoulders. "Cheer up," he said, "don't worry."

"But I can't help worrying," she wailed.

"If it isn't authentic," he said stoutly, "we've had a lot of fun out of it anyway, haven't we? Don't look so tragic."

"But I feel tragic," she told him, "and I'm so all of a dither that I shortchanged a customer this morning and when one woman asked for mythology for children I handed her a *Golden Bough*. . . . I think I'm gradually going nuts," she admitted sorrowfully. "Will you call me up first thing, after you see them?"

"You'll be here," he said. "We might as well hear the verdict firsthand — and together."

And so on the following evening Val was there. And there were the three grave experts, one long and thin, one short and fat, the third just middling. They should have been bearded, she felt, but they were not. They were like three doctors in consultation, examining, re-examining, conferring, probing. One of them owned an authentic *Tamerlane*, which he had brought along for comparison. Ted stood watching, and Val stood beside him. She had her hand on his arm and her strong little fingers were hard and almost hurting in their grasp.

And when it was over the most expert of the experts removed his glasses and swung them from a black ribbon between his long fingers. He beamed on Ted.

"I congratulate you, Mr. Morrison," he said, and it was an accolade.

Here, I regret to remark, Valentine shrieked; not a loud, but an authentic shriek. "I do beg your pardon," she apologized, blushing.

But the experts understood. There had been times in each of their strange, molelike, delving, dusty lives when each had felt like shrieking . . . whether with triumph or despair.

Before they left Ted had received his first offer. Fifteen thousand dollars.

It was a lot of money. Cash money. Ready money. Certified check. Ted gulped and looked at Val. Almost imperceptibly she shook her head. He grinned at the gentleman who had made the offer. He said, "Thanks — that means a lot to me but —"

"But not enough?" opined the gentleman

shrewdly. He sighed. He could have sold it for at least twenty.

"No," said Ted, reading the gentleman's mind without difficulty. "I'm sorry."

"You're sensible," said the expert, with disarming friendliness, "but I must remind you that people aren't buying books —"

"You're telling me!" said Ted.

When the experts had departed Ted seized Val in his arms and they executed a remarkable little dance about the bookshop. It was one of those symbolic dances which, had you seen it upon a Broadway stage, would have been entitled "Spring Is Almost Here" or "Business Is Picking Up." Finally Val released herself and dropped into a chair.

"What are you going to do with it now?" she inquired. "You can't put it in the bank at this hour."

"This dragging it in and out of the bank is a nuisance," said Ted, "and this safe's not impregnable." He gave it a contemptuous kick as he passed it, hurt his toe and spoke profanely. Val giggled. He suggested, "Look here, suppose we take it to your house for tonight?"

He foresaw that *Tamerlane* was going to be more trouble to him than a helpless baby or the litter of kittens with which Keturie would soon present him. He groaned, "We'll sell the darned thing," he said firmly, "and get rid of it."

The safe in the Loring household was large and solid and concealed. And into the safe went the *Tamerlane,* to stay there until the following day when it would go back to the bank.

Val said, before they parted:

"Everyone will know by tomorrow. It will be all over the trade . . ."

"I suppose so," said Ted. "Darn it," he said suddenly, "I'd like to keep it."

"Ted!" She looked at him in horror. "Don't tell me it's got you too?"

"Too? What do you mean?"

"I've been feeling the same way."

Ted looked at her. He said, after a minute, "Well, we can't afford to collect books. We've got to sell them. Can't have your cake and eat it too. Not yet, at any rate."

"I know," said Val, sighing, "but I've become attached to it."

She walked with him through the hall to the door. Ted glanced up absently as if he expected to see a spray of dark green leaves with waxen white berries, like jade, among them. But the mistletoe was not there.

"Have you told Flora?" asked Val casually.

"I called her up," answered Ted. "She isn't back yet. I got the lecture bureau people, she'll be home tomorrow."

"Oh," said Val, and presently went on upstairs to write to Bill. She hadn't written Bill
for nearly two weeks.

# Chapter XII

Ted was going to see Flora. He went, figuratively speaking, with his hat in his hand and his money in his pocket. Not that it was actually in his pocket for the *Tamerlane* still reposed in the safe-deposit box. But there had been other offers and on the afternoon of this particular day a message had reached him indirectly from, of all places, Hollywood, California. It appeared that a certain very brightly shining star, a deep-chested gentleman whose shadow across the screen caused the box office pulse to beat in silver tune to the hearts of infatuated maidens, had built himself a house and a library and was intent upon book collecting. He had an agent in New York who kept him apprised of rare items and to do that agent justice he was an honest man with a love for books — he even read them. The star, it seemed, had wired him that without this *Tamerlane* item it was highly probable that he would not live to make another picture. He already owned a first folio Shakespeare and coveted a Gutenberg Bible. And so the agent had telephoned Ted and Ted had rather patronizingly granted him an appointment for the following day. "It doesn't do to be too eager," he told Val.

He was thinking of the motion-picture star when he rang Flora's bell. She had moved from her original quarters and was inhabiting half of a thin little house over near the East River. It was a charming house, what there was of it. You entered and stood in a square hall the size of a postage stamp, while just before you narrow stairs led upward. On the second floor there was a living room and a dining room and a little kitchen; on the third, the bedrooms.

Flora ran down to open the door herself. She was, he saw, in one of her most vivacious moods. She tugged at him with her pretty hands and drew him up the stairs, talking all the time. It was marvelous, she said, it was terribly exciting. But how could he bear to sell the book? Perhaps Poe had held this volume in his fated hands, perhaps his strange eyes had looked upon the very pages.

There was not much light in the living room. There was a black-gray diffusion from the river, and the pale glowing of an alabaster lamp or two did little to dispel it. The room itself was gray, rough gray walls, dark oak, with strange notes of sudden violent color shrieking from couch or bookcase or wall hanging. There were violets in low silver bowls.

Flora wore a frock the color of the violets and her yellow hair, as she shook her small head, belled out about her face. She drew Ted to the couch, and sat beside him. She said, "We've drifted apart, somehow."

She had a lyric voice, very moving, high, faintly elfin. Ted replied, feeling immeasurably earthy:

"It hasn't been my fault."

She drew away from him and looked up into his face. She accused him instantly:

"You can't *bear* my success." As he said nothing for a moment, she went on, "It hasn't changed me, Ted, not the essential me." She touched herself lightly on the breast. "Can't you see that?"

He had been terribly in love with her. This much he knew, and of this he had been thinking for the past months. But his love for her had been all bound up with things which no longer seemed to exist, not for her at any rate; with smoky rooms and young excited voices arguing, and great plans taking nebulous shape, and the sting of acid red wine and the brave dreams of a world made clean for young lovers and made safe for people who struggled to survive.

"We've been all over this before," he said. "Your success . . . that doesn't matter."

"What do you mean?" she inquired sharply.

"I mean, it shouldn't matter — to us. It did, to me, because I had nothing to offer. But when we were both poor —"

"I'm still not very rich," she interrupted.

"I know. I meant when — Oh, you know what I mean, Flora. Back there two years ago . . . it was different. Then you became Flora Carr."

"I've always been Flora Carr," she said proudly.

"Please," Ted told her with something very near impatience, "please, don't willfully misunderstand. Of course, you've always been Flora Carr. But now you're a symbol, you're darned near a legend," he added, as if astonished, "and lately I haven't been able to get at you at all. When I come to see you here a half a dozen people come in — you're — you're surrounded. You aren't yourself."

She said dreamily, "I'm never myself. What is one's self, really? As altering as the winds, as the river."

Ted was extremely irritated. This was the sort of little speech — quite, one hoped, extemporaneous — which had once charmed him utterly. But now he wanted to take her by the shoulders and shake some sense, some straight talking into her.

She said, as he did not speak, "Ted, I love this little house. It is as narrow as the grave."

A slow, delicious shudder ran over her. "I lie in bed sometimes, very straight, feeling tall, beeping myself quite still. I tell myself, some-day you will lie like this and hear nothing. You will see nothing and feel nothing. It will be a very narrow house, Flora."

He said crossly, "Evelyn Scott wrote a book with that title once, didn't she?"

Flora closed her lips in a thin rosy line. If Ted was going to be disagreeable . . . She leaned forward and took a cigarette from an ivory box and lighted it. "You didn't come here to be unpleasant, did you?"

"No," agreed Ted. What was the matter with them both? He put his arm about her and she suffered it. She was slender in his grasp, a wisp of a woman. "No, I came here to ask you to marry me. Don't speak, don't say a word till I've finished. When we were poor you said it was impossible . . . impracti-cal. And then, afterwards, I couldn't ask you — you were beginning to make money; I had all I could do to keep the shop going. Besides, you made it pretty plain that you weren't in-terested in marriage and —"

She broke in. "I thought you agreed with me." She opened her great eyes on him, shin-ing, reproachful.

He was excessively uncomfortable. He hadn't been really comfortable about Flora for a long time. When they had been so much together in the Village they had shared a seemingly desperate and very young love of bitterness and sweet much mingled, and of frustration . . . a love which talked a good deal. Surely he agreed with her theoretically that law and church could not make love really legal. Its legality lay in itself. And he had reiterated that he agreed with her — that time in Boston. But had he? He remembered her saying to him, laughing a little, "Dear Ted, I'm afraid you were born with a sense of sin."

This speech had infuriated him at the time. Probably because he was afraid it was true. He had come back to New York trying to believe the things Flora had said to him. "This reaching out for each other across the wastes of terrifying life, this is the essence of poetry, Ted, this is beauty."

That she could make phrases in such a situation was part of her nature. Perhaps the phrases would have meant something to him had they been spoken in a different setting. But in a hotel bedroom!

If, back in the other days, this had happened to him, he might have felt differently about it. They had stood, in those Village days, on an equal footing. But he had been younger, not only in years, and Flora younger still . . . and, he believed, frightened. There had been great reverence in his feeling for her then, and surely he had been frightened too? A couple of youngsters saying brave things, shouting them — groping, wondering.

Now he said:

"I did — I do — agree with you theoretically. But it doesn't work out. Possibly I made myself agree with you because I knew you were going places."

"Going places — you mean the lecture tours?"

"Of course, I don't mean the lecture tours! I mean, from one success to another . . . it's just a phrase."

"Oh, slang," said Flora. She added thoughtfully, "You're a good deal slangier than you used to be, Ted; that's Val's influence, I suppose."

"Don't be absurd," he said brusquely. He remembered vividly how uneasy and short he had been with Val after his return from that Boston trip; as if — as if he'd been ashamed, as if he couldn't endure to look at her comic little face, as if he were hiding his discomfort by being disagreeable.

"Not that it matters," said Flora. "Well, go on."

He didn't want to go on, he found. He floundered a little. Who was it said, "His honor rooted in dishonor stood"? Tennyson, of course. People didn't think as much of Tennyson these days but . . . He pulled himself back with an effort. He said gravely:

"I hadn't, I suppose, any real right to ask you to marry me then, so when I did and you refused, well, it was what I'd more or less expected. But now things have changed. I'll have the money from the sale of the *Tamerlane*. Half of it, that is," he added hastily.

"Half of it! Why half?" she asked.

"Well, Val found it," he answered. "I told her it was half hers, really."

"That's ridiculous surely. She isn't going to take it?" demanded Flora.

"She says not, but —"

"Don't be quixotic, Ted," Flora told him. "What if she did find it? It was yours, it had been left to you —"

"I know, but I feel that she —"

"She won't take it, she's too sensible," Flora decided. He wished to heaven she'd let him finish a sentence. He felt as if he were talking Choctaw.

"How much do you expect to get for it?" she asked him quickly, before he could speak.

"I shall ask thirty thousand," he told her. "I've a possible buyer now who might be persuaded to meet that price."

"Thirty thousand!" She moved closer to

him on the couch and laid her small head against his shoulder. She said again, dreamily, "There's the most divine place, in Vermont. It could be bought and remodeled for, oh, for fifteen thousand or even less. There are acres and acres . . . fields and brooks and old tumble-down stone walls and a little lake, of a most celestial blue. There are old trees and there are older mountains and there's a great fireplace — it would be marvelous."

"But, Flora, I hadn't intended to buy property. I thought, with this behind us, safely invested, most of it that is, we'd have an anchor to windward — and I meant to enlarge the shop —"

"No," she said definitely, "we'll buy the farm and live there the year round. There's lots of room. We could have the most amusing people come to visit. It would be a heaven for me to come home to —"

"I thought you said, all year round."

"I have to fulfill my lecture contracts."

He said, after a minute:

"And what am I to do? Stay in Vermont and run the farm while you go off lecturing? How do you expect me to earn a living?"

She laughed at him then. She said, "Really, darling, you are too quaint!"

"You want me to give up the shop?" he persisted.

"No," answered Flora, after sufficient thought, "no, of course not. Not if it amuses you. Keep the shop. You could get away week-ends, engage a regular assistant . . ."

"What do you mean, a regular assistant?"

"Don't parrot me," she said sharply. "You know that Val's only playing at bookselling. Get an older woman . . . or another man. Not that I'm jealous of little Val," she said, smiling, "even if she is in love with you."

"She isn't," he denied instantly and was alarmed to feel his heart turn over, "that's nonsense, Flora. She's engaged to Bill Rogers."

"What difference does that make?" asked Flora in her high silken voice.

"Skip it," said Ted, "for the time being. Then you will marry me, Flora?"

"Are you so determined to make an honest woman of me?" she asked him.

He had no reply to that. Because it was true. Or perhaps he was determined to make an honest man of himself. Yes, that was nearer the truth. He said to himself, I am in love with her, I've been in love with her for years. But it didn't make sense. Sitting there, he felt only an exasperated affection, a sort of habit devotion, and a wild, wholly conventional desire to marry a woman who had granted him, just a thought too graciously, her favors.

"I wish you wouldn't say things like that, Flora. I've wanted to marry you for a long while. Now for the first time it seems really fair to you."

She said, "I don't know. I — I am deeply fond of you, Ted, but I don't believe in marriage."

"Yes, you do," he contradicted her stoutly. "That's just conversation. Book talk. Of course, you believe in it. In stability, in a home, in children."

"Children!" She shuddered again, not as deliciously. "Not children," she cried dramatically. "I couldn't, I wouldn't. They would *destroy* me!"

She could think of herself, indeed had often thought of herself, as a lover. Never as a mother. Great romping, demanding children! She couldn't think of them without horror. She could set them down on paper in the most living and delicate pattern. Her poem "For Alice, who died young," was one of the loveliest and most touching things she had ever written. She had felt it, she had wept over it. This child whom she had never known was as real to her as the man sitting beside her. Possibly more real. This child was her child, she had conceived it, had carried it through the slow heavy period of gestation, and had been delivered of it in agony and tears.

And she thought of herself also as a child, not quite of this world, stooping to the warm, glowing savage things of earth, yet forever virgin. Perhaps she was right.

She put her fragile arms around Ted and leaned closer to him and whispered to him, intimately. The blood thickened in his veins, was loud in his ears, as he bent to kiss her. She had an expert power to stir him, but with the light, yet seeking pressure of her mouth upon his own he was aware of some unrecognized misery, in which there was no delight.

Flora drew away from him. She was smiling secretly. "But, if I marry you — *if*, I say — you must understand that I must be free?"

She had her conventions, too. Freedom was one of them. They had talked of freedom between married lovers, or lovers unmarried, in the old days. They had talked of it since. It had always seemed comprehensible to him then but not now; not quite. He asked:

"Just what do you mean by — ?"

Someone had unlocked the narrow front door with an accustomed key and they had not heard the door open. There were footsteps suddenly, and loud, upon the stairs and a voice said, "Darling — I came back so much sooner!"

Flora was sitting away from Ted, delicately upright. She was quite unstartled. Color rose

228

to her cheeks, the color of excitement. In the doorway a young man stood, smiling. His smile faded a little. He said, "I'm sorry —"

"Don't be," said Flora, and laughed at him. "Come in, Peter. This is Ted Morrison."

This Peter Davis, Ted saw instantly, was a handsome young man, the golden youth of the loveliest poems existence. Tall, extremely fair, extremely vital . . . and perfectly unabashed. He came into the room and shook Ted's hand. He sat on the arm of the couch and laid a small, unself-conscious kiss on the very tip of Flora's ear. He said, "If you knew how I hurried . . . I canceled my last two appointments."

They talked, and Ted felt himself ignored. Davis, it appeared, painted portraits. He had been out of town for a month, executing a commission in St. Louis. Ted remembered that Flora's last lecture had been in St. Louis.

He sat back against the corner of the couch and said nothing. He could feel himself growing more and more stolid and sharp-cornered like an uncomfortable chair. Flora said, after a little while, "Look, Peter, I didn't expect you back so soon. Ted came to talk to me, very gravely, about most portentous matters. So run along, do — I'll telephone you."

Peter ran along, with the utmost good grace.

When the farewells had been said and the downstairs door had closed, Ted turned. "Is that what you meant by freedom, Flora?"

She replied, "Why not?" and looked at him, level-eyed.

"Or," asked Ted, still conscious of his heavy hand but unable to avoid it, "were you thinking of marrying him, too?"

"That would be bigamy," said Flora, with her sudden, childlike chuckle. "Marry Peter!" She flung back her head and laughed. Her throat was long and slender, with shadowed hollows. "Heaven forbid," she said. "He's marvelous . . . he gives me something . . . a vitality, a glorious lightheartedness . . . but men like Peter are merely interludes, Ted."

"He has a key to your house," said Ted.

"I hate doorbells," Flora told him. "Many of my friends have keys. It doesn't always mean anything."

"I see," said Ted. He wasn't going to ask if Davis "meant anything." Perhaps he did not, it was even likely that he did not. The "darling" didn't mean anything, either. Everyone called everyone else darling nowadays. It was easier than remembering Christian names or surnames you had heard only once or twice. But —

Not that he had anything against Davis.

"Is Davis one of the amusing people you'll

want to fill your house with, in Vermont?" he inquired.

"Now," said Flora, "you *are* being nasty!" She got to her feet and walked over to the windows and stood looking out on the dark life of the river. She said, without turning:

"I can't imagine what's got into you. You've gone as stuffy and as commonplace and as conventional as . . ." She groped for a simile and found none.

Ted rose and followed her to the windows. He stood just behind her, not touching her at all. He said:

"Perhaps I have. I don't know anything about this key to your house business and Davis — or a dozen like him. Only no one can have a key to *my* house."

She flung around on him then, and leaned back, arms wide, hands clenched about the soft stuff of the draperies.

"I won't live in your house," she said, "if it's a prison. I couldn't. I couldn't breathe."

"All right," said Ted, after a while.

A little later he was out in the street. There was still frost and a cold wind, in March. He turned up his overcoat collar and walked west, his head bent against the sting of the sharp air. That was that. Flora, he thought, was probably picking up the telephone.

What had happened to him? he asked himself. He knew. A potential thirty thousand dollars had happened to him. Security, if there was such a thing, within his grasp. Foundations on which a man might build.

For Flora he felt a curious, grudging admiration. At least she didn't veer with every breeze, not basically. She had the courage of her convictions. She had changed her mind about starving to death, unrecognized, but she hadn't changed it about a number of other things. Possibly she never would.

He asked himself, making his way, his back to the wind, which blew damp and cold from the river, Is it possible that all my convictions were born of hunger and disappointment and worry and resentment against people who had more than I had?

This problem interested him so much that he almost forgot Flora. He hailed a bus finally and went on downtown to his room. By the time he reached there, he had exhausted, without coming to any conclusion, all his arguments with himself. Flora's picture stood on his bureau. He couldn't escape her, once he was back home again. He sat down on his bed and thought of a farm in Vermont and Flora sitting, like an elf-made mortal, in the corner of the stone fireplace he had never seen and now would never see. He thought of the people crowding in and out, the circle she would draw about her, the idolatry she would attract. He thought of a farmhouse door with a great many keys and of himself in the book-shop, wondering. And he got to his feet and laughed aloud, with a most extraordinary sense of relief. Flora wanted to be free, did she? Well, she was free. And so, by God, was he!

# Chapter XIII

Val came into the shop and looked around it and hated it. Everything about it displeased her. The bright array of books in their colorful jackets smugly parading the shelves, the tables laden with small gifts in glass, china, leather, the windows with their display rather brilliantly arranged by her own two hands, the tall and the squat vases containing flowers. She glanced through into the back room where Ted was kneeling before the fireplace and coaxing a cheerful flame into being. She hated the back room, too. And Ted.

Stupid place, she said to herself. Who wants to read books anyway? Who cares what gruesome, loathsome, picayune authors set down on typewriters, who cares what publishers buy? I don't! And as for those silly gifts, would anyone in their right minds want 'em? I wouldn't! And as for flowers, nasty, sneezy Pollyanna things, I detest them!

Yes, she despised the shop. She was bored with it, she was fed up. She would resign and go home again and become once more the pride of the Lorings, a well-behaved little girl with green eyes and dark red hair who did a little charity work and went to teas and luncheons and waited for her fiancé to come back from the South Seas and marry her at a very fashionable church, red carpet, awnings, gaping populace, ivory satin, her mother's rose point and a hymn book — or was it a prayer book? — bound in white leather.

She hated the shop because she loved it and because it was so very much her own and because she knew as well as she knew anything in this world that if Ted didn't throw her out Flora would drive her away eventually. They would pay her a nice legal interest on her investment and they would say, Run, don't walk, to the nearest exit.

All this time she was approaching the archway to the back room and now she stood there, in nice, rather shabby tweeds, with a feather in her absurd hat. Ted looked up. He said, "You're late," genially.

"Well, what of it?" replied Val in the tone of voice which can be properly described only as a snarl.

Ted came to his feet and looked at her with a tolerant solicitude which utterly infuriated her.

"Come, come, my pet," he remarked, quoting from a certain very popular play, "what has upset it this morning? Did it get out of bed on the wrong side? Bring on your dolls, I'll mend 'em."

"You make me tired," said Val viciously, "and the shop makes me tired. I could scream. I'm all set for a nice nervous breakdown . . . or would be if I could afford it," she added wistfully. "Nice tip-toeing doctors, anxious family, three starched, good-looking nurses, trays, window shades drawn . . ."

"What's the matter with you?" asked Ted, dropping his my-little-man tone.

She put out her foot and kicked the fire screen. It fell over with a clatter. There were tears in her eyes and the beginning of laughter on her lips.

"Hey!" exclaimed Ted, galvanized into action. He picked up the fire screen. He said soothingly, "Go to bed."

"Here?"

"No, you dope. Go home. Take the day off. Go to bed. I'll lend you a book."

"I hope I never hear the word 'book' again!" said Val.

For it had happened. It was her fault. The agent of the ultrawealthy motion-picture star had purchased the *Tamerlane.* Depression price, but more than the other offers. Twenty thousand dollars. The money was in the bank, and the *Tamerlane* was speeding west.

Val jumped up so suddenly that Ted almost fell out of the chair he was now occupying, and ran to the housewifely corner where she hid her dusters. She went into the main room and started flicking books with a practiced hand. She moved a glass dog back two inches and a china giraffe forward one. She cast her eye at the greeting cards. It would soon be time to put out the Easter display. She said in a muffled voice, "We'll have to reorder Flora. We simply can't keep her in."

Ted had followed her and was standing at his desk. "She'll be glad to hear that," he commented casually.

"Well, why don't you tell her?" snapped Val. She was behaving like nothing on earth but your neighbor's children, and she knew it.

Ted was sincerely alarmed. One of the pleasantest and most exciting things about his partner was that she was not monotonous. You fought with her, you wanted to punch her little snoot, but she did not bore you. You couldn't say to her, "You're not at all like yourself today," because she wasn't the same two times hand running anyway. But this mood was one he had not encountered before. He hadn't provoked it, of that he was sure. She must be sickening for something.

He went over to her and took her hand. She snatched it away.

"What's the big idea?" she demanded.

He took it again, firmly, and put his other

hand on her forehead. Val shrieked. She added, "Have you gone completely gaga?"

"No. But look here, Val," he said, dropping her hand and removing his own from her brow, "you don't *feel* feverish."

"I do too!" she denied.

"Have you a pain anywhere?" he asked her anxiously.

Val flung the duster in his face, laughed and cried all together for half a minute while he fluttered about her wholly incapable of anything but soothing pats and "there, there"; whereupon she whirled away from him and departed to the tiny lavatory in which she bathed her face, powdered her nose and reddened her lips. Then she came out again.

"I'm all right now," she said composedly. "I just had an attack of the vapors."

"Do take off your hat," urged Ted, "and stay awhile."

She did so, and sailed it across the room, to hang precariously on the tilted racks of greeting cards. He asked, as she sat down on a straight chair and folded her hands, "Look here, what's got into you?"

"Nothing. Don't mind me, I'm a nut. I haven't been sleeping."

Ted thought, Rogers? I wonder. He had a vision of Val sitting up half the night writing to Bill Rogers, tracing his possible course on a wall map. He asked, "Haven't heard from Bill lately, have you?"

"No," said Val, "I haven't. I saw his mother last night. She's bothered. He left the base some time ago to go somewhere. He was pretty vague about it all. We keep on writing. When he gets back to the base he'll have about a million letters and news as stale as week-old bread. This should be his last excursion; when he returns to the base he's supposed to start for home."

Her voice shook, a very little. Ted found his own feelings mixed. He was aware of instant compunction for her and an utter dislike of Mr. Rogers. Damned fool, running off to some unlikely place for no good reason and making a good kid like Val unhappy, to say nothing of his mother, for whom Ted cherished a real admiration.

"I'm sorry you've been worried," he said gently. So gently that Val looked up quickly to discover if this was or was not a gag. But it wasn't a gag. It was genuine. He looked sorry. He patted her shoulder and gave it a little squeeze. He said, "Buck up, old thing, he'll come back all right."

Val thought, If he goes on being nice to me I'll be hysterical again. She sniffed audibly. She said, "I sound like Miss Smithers," and gave him a childlike, somewhat diluted smile. She thought, Let him think it's Bill; of course, that's fine, and it is Bill, really, part of it, but not in the way he thinks.

Having made up her mind to be indirectly dishonest, she was of course completely frank.

"It isn't really Bill," she said. "Never mind, Ted. I'm just a little unbuttoned. Or is it undone? I'll do myself up again. It must be the spring coming on although I must say today doesn't look very much like it. To say nothing of no customers."

"We'll get 'em," prophesied Ted cheerfully, much relieved that she had somewhat recovered. Too proud to admit she was worried over Rogers, was she? Game little critter. Or perhaps she didn't like him, Ted, well enough to confide in him. He thought briefly of Flora's astonishing statement: "Val's in love with you." He put that aside hastily. Poetic license.

"You seem pretty cocksure this morning," said Val suspiciously.

"I am. This *Tamerlane* business has given us a lot of publicity. Watch the people flock in out of curiosity. Once we get them here we'll sell them or bust."

"Where's Keturie?" asked Val suddenly.

"I haven't the least idea," answered Ted. "Come to think of it, I haven't seen her this morning."

"That's funny," said Val. She went outside for a moment and presently came back to report. The janitor hadn't seen the cat either. And it wasn't at all like Keturie to be absent of a cool morning when there was a wood fire burning. She liked fires. She would curl up with her tail about her and her paws folded under her and look for hours, it seemed, unblinkingly into the fire, thinking her feline thoughts.

A customer arrived, walking briskly. An elderly man, an amateur collector whom Ted knew well. He had bought books off and on from Ted since the shop opened. But now because Ted had found and sold a *Tamerlane* he seemed to have more respect for that young man's judgment. He came in armed with a notebook and Ted took him to the small office room and delved among his shelves for certain trade encyclopedias.

Val went into the back room and stood looking out upon the rather bleak backyard which belonged to the shop. You could do things with it in the spring and summer, she thought. Plant things, make it attractive. But she wouldn't be here next summer. She'd be on a steamer somewhere bound for round-the-world. Or did Bill plan a honeymoon trip on the yacht? She hoped not. She'd be seasick, as sure as sunrise.

Flora could amuse herself with the back-yard.

Val turned, listening. She had heard a strange, forlorn sound. It seemed to reach her, rather eerily, via the radiator. She thought, It's Keturie . . . in the cellar!

She flew out of the back room past the desk, Ted and his startled customer, out of the side door into the hall and down the cellar steps. It was, as she had suspected, Keturie, making her mournful plaint and accepting her pre-ordained doom fatalistically. Even cats know that tribulation follows escapade and pain follows pleasure.

"Golly," said Val, sincerely frightened, "you poor little devil."

She almost asked, "Shall I call a doctor?"

But Keturie was doing nicely, thank you.

The customer upstairs departed. He had left a substantial order. Ted was to act as his agent in the matter and buy him this and that and the other thing. Mr. Morrison was sure he understood? Ted was sure. He bowed the customer out and betook himself to the head of the cellar stairs immediately thereafter.

"Val," he called. "Val, are you down there, for heaven's sake?"

"Don't come down," cried Val hastily, feeling that a man's place was not in the delivery room. "Stay away. She's all right."

242

"Who's all right?" asked Ted, wondering if Val had been authentically bereft of her senses, this time.

"Keturie. We're grandparents!" shouted Val.

"What!"

"She's having kittens," said Val, "you idiot. Go back and mind the shop, I'll be along presently."

Dazed, Ted went docilely into the shop but every so often he ventured back to the stairhead to ask aniously, "How many?"

"Three . . ."

"Four . . ."

"Five!" reported Val triumphantly, at last. She came up the stairs looking excited and frightened and elated as one should look who has come to grips with life, as it were. "Five."

"Lord!" said Ted helplessly.

"They're pretty cute," decided Val, "that is, not yet. I don't like 'em so new. But they will be."

She wandered into the back room, sat down and absently accepted a cigarette although as a rule she did not smoke during working hours and, indeed, rarely at any time.

"What'll we do with them?" asked Ted.

"We'll wait till they're old enough to leave her," Val answered, "and they can live in the cellar till then. Then we'll call the S.P.C.A."

243

Ted looked at her, affronted by woman's practicality and callousness. To be sure, he couldn't have five kittens and a mother cat leaping around the place, it would disconcert customers and discourage trade but —

He was fond of Keturie. He felt moved at her plight. A mother for six weeks or so and then, a cat — Cornelia mourning her children.

"But won't they be destroyed or something?" he asked plaintively.

"Of course," said Val, "if no one wants them." She added, "It would be fun to keep just one. Keturie will be more grown up now. And a kitten's a lively thing to have around."

"Well, why can't we?" asked Ted, conceding the one. One out of five. Just like the advertisements.

Val said in a hurried little voice, "Well, Flora doesn't like cats, you know."

"*Flora* doesn't like . . ."

He was gaping at her, the perfect village oaf at the county fair, his glasses down on his nose, his mouth unbecomingly open. Val explained hastily:

"Oh, I know. I thought most of them did. Poets, I mean. Cats are — exciting and legendary and mysterious, aren't they? But she doesn't. Keturie jumped up on her lap one day. Flora didn't do anything about it or say anything. But I could tell by her expression

. . . No, we'll give them all away and you'll have to get rid of — of Keturie too, Ted. Because now that she's done this once, she'll do it again. A couple of times a year. More, maybe," said Val, slightly confused but sticking to her zoology.

"But what in thunder has Flora got to do with it?" asked Ted once he found he could shut his mouth and reopen it in order that words might issue therefrom.

"Well, she'll be here, I suppose. Oh," wailed Val suddenly, "you aren't *really* thinking of giving up the shop!"

The door opened. A customer came in. Val rose. Ted rose. He stood over her. He paid no attention whatever to the customer.

"Look here, you've got to explain yourself. Make it snappy," he ordered.

She said baldly, "Now that you've got this money you and Flora will be getting married, won't you?"

Ted turned away. Val watched him advance toward the customer and now it was she who stood agape with amazement. He could at least answer a civil question, she thought angrily.

He did answer it.

"We — certainly — are — not!" he said quite loudly and spacing his words. The customer dropped the book she was examining as Ted approached her with his most engaging smile. "Is there anything I can do for you?" he inquired blandly.

Val fled once more to the back room. It was spring, it was summer, the nonexistent trees in the naked backyard had put forth rosy blossoms. Keturie could keep all six — five — kittens if she wished. Well, maybe she'd be content with one. The bookshop was probably the swellest place in the world. She wanted to send greeting cards to every person of her acquaintance. She had never seen anything as charming as the red roses in the dark blue vase with the handles.

"Miss Loring," called Ted severely.

She came demurely from the back room and walked toward him. She held her head and her color high. "Yes, Mr. Morrison?" she murmured inquiringly.

"Have we a cookbook called *Get Your Man?*" he demanded.

When the customer had departed with a cookbook which was guaranteed to please a husband, Val collapsed into a chair.

"Ridiculous," she gurgled, "utterly absurd ... I mean, as if she could! Oh, dear," said Val remorsefully, "poor old thing ... I shouldn't have said it."

But Ted was not thinking of the customer, who had been too obviously knock-kneed and whose left eye had wandered wildly. He said,

"Look here, about Flora and myself —"

Val stated, "You're not getting married," with an air of finality.

"No," said Ted, "we're not. We — Oh, hell," he muttered, torn between something approximating the truth and chivalry, "we neither of us want to," he ended feebly.

Val, on a tone of pure rejoicing, said, "I'm glad . . . I mean if you're sure you don't want to. But — if — if you're just being gallant, with a breaking heart or something . . ." She halted and then added seriously, "If you're sorry —"

"Well, I'm not," he shouted, glaring at her. "Do I look sorry? It — it was just one of those things. We'd outgrown one another," he said firmly.

"Keturie," murmured Val, "may keep one kitten. A son. Unknown Junior."

She had no right to feel so alive and happy and tingling to her fingertips. Or hadn't she? Perhaps just because of good-comradeship she did have a right. For Flora wasn't the girl for Ted at all. She was brilliant, she was attractive, but she wasn't for Ted. She needed a different type of man, less sensitive — not that Ted was a touch-me-not, shrinkable and wistful, perish the thought — less proud. No, she wasn't Ted's girl.

Val thought happily, Next summer I'll make

him do over the backyard.

But next summer she wouldn't be here. She rose and went into the back room, to get out the account books. She ran her eyes down the figures of its columns. They had done very well. Ted was to lunch today with some expert or other, he had come swiftly up in the world since the *Tamerlane* episode. She would have something to eat sent in, she thought, trying to keep her mind on mundane matters.

Ted came in and stood beside her. She looked up from the desk. Her fingers were inky with figuring and her hair a little disordered. She had not put on her smock. It had been a rather cockeyed morning.

He said abruptly:

"I suppose you and Bill will be planning to —"

"I don't know, Ted. It isn't certain when he gets back," Val interrupted him.

"But you said something about getting married — in the summer."

"I know I did." She bit the end of the pen and stared into a pigeonhole. "But perhaps not. In the fall . . . or winter," she added vaguely.

Ted said, "You can't expect him to keep putting things off."

"No," agreed Val, "no, I can't."

He went away after that. And later, during

her lunch hour, with a sandwich too dry and a malted milk too sweet, Val asked herself what was the matter with her, she was becoming as changeable, as moody as an adolescent. She didn't have to ask herself more than once. She knew.

She thought, I can't marry Bill, feeling as I do about Ted. I hoped I'd get over it. I was sure that I would. But I haven't. I'm getting worse. The darned old disease just won't run its course. When Bill comes back, I'll tell him. It isn't fair to him, it isn't fair to me.

She munched the sandwich, choked slightly when forced to answer the phone, and drank the malted milk. Once she went down to see how Keturie was getting along. It must be amazing, she thought, peering into the corner, where having made herself comfortable among old boxes and wisps of newspaper, Keturie lay and washed her children, to be one self-contained cat one moment and then, at practically the next, the mother of five. Yet Keturie had shown no astonishment, merely resignation. Now she looked rather prideful.

I can't bear to hurt Bill, thought Val, I'd feel better about it if I hadn't gone into it with my eyes open . . . well, partially open at least, much more so than those kittens. I knew what I was doing, I was furious at Ted, and hurt and — and . . . No, if I could go to Bill in good faith and say, "When I sent you that wire I honestly believed that we belonged to each other —"

But this was so much worse. To have to say, "I never really was in love with you, Bill, I've known it all along."

But she had to do it, for his sake, and for her own.

Ted, she thought, working at the account ledger again, Ted doesn't give a whoop for me. Oh, he likes me well enough, better than he did. So you can't honestly accuse me of breaking with Bill just because Ted and Flora are all washed up and there's a chance for me. There isn't a chance.

She felt pretty sorry for herself after that. But sitting there presently, the pen idle, her eyes on the disorder of the desk, she began to recapture that ridiculous, unseasonable spring fever. She could go on and on, she thought comfortably, year after year, minding the bookshop, watching it grow, fussing with the backyard, seeing Keturie through her periodical maternities, quarreling with Ted, making up again. Of course, she pondered, every new girl whom Ted met would ring a little alarm bell in her brain. But he hadn't met anyone new — not yet.

Ted came in. The expert's luncheon had been swell. Three very erudite critics, the owner of one of the more prosperous book-shops in town, an editor of books published by a famous private press, and himself. Book talk, lots of it, the sort you could get your teeth into. So he returned to work, late, with an all-conquering sort of air as if in the next batch of books he took over another *Tamerlane* would surely turn up.

"How's Keturie?"

"She's fine. I think the kittens are going to be part gray and part black. One looks tor-toise-shell-ish, though."

"Good heavens!" said Ted blankly.

Late in the afternoon Keturie made a personal appearance. She was accompanied quite involuntarily by one of her children. Walking proudly, Keturie laid the atom at Ted's feet and then returned to get another. She did this five times, until the rug in front of the fireplace was completely covered by progeny. Ted moved away from them, a little affronted. He didn't care for them, he told Val, who was down on her knees beside them.

"You will," she said, "wait till they can get about and do lots of expensive damage in the shop. You'll love them then."

Keturie sat by and washed her whiskers. She had seen her duty and had done it. She was attached to Ted, more perhaps than to Val. She looked up, green-eyed, for applause.

The telephone bell rang sharply.

Val jumped up to answer it. "Never mind," she told Ted, "I'm expecting a call — about those reorders yesterday which haven't been delivered."

Looking down at Keturie, now rubbing her head against his shoe, Ted waited benevolently for Val to return. He was at peace with the world. Or almost. He had twenty thousand dollars in the bank, the bookshop was doing better business, he and Flora understood one another. If there was something that nagged at him, that kept him from being a completely happy person he ignored it for the moment.

He heard Val's quick voice answering the telephone. He heard her voice change. He heard her say sharply, "No . . . *no* . . . I don't believe it!" And then, "It can't be . . . there must be a mistake somewhere."

Turning so suddenly that he threw Keturie off balance, at which she complained mournfully, Ted went into the other room. Val was standing by the telephone. She was white and her lips shook.

"What is it?" he asked her urgently. "What's the matter?"

She moved over to him and put her head down on his arm like a child in grief. She said, "It's Bill. Mother phoned, she'd just heard from Mrs. Rogers. They think he's lost, Ted. There's been no word, and they've found — wreckage."

# Chapter XIV

She was not crying; she had excellent control of herself, but she was ashen to an alarming degree. He put his arm about her and took her back into the other room, put her in a chair and went to his desk and looked in the drawer for that pint of whisky someone had given him, here in the shop. He found it and got the cork out and poured out a hooker into a paper cup and carried it to her. "Drink that," he ordered.

"But I don't want —"

"Drink it."

She drank it, sputtered and made a terrific face. Ted brought her some water.

"Now," he said when she had handed him the crumpled cup and was lying back in the chair. "Now, tell me what you know."

It wasn't much. Bill's mother, secretly becoming more and more frightened, had started sending out cables of inquiry. At the island where Bill had made his base they knew nothing. Then came the cabled story of wreckage washed up somewhat off Bill's proposed course . . . a battered piece of timber marked with the yacht's name.

"He'll be all right," promised Ted frantically — he'd say anything to take that stricken look from her, "you'll see if he won't. He'll turn up, in time, right as rain."

She said, "I'm thinking of his mother."

The big diamond was a little loose on her slender finger. She turned it around in the way she had and then stopped and stared at it. Bill had given her the ring. She'd taken it. She'd worn it, under utterly false pretenses, but she had been going to give it back to him again. Now she could never give it back.

She began to cry.

Ted put a great handkerchief in her hand. He made funny noises supposed to be consolatory. Finally he knelt down in front of her, careless of any customers who might come into the shop, and begged, "Please, Val, don't. There isn't anything I can possibly say — I wish I could."

She put her head down on his shoulder and his arms went around her with the utmost naturalness. And she cried there, comfortably, for a while.

After a time she stirred and wiped her eyes and blew her little nose. She said, "Sorry."

She was game, all right. He'd thought that before, he'd think it again. He felt a sudden unpleasant pang of envy of Bill Rogers, who could inspire courage and grief in Valentine Loring. He said awkwardly, "You — you'd better go along home now. Your mother will be looking for you."

She nodded and rose and went past him to get her coat and her hat with the feather in it. She looked pretty forlorn, he thought. Even the feather seemed to have lost its perkiness. He offered, "I'd better come with you."

"No," she said. "I'll be all right."

"I'll call a taxi."

"I'd rather walk, Ted."

"Don't come back tomorrow," he said, "I'll get someone in."

"I'd like to, if I can," she told him, "I'd rather be working."

He went with her to the door and watched her trudge up the steps and walk down the street, all the spring gone from her tread. He saw that she clutched his handkerchief tightly in her hand. He cleared his throat. Damned shame, things like that oughtn't to happen to Val. She wasn't built for tragedy, she was made for laughter and gaiety and lightness. He was grave thinking of Bill Rogers, whom he had always liked even while he resented him, his money, his ease, his charm. It seemed incredible — so vital a person. What had gone wrong, what had happened?

Val, walking against the wind, not feeling it on her face and throat, went slowly. She dreaded going home, to her father's awkward tenderness, her mother's arms. More than anything she dreaded seeing Mrs. Rogers. She felt that she had no place beside the older woman in her rebellion and sorrow, no place as Bill's betrothed, at any rate.

She was terribly shaken and she was miserably unhappy. She was so fond of Bill. She loved him, she would do anything for him — except be *in* love with and marry him. Her best friend, she told herself, in the worn phrase. He'd loved her so much, been so patient with her, so absolutely loyal. He'd never — how did they put it? — never even looked at another girl.

But she couldn't mourn him the way his mother would expect her to mourn him. She couldn't pretend to be completely crushed. She wasn't. She had cared for Bill Rogers all her life and now she would never see him again. But —

If it had been Ted?

Sharp and clear as lightning in a summer sky. If it had been Ted. She stood quite still in the middle of a crossing while the lights changed and cars rushed toward her and a wild-eyed officer shouted at her. She came to her senses with about a second to spare and ran for safety. If it had been Ted —

Even to think it made the world go quite empty and black. She thought, That's it, that's been it all along. I could even bear to have him marry Flora or anyone, but I couldn't bear never to see him again.

This, then, was her man, Ted Morrison, his lean and lazy inches, his bright blue eyes, his absurd glasses, his enthusiasms and stupidities and absurdities. She had known it ever since the day she slid down his front steps and offered to be his valentine, brazenly and with laughter.

No amount of forcing herself to think her feeling for Ted would pass, no amount of enumerating all Bill's good qualities and their happy times together, could alter the matter.

She reached her home and went in, trembling a little with that sick excitement which comes before one faces something one has been dreading. Her mother met her, very gravely. She put her arms about her just as Val knew she would. And after a time she said gently, "You'd feel better if you'd cry."

Oh, she could cry, she could weep for Bill and the waste of his youth and the long years ahead which he would not know; she could weep for Bill and all their comradeship, wholeheartedly. But she could not weep for her lover.

Her father came in later. She saw by his face that her mother had telephoned him. He was stumbling, manlike, inarticulate. She kissed him, leaned her wet cheek against his cheek. She said, "Why did he have to go on that stupid trip?"

Mrs. Rogers wanted to see her, Marcia Loring said. Did Val feel up to it? They'd go around after dinner.

Val didn't want any dinner. But they urged her to eat and she made a valiant effort, crumbling her bread, drinking her hot soup, choking down a bit of steak. Now and then she spoke, firmly. "It isn't authentic, is it?"

"I'm afraid so, darling."

"But they might have been wrecked and saved."

The plank which had come ashore had shown signs of being in the water a long time, they told her gently.

She said, after a while, "I won't believe it. Not yet. I don't see how his mother can. If I were his mother I'd *never* believe it!"

It would have been funny if it hadn't been so sad, thought Marcia, her eyes filling, the small person sitting there, her cheeks bright with sudden color, defying fate, defying the elements, defying the proofs of tragedy and of loss.

After dinner they went to the apartment Bill had shared with his mother. It was a lovely place, restful, spacious, quiet. Mrs. Rogers was lying down, the grave manservant told them. He'd been with the family a long time, he had his own grief. She would see Miss Valentine.

So they left her there for a while and she went alone into the room she expected to find darkened. The servant had erred. Bill's mother wasn't lying down, she was sitting quite erect at her desk and all the lights were burning. She turned a hard white face on Val and her lips looked as if she had been biting them, they looked ragged and sore. Her eyes looked sore too, with red rims.

Val went over to her and knelt down beside her and put her arms about her. "Don't you believe it — you *mustn't* believe it."

"I don't," said Bill's mother, "I won't. But I'm frightened, Val, I'm frightened almost out of my senses." She took the girl's shoulders in her two small hands and shook her, hard. She said, "You — love Bill too, don't you?"

Val said, "Yes," very low, and turned her eyes away. They brimmed, but that was not why she did not want Bill's mother to look into them.

Mrs. Rogers said, after a minute:

"He was insane about you. He — he *is* insane about you. I will not speak of him in the past tense, I will not. But you — you weren't in love with him, Val," she said clearly, "you were just very fond of him. I did you — and

260

him — a great wrong last summer."

Val didn't understand that, but she did not ask any questions. She waited, her hands wet and her face burning. Mrs. Rogers went on presently:

"I wanted him to have you because he wanted you so much. I — I've always been jealous of you, Val, ever since you were a little thing. Not meanly. Don't think that. I loved you too, not only because Bill did, nor in spite of the fact that Bill did. But for yourself. I'd have let him marry you, knowing in my heart of hearts that you didn't care for him as he did for you. It would have been a grave injustice toward you both. But I couldn't bear to see him denied. And I thought, She's fond of him, she's very young, she will come to love him, in the way he wants . . . for I was selfish about it. Perhaps I thought, I'll always love him best, and someday he may know it. Perhaps I believed that if he married a girl as much in love with him as he was with you, I'd have no share in him."

She put her arms down on the desk and laid her head upon them and wept, soundlessly.

Val got to her feet. She stood there with her hand on the older woman's shoulder. She said clearly, "Yes, you're right, of course. When he came back, I was going to tell him.

Between us we would have made a mess of his life; and mine too, I suppose. So, when he comes back," she ended, "I'll tell him."

Mrs. Rogers raised her ravaged face. Her eyes were somber. "*You* don't believe he will come back."

"I do," said Val slowly.

His mother said, "I'm doing everything I can. There'll be boats searching . . . and planes. Everything money can buy and human ingenuity conceive. I cannot believe it." She looked up at Val and struck her hand violently upon the polished surface of the desk. "If I believed it I should lose my mind," she said. "I've been an idolatrous mother. I've not shown it — much. I've kept it hidden. I — I was like the savage mother who pretends that after all her child is not very remarkable lest the gods overhear and snatch him from her. I've never interfered with Bill, and his life . . . that is, until I interfered with you," she corrected herself slowly. "I've always stood aside . . . given him laughter and a light sort of good friendship. He wanted it that way. But —"

She broke again, briefly. Then she rose and put her arms around Val.

"I don't know why I can't hate you," she said, as if in wonder, "for — for planning to hurt him, so terribly. But I don't. You're an honest little thing, Val."

Val's father came back for her and took her home. They talked, with Marcia, in the living room, until late. Val said, "She doesn't believe he's dead. I don't either."

Across her bent, red head they regarded each other sorrowfully, rebelliously. This was their child and they could not help her. The paper that day carried front-page headlines, screaming and black. Val read Bill's name with a sense of bewilderment. It didn't look real in print, that sort of print, although she had seen it a good many times staring at her from the pages of a newspaper. They ran a picture of him, and one, rather smudged and quite hideous, of herself. There was a reference to their engagement. There was a picture of the lovely ship which had betrayed him, and there were pictures and stories about the young men who had been his shipmates. There was a list of his clubs, his college associations, his privately printed books.

If Bill ever sees this, thought Val, he'll be annoyed and a little amused.

She said as much to Ted. Ted, very tender with her that day, asked gently, "You think he will see it, Val?"

"I do. His mother does too."

Oh, the pitiful tenacity of women, Ted thought. He said quietly, "You mustn't get your hopes too high, Val. Neither of you should. It would make it so much harder."

She crumpled the paper and shook it in her hand. It made a harsh rattling sound.

"But we must, can't you see that? There isn't any real proof. He could have reached an uninhabited island, he could have been picked up by a passing boat. Perhaps they have all been saved and can't send us word."

But the days went on and the word did not come. People began to speak of Mrs. Rogers in muted tones, over the teacups. It was insanity for her to cling so long to hope. Surely a memorial service . . . ? But she would hold no memorial service. She went about her business quietly, keeping in touch with the rescue boat she had chartered, with the planes, and without, so far as her friends could see, any lessening of hope. At first Val was with her a good deal, and then not as much. For long silences would fall between them and the older woman's drawn face and eyes seemed to reproach her, seemed to cry out at her, You are not experiencing what I am experiencing, you aren't worthy to have been loved by him.

People talked about Val too. She went to work. She did not wear mourning. She did not comport herself as a grief-stricken girl should, nor did she shut herself away from her friends. It was unconventional, to say the least. But, then, this generation was remarkably hard and unfeeling.

Now it was spring and the young leaves were tender and green in the park and there were tulips dancing in window boxes. The bookshop had gay flowers, like sunlight, in the blue vases. And business was brisk. So brisk that Val once said ruefully to Ted, "I believe I'm attracting business too, from people who didn't know me — who read about me and Bill."

"Damn them," said Ted, with more fury than one would expect from a shopkeeper whose sales were better than normal bad times would warrant.

"That's all right, Ted, don't mind. I don't. Bill wouldn't either, if he knew. He'd laugh and say, 'Glad to be of service.'"

It was one of the things he had often said, in a silly pretended stiff way, with his eyes amused. She remembered once, the first time he'd ever kissed her she'd slapped his face and he'd said just that.

Ted looked at her quickly. The weeks had gone by, and no news had come. Was she, too, beginning to believe with the rest of the outside world — which was no longer much interested — that Rogers was lost and that he would never return?

She was beginning to believe just that. And

when May came and June, she did believe it. By this time they would have heard, they were sure to have heard. Going to see his mother, she thought, If only someone would make her see too. She's killing herself, for nothing. She had a fleeting, irrational anger against Bill, whom she had loved and for whom she felt an enduring sorrow and self-reproach, that he should have done this and so terribly devastated the woman who loved him.

But Mrs. Rogers was firm. She would wait and she would hope until she died. That much was perfectly evident to Val. She would go on, keeping up the futile search. She was talking now, now that the first boat had come back reporting nothing, of chartering another and going herself.

"But you mustn't, you aren't well enough, what does the doctor say?"

"He says it will kill me, but doctors are fools," said Bill's mother with her shadowy smile. "This not knowing is what kills me. Oh," she said hastily, "I didn't mean that. I know, of course, I know. I've never stopped knowing." She swung about in her chair and faced Val directly. "You feel that way, don't you?"

"Of course," said Val, without conviction.

"No," said Mrs. Rogers, "you don't. You've come around to thinking . . . like the others. Yet you can't believe that anything would really happen to Bill," she said, "not to *Bill?*"

She could see him, vital, strong. Nothing could happen to that vitality and that strength. She knew it perfectly well. She had told herself in times gone by that if Bill had gone to war he would have come out unharmed. Thank God, he had been too young to go. But if he had . . . the bullet hadn't been made which could find him, his mother thought.

She would not open the Southampton house. If she did not go out with this second chartered boat, she would go to the mountains or stay in town. She could not bear to see the ocean. It had been, of course, a different ocean . . . but what if she went down there to the dunes and lay awake at night and listened to the water beating inexorably on the shore? No, that she could not endure, no one could ask it of her.

June was very warm. Val, walking slowly away from Mrs. Rogers' apartment that Sunday morning, thought longingly of the country. But the heat wave would pass. She thought, Now that she feels I no longer believe he'll come back, she doesn't want to see me again. She didn't say anything but it was clear enough. That's why she wanted me with her so much, before. Because I believed, as she believed, that he would come back. Now she knows that I don't.

It was the first time she had actually admitted it to herself.

She admitted it to Ted, a day or so later. She said suddenly, "I've given up hoping, Ted. I wish she would. But she won't."

He muttered something. She didn't know what. She knew that he was terribly sorry for her. He had been unutterably kind all these weeks. Sometimes she wished he would not be so kind. She would have liked to have seen him in one of his irritable moods, she would have loved to have him fly out at her, when she made a mistake — she made mistakes more often than once. But he didn't. He handled her as if she were made of the most fragile glass. She couldn't shout at him, couldn't say, "You needn't, I'm flesh and blood, I'm human . . . and I'm not devastated by Bill's death. I was terribly fond of him, I miss him, it still seems incredible to me, but I'm hot heart-broken. How can I be when he didn't have my heart?"

No, she could hardly say that to Ted, either in a shout or in a whisper.

Toward the middle of the month the heat wave passed and it was cool again, there was life in the air. Even Keturie, who had been sulking of late, came to herself and began to romp with her one rescued kitten as if she were Junior's age. And indeed she was not much older than her fantastically marked, amusing son. They had a grand time together racing through the shop and upsetting things generally until finally Val banished them to the backyard. She was no longer afraid that Keturie would run away and she was certain that Keturie would keep Junior well in hand. She was standing at the window, laughing at them, when Ted came in to see what it was all about. He regarded the two blobs of fur in the backyard with a lenient eye.

"They're cute," said Val, "they're lambs."

"Cats."

"Lambs. What would we do without them?" She looked around the shop. "The shop's nice too," she said, "we're lucky."

They were lucky. He was lucky. He regarded her, her tousled hair, her hands in the pockets of her smock. Sunlight came from the windows and fell upon her hair and her face. He thought, I wonder if she's getting over Rogers?

But, of course, she wasn't, she was too loyal. If — if women got over things like that so soon, he'd never have any respect for them again! And yet . . .

He thought, *I'm in love with her.*

He thought it just like that, suddenly,

baldly. He couldn't believe the accurate evidence of his senses, his eyes contentedly beholding her, his arms which ached to hold her, his heart thumping unmercifully in his breast. Had he been in love with her all along? He didn't believe it, he refused to believe it! He had disliked her and liked her and found her good entertainment and amusing and attractive . . . oh, very attractive.

But in love with her?

Never, said Ted to himself, it happened just this minute.

He turned and walked away from her without a word and busied himself needlessly at his desk. Bill Rogers. He stood between them, himself or his ghost. But perhaps she was over it?

He didn't know. He couldn't find out. He dared not. They'd just have to go on as they were, for a while at any rate.

But Flora had said . . .

Flora was crazy.

Perhaps she wasn't so crazy after all.

He hoped that she wasn't.

He smote the desk and the paper on it jumped and the pens and pencils rattled and a box of clips fell on the floor. Val came in.

"What on earth are you doing?" she asked disapprovingly.

"Nothing, just breaking up housekeeping.

Let's go out to dinner tonight."

"But —" She hesitated a little. She hadn't gone out publicly except with her people since Bill's death . . . so much she granted to the conventions.

"Oh, somewhere quiet. You're looking very pretty this afternoon," he said, and caught his breath because it was so true and because he was aware of it in the fullest sense for the first time.

Val walked over to the desk and opened a drawer. She took out the pint bottle. No, nothing was gone from it except her own small hooker. She replaced it.

"You've been drinking," she said severely, "but what?"

# Chapter XV

Her heart was behaving without decorum. It wasn't the first time in her life that a peronable young man had told her she was very pretty and it wouldn't be the last. Be quiet, you absurd thing, she ordered that accelerating machine which shortened her breath and otherwise distressed her, what's the idea of acting up?

Ted said:

"No, I haven't been drinking. Shut that drawer, will you? First thing you know we'll have a temperance customer in here and she'll go away mad."

Val closed the drawer.

Ted regarded her approvingly.

"And now," he remarked, "you'd be even better looking if you washed your face."

She said, "Oh!" in a small and furious tone and hastened to the nearest mirror. She did have a slightly speckled look . . . a smudge here, the merest suspicion of an ink spot there. She excused herself, after a moment, with great dignity. "It's the pens. Isn't it possible to have a pen around here that doesn't leak?"

Ted began to laugh. He was still laughing

when he went forward to wait on a customer. Val, in the lavatory, scrubbed her face till it shone and then dulled the gleam with powder. She caught herself smiling at her reflection and then tucked in the corners of her lips gravely, putting the smile to bed.

The customer bought some note paper, a dozen wood and paper cigarette holders and hesitated over a book. Ted, waiting patiently, reminded himself sardonically that this was supposed to be a bookshop not a notion counter. He had always refused to admit himself reconciled with the side lines Val had introduced, no matter how lucrative they had proved to be.

That young person, humming casually if slightly off key, strolled out into the shop again, woke up her smile for a moment and turned it full on the customer, an elderly lady in pince-nez and boots of the congress-gaiter type. The lady smiled in return. Val departed to the back room and the customer hissed at Ted:

"Isn't that Valentine Loring, whose fiancé was lost? Poor girl, how dreadful for her. Such a fine young man too, one hears."

"That's my partner, Miss Loring," said Ted shortly. He had forgotten the silent part of it. He was willing to shout it. My partner!

The customer clicked with tongue and impeccable synthetic teeth. "Dear, dear," she said, "so brave."

Her voice trailed off. Evidently she was one who read the papers and hung eagerly upon the reported doings of the great and the near-great and the merely news-making. Ted recalled now that she had been in before, several times, since the disaster, but probably not when Val was in evidence.

He wrapped her cigarette holders and the note paper, refraining from a wild desire to throw them at her head. Why does she want the holders, he mused, surely she doesn't smoke?

She was still poking about the books. Val had seen to it that there were several comfortable chairs in the main room of the shop, with an ash tray sewn on a strip of leather across the arm of each. In a moment of pure — or almost pure — mischief Ted offered the lady his case. "If you'd care to sit down and rest . . ." he suggested.

The customer glared, clutched her parcel, said firmly, "Young man, I never smoke," and fled. Ted laughed again. Val came out of the back room where she had been picking up the newspaper. Unknown Junior had evidently been reading. He hadn't liked it apparently, perhaps the tone of the editorials displeased him or else he belonged to another political party, for it was torn to shreds.

"What's the joke," she said, "or is it private?"

"I couldn't possibly tell you," he replied gravely, "you're far too young. But I think we've lost a customer."

"Now that the notes are paid," suggested Val, "and the shop can worry along, don't you think you'd better let me do all the waiting on casual droppers-in anyway? You can sit in the office and prop up that great brow of yours with that spirit hand —"

"Do I look like Mrs. Browning?" he inquired, pained.

"No, more like Flush. To continue, you can sit there and look erudite and come out of hiding only when we have someone who wants something which is up your alley. We can't afford to have you frightening away customers, making funny faces and funnier noises — even if there is money in the bank."

"That reminds me, where shall we spend it, tonight?"

They decided on a little restaurant on the East Side. In the dear old days it had been a prosperous speakeasy of the better kind and it still flourished, legally. It possessed a remarkable if somewhat abusive parrot and a nice flight of stone steps. There was a pleasant semigloom about it, excellent food, music which was not too obtrusive, at least early in the evening.

Val's mother said, "Well —" rather dubiously when Val told her that she was going out. She spoke to Mr. Loring later, after Ted had rung their doorbell and he and Val had departed. "I suppose it's inevitable," she said, sighing.

"What? Oh. . . ." He woke from his newspaper with a start. "You can't expect the youngster to sit home in mourning indefinitely," he said tolerantly.

"I know. But it hasn't been very long. Besides," said Marcia, "she assured me that she doesn't believe Bill is dead."

"Then she isn't in mourning," said Mr. Loring, too reasonably, "so it's all right either way."

Dinner was fun. They talked gravely about the bookshop and its possibilities. They argued. Ted was all for moving from their present quarters in the autumn to a larger establishment. Val could not see it. They could, she thought, handle what they already had. More, now. It was foolish, it was shortsighted. Better continue a small business which paid them, and which might pay them even better when times picked up, than to undertake anything larger . . .

which would become a source of worry and sleepless nights . . .

"Look, there's Flora!"

It was Flora. She had two young men in tow and a very plain middle-aged woman. They sat down at the bar and ordered their cocktails. Flora was looking well. She had put on weight. It had recently been announced that she would do a series of sponsored readings over the radio.

"Who's that with her?"

"Haven't the least idea," said Ted, looking in vain for Peter.

Flora saw them, exclaimed on a high note and came over to their table. She kissed Val, rather to that young woman's astonishment, and smiled a little mockingly at Ted. The smile contained all the elements of I-told-you-so and made Ted wonder, suddenly, if this was not the explanation of Mona Lisa's subtle expression. He had heard it laid to everything from unrequited love to colic, but now it seemed to him that he had solved the riddle.

"Ted darling!" cried Flora, with exaggeration, "and Val!" She struck a becoming attitude. "How nice to see you." She added, "You're looking better than I expected, Val."

"It was sweet of you to write me," Val told her rather stonily. And indeed Flora had written her a charming, sad little letter at the time of Bill's death. For that was how Val was thinking about it now, although she would not admit it openly — Bill's death.

Flora patted her shoulder and said deeply, "I understand."

Understand what? wondered Val silently.

Presently Flora explained her companions. "Major, the columnist, and David Ring — you've heard him on the radio?"

"Who's the girl?" asked Ted.

"My secretary," said Flora, "Angelica Austin . . . she's marvelous . . . I couldn't exist without her."

When she had gone Val twinkled briefly at Ted.

"She picks 'em plain," she said, "which has its source in wisdom."

"Meow!" said Ted.

They laughed together, more heartily than the occasion warranted. But it was pleasant to be able to laugh about Flora. Ted thought soberly, however, that when the time came to talk to Val of things other than cabbages and kings he might have to speak of Flora without laughter. This worried him considerably. If you kept silent you were being chivalrous and unfair. If you spoke you were being honest and no gentleman. These problems were difficult and even the newspapers and the etiquette books could not solve them for you.

It was late when he took her home, and Val was sleepy. She yawned in his face, which disconcerted him. "Sorry," she excused herself, "not used to being up so late."

After he had gone she went up to her room. The family slept, the house was quiet. On her desk was a message from Mrs. Rogers in her mother's handwriting. "She says to tell you she has had a letter from Bill. . . ."

Val read no further. Her knees shook under her and gave way, she sat down limply on the side of the bed, the nervous tears in her throat. Her first and instant reaction was an overpowering gratitude. He wasn't dead. He was alive . . . he — She read on after a moment, and the sheet of note paper shook in her hand. She had misread it. "A belated letter from Bill . . . weeks and weeks back. It must have been mailed just before he went out on that last trip. She would like to see you tomorrow night if you can arrange it. . . ."

Oh, poor woman, thought Val, in an agony of sympathy, poor woman . . . after all this time . . . a little, lost letter . . . how horrible.

Her drowsiness fled. She undressed and went to bed and lay awake for a long time thinking her unhappy thoughts. The telephone rang just as she was dropping off to sleep. She went out into the hall where there was an extension and answered it. The downstairs instruments must have been switched off for the night, she thought, picking up the receiver.

It was, she ascertained after bewildered questioning, a policeman. There was a fire in the building which housed the bookshop. They had just reached Mr. Morrison . . . the janitor had given him the names.

Val hung up and ran back to her room and redressed, hastily, sketchily, and flung on a coat. She slipped some money and a front-door key in her pocket and went hurriedly but softly down the stairs, holding her breath. If her parents woke up they would stop her.

She would get there faster than Ted, she was so much nearer. She hailed a night-hawk taxi and got into it without any trepidation and gave the address. Her hands were ice cold and damp. She clenched them together. Please — not the shop —

There was the usual crowd gathered about the building. There was a radio car and policemen and the fire engines, the great red juggernaut affairs with the firemen swarming about. She heard the sounds of axes, the sound of water hissing on flame. The janitor hopped on one foot and then on the other. He had forgotten his slippers. His wife was huddled on a nearby step surrounded by such belongings as she had managed to save and her three excited children. No one else lived in the building. The fire had started in the basement.

Val tried to get through the lines and was stopped instantly.

"Who are you?"

"Valentine Loring . . . Mr. Morrison's partner," she told them. "Please let me through."

But they would not. They said firmly, "Now, miss, it don't do no good to take on like that. It's under control, see. . . ."

"But the shop —"

As far as she could find out, the shop wasn't on fire, not yet. It had all begun in the old rags and newspapers and things in the basement. The policeman eyed the janitor with severe regard. "Maybe he'd had some old oil cans lying around."

The janitor trembled and swore that he had not. "Spontaneous combustion," someone said wisely, "the man ought to be shot, no more sense than a cat!"

*Cat!*

Keturie and Unknown Junior . . . probably asleep in the cellar. And the cellar was burning.

"No, you don't, miss!" said someone else, kindly but implacably.

Val said something, half sobbing. They listened. Someone left . . . someone in the building. "Here, speak up, can't you, we don't understand."

"Oh, a cat! Well, I wouldn't take on if I was you, miss. Cats is smart, she's probably found her way out . . . maybe she wasn't in — cats never sleep in, 'specially on summer nights," they explained.

"But —"

The fire was still burning although halfheartedly when Ted arrived. He was hatless, as Val was hatless. He was also breathless. He broke through the gathered company and ran straight to her.

"Val, for heaven's sake!"

"Oh, Ted," she wailed and clung to him, "isn't it awful? I mean . . ."

Someone in authority spoke to him.

"Mr. Morrison? It's all right, they've put it out, practically. I don't believe there's much damage."

Ted looked through the graying gloom, still redly lit, at the broken windows, the streams of water. Books suffer from water as much as from fire. He shook his head. Of course, they were insured, the insurance would probably cover it, but —

Val was saying urgently, "Ted, it's Keturie. I — they won't look for her."

Ted said, patting her, "She's probably out, Val, I wouldn't worry."

"I do so worry!" said Val violently. Her face was twisted with grief like a child's. "I can't bear to have anything happen to her, she's — she's part of the shop, Ted!" She stamped her foot at him. "Don't stand there gaping at me!" she commanded furiously. "Can't you *do* something?"

She broke away from his detaining arm and went over to the shivering janitor. The janitor's quarters were in the basement across the way from the shop, down half a flight of stairs. She shook the man's arm till he turned a bewildered face to her. "Have you seen the cat?" she demanded.

It took her several minutes to make him understand. Then he shook his head. No, ma'am, he hadn't seen any cat . . . he had enough to worry about without thinking about cats. And now they were going to blame him. As if he hadn't kept the place clean as the next man. He hadn't left no oily rags around, no, not him.

Val said furiously, "Well, that settles it, I'm going in!"

She was pretty quick . . . but Ted was quicker. He caught her and shook her hard.

"What in hell do you think you're doing?" he asked her.

"Let me go!"

"I will not!"

She was crying, from sheer rage. He shook her again. Hysterical, was she? Well, he'd fix that. He slapped her soundly, and thrust her into the arms of an interested male spectator. "Here, hold her," he ordered grimly.

No one stopped him. Perhaps they were too astonished. Perhaps it was because, although neither Ted nor Val knew it, the fire was just about over, while smoke still poured out, thick and suffocating.

Val, when she caught her breath screamed, "Ted!"

"Hey, hold on there," expostulated the man in whose arms she struggled, "quit kicking my shins."

"Where'd he go?" she cried.

"After your cat. You wanted him to, didn't you?" asked the man. He had little use for women. He was henpecked at home and it gave him a great deal of abstract masculine pleasure to control, if only by pure physical force, this unknown female.

"But I didn't mean . . ."

"Women never do," said the man gloomily, "and still men have to suffer!"

He was so pleased at that that he relaxed

his grip. Val slipped away from him and made for the nearest policeman. He was standing talking to the agent for the property, who had just arrived. They both stared at Val with some astonishment.

"He's gone down there," she said, without preamble.

"Who has?"

"Ted," she answered exasperated. "Why doesn't one of those firemen do something about it?"

"The fire's out," said the policeman soothingly, "it didn't amount to much, sister. Hadn't you better run along home to bed?"

"But there's *smoke*," said Val tearfully, "he may be unconscious." She gave the large stolid arm of the law a determined push. She had never had much use for the law anyway. "Why don't you *do* something about it?" she demanded. "Why do we pay taxes anyway?"

"That's what I want to know," admitted the agent glumly. "I've been wanting to know that for a long time. You tell me."

The engines were snorting. The snaky hose was being reeled up preparatory to departure. The agent moved over and pierced the janitor with a stern eye. The janitor was in a state bordering on collapse. He would presently return to his humble dwelling and find it unmarred by fire but with running streams of water, and neatly axed here and there. But if there was a bed, damp or not, he craved its shelter. Tomorrow would be time enough to answer questions with investigators and adjusters and all the aftermath of fire.

The engines snorted away. The fire chief's car pulled out first, its bell clanging. No one noticed Val.

She met Ted coming up the basement steps. He was as black as a top hat and his eyes were running and he sneezed furiously once or twice. He had Keturie in the bend of one arm, far too tightly. She was complaining bitterly. Unknown Junior hung out of one pocket, his eyes baleful and his voice raised to join his mother's.

"Take the damned thing, she's clawing the life out of me," said Ted and thrust Keturie into Val's arms.

"Ted . . . you fool — you might have been killed."

"Well, you wanted me to fetch 'em, didn't you?" he answered crossly, and sneezed again. "The place is a mess," he reported, "never saw anything like it!"

His feet were wet, his socks were wet, his trouser cuffs sopping.

"You'll catch your death," said Val, remembering his recent near-pneumonia and forgetting the season.

"Smoke gets in your eyes, all right," said Ted grimly. "I hope I never hear that song again."

"Come on," she said and tugged at his arm, "you've got to get home."

"I'm staying here," said Ted. "You take the menagerie."

"There's nothing you can do now," she told him, "and the fire didn't reach the shop."

"No, but the water did." He sneezed once more. Val pulled him over to the curb. The crowd had almost dispersed. One or two people looked at them curiously and laughed. A taxi drew up.

In the taxi, with both Junior and his mother in her lap, Val said:

"If anything had happened to you —"

"Would you care?" he asked. The sentiment was a little spoiled by a sniffle. He rubbed at his eyes with a hand and said, "Damn!" explosively.

Val gave him a handkerchief, a small, silly handkerchief with black Scotties on a red ground. He used it. She said, "You know I would."

"Val . . ." he said. He put his arms around her. Keturie squeaked and Junior wailed. Neither Val nor Ted heard them. "Val," he said, "I know it's too soon — but I do love you — so much."

287

When he kissed her she could smell and taste the smoke. That didn't matter. She kissed him in return, with intensity, with a passion which shook him terribly and made him both triumphant and humble. She said, "We belong together . . . I've always known it."

"Darling . . ."

"Meow," remarked Keturie and scratched Val, but she did not even know it.

The cab stopped. After a while the driver peered in and asked benevolently, "Getting off here?"

"Yes. No. Wait for me," said Ted, dazed.

They went up the steps together . . . a gentleman with bedraggled garments and a black face; a lady whose face was pretty well smudged, and who had two cats clutched firmly in one arm.

Once at the door Val discovered that she had lost her key. There was nothing to do but ring. She rang the bell. She stood there waiting, one hand in Ted's. She withdrew it as the door opened.

Mr. Loring, in his pajamas, gaped at them.

It was almost dawn. He said, "What . . . Val . . . at this hour . . . what in heaven's name has happened to you?"

Val said happily, "Nothing. I mean . . . there's been a fire in the bookshop but —"

Mrs. Loring, who was in deadly fear of burglars, but who could not permit her husband to run any danger without her, was coming down the stairs. She reached the bottom step, took one look at her daughter — disheveled and dirty — and for the first time in her life fainted.

# Chapter XVI

There was considerable commotion. Val and Ted knelt down beside Mrs. Loring instantly and Mr. Loring complained vaguely, directing his distracted comment to Ted . . . "as if you hadn't caused *enough* trouble!" a remark which later in the morning gave that young man considerable pause. Val, with her mother's head laid flat, according to nursing Hoyle, ordered, "Get some water, somebody, don't stand around doing nothing!" But by the time the water arrived Mrs. Loring had recovered. She sat up and said faintly, "I'm so sorry — but really . . . you looked — !" She regarded her child again and said more briskly, "But fainting won't help. What's happened?"

Val told her. Mrs. Loring sighed, "I suppose I've made a fool of myself," and with her husband's agitated help got to her feet. She explained, holding to the banisters, "I couldn't imagine . . . at this time in the morning —"

"I was home hours ago," Val told her, "when they called me and told me the shop was on fire."

"Oh, dear," ejaculated Mrs. Loring, and sat down on the stairs. "Not a step do I move until you tell me all about it," she said suspiciously. It occurred to her that beneath soot and smoke both Val and Ted were remarkably radiant for a couple of business partners who had undoubtedly suffered a severe financial loss. Indeed, Ted was inclined to be almost facetious. Not much fire, he assured her, if a great deal of smoke, to say nothing of rivers of water. As soon as he got a wash and a shave and a cup of coffee he'd go back and ascertain the damage. "Marvelous publicity," he announced further, "successful shop goes up in smoke!"

After a little while during which everyone talked at once, Mrs. Loring, escorted by her husband, went back to her room. Ted was given the freedom of the guest room bathroom, a borrowed razor, a clean shirt, bathrobe and slippers, while his bedraggled trousers, his socks and shoes were taken away to be dried. The invaluable Frieda, roused by the excitement, appeared in curl papers, firmly grasping a poker. It was evident that she took it upstairs with her every night from its place beside the old-fashioned range. She grasped the situation, however, just as firmly in a brief space of time and presently marched herself to the kitchen to light a fire and dry out Ted's belongings.

Ted looked, thought Val, washed, brushed and dressed and in as much of her right mind as is possible in a completely happy human being, exceedingly silly and rather nice in the bathrobe, which was a bit too short for him. He had long legs and when he strode about and the bathrobe revealed a glimpse of shorts and garters, she giggled somewhat self-consciously. No man is beautiful in BVD's, she thought sorrowfully.

Presently there was coffee, at which Mr. Loring joined them. Mrs. Loring begged to be excused. She was still a little shaky. Perhaps Val would go up and see her afterwards and explain more coherently the doings of the past night?

Ted, dried and pressed and himself again, told Val, "it is my rooted conviction that no man can comport himself with dignity without his trousers except Alfred Lunt in *Reunion Suit in Vienna* — or whatever it was called" and departed for the shop. Val had no time alone with him. She called after him in the hall, "I'll be along in an hour or so," and went up to placate her mother. Her mother, much ashamed of her recent display of weakness, was inclined to be severe. "You had no business chasing out like that," she said. "I thought your father was the only one in the family who ran after fire engines . . . and I hoped he had outgrown it."

"But it was the shop!" expostulated Val.

"Well, what could you do about it?" asked her mother, unanswerably.

When Val reached the shop again people were still milling around, the agent, the owner, the disconsolate janitor. Ted was haranguing them all in the smoky hall. "Come in," he said politely to his partner, "and take sides. Which will you have — a golden apple or a silver grapefruit?" It was, she saw, to be a tug of war.

They were there most of the morning. The damage in the shop itself was comparatively slight. But smoke had done a good job on the walls and ceilings. They looked like the newest type of decoration. "It has to be done over," pronounced Ted inexorably.

By noon the details were more or less settled. The shop would close for repairs. There would be work going on in the cellar meantime and the janitor's little two-by-four needed some attention. Meantime, as there was to be some rebuilding and the two other small shops on the street level — one was lace and the other was gowns — had also suffered some damage and the owners were talking happily of breaking their leases, why not alter these to suit Mr. Morrison? He would take them, if they were thrown into one and thus make a duplex of his simplex, so to speak, upstairs and down.

"But, Ted —" whispered Val.

"Hush up," said Ted, "we've got 'em by the short hair. They'll do anything to keep us. We'll reopen as soon as the place is repainted downstairs and next autumn we'll have the upstairs place as well."

"We won't need it," said Val.

"Yes, we will," he contradicted. "There isn't enough room, you know that. We'll do gifts — and cards and fiction and such upstairs and keep the downstairs shop for the fine editions and firsts and the prints and all that. It will be cheaper than moving out and looking for a bigger place."

He regarded her. They were momentarily alone, but not sufficiently. He said, "I'm starved. How about lunch?"

They lunched very early at a little teashop around the corner. The food was execrable and the service worse, but the food seemed to them far better than any they had ever eaten and they ignored the service. He put his hand over hers on the table.

"Sure you meant it? Sure it wasn't just the excitement of being burned out?" he inquired.

"I meant," she assured him, "but —"

"But what?"

"We can't tell anyone yet," she said soberly.

"Why not?" he shouted at her. "Aren't

ashamed of me, are you?"

"Don't scream," she said severely, "or I shall be. No, listen, we must be serious. It's — too soon, Ted. I can't upset the family. I can't hurt Mrs. Rogers like that."

"Nonsense," he said, "I know how you feel. But look here, Val, do you mean to say you're going to keep me waiting? I thought we'd get married right away . . . perhaps not tomorrow," he conceded generously, "but next week. And go away for a little and then come back to work. The shop would be ready by then," he reminded her.

"I can't, Ted. What would people think?"

"I didn't know that you were so conventional . . . I mean that you'd care what people thought."

"I don't, as a rule. But this is different . . . I was engaged to Bill."

"Were you so much in love with him?" he asked her slowly.

"You know that I was not. I was awfully fond of him, Ted. If you hadn't come along. But you did . . . and so . . ."

"Why did you engage yourself to him in the first place?" he demanded.

"I thought that — you and Flora . . ."

Flora.

Ted pushed his plate aside. He took her hand again. He said, leaning forward:

"About Flora . . . I —"

"Please," said Val, a little pale, "please don't tell me anything, Ted. I'd rather not hear. I suppose that's pretty reactionary of me, but I don't want to. Just as long as I know it's over."

"It was over," said Ted very gravely, "before it really began." He looked up at her, his eyes incredibly blue. "I've been in love with you for a long time," he told her, and forgot that up until this minute he had believed it to have been a matter of less than twenty-four hours.

She said, "We'll make a crazy couple. We'll probably fail. Oh, not as a couple, but in business. I do think we're taking on a lot, Ted."

"I don't," said Ted. "You wait and see."

The curious courses came and went. They ate, unknowingly, they drank extraordinarily weak tea and toyed with a pallid gelatine affair topped by a blob of whipped cream. After which Ted paid the check, far overtipped the adenoidal waitress, and tucking his girl under his arm went out on the street again. There he hailed a taxi and gave the immemorial order, "To the Park."

They sat in the Park near the lake on a stiff green bench and forgot that other people were also entitled to use the Park. So far as they were concerned it was inalienably their own, their private pleasure grounds. But no one could have taken them for lovers, at first glance. For one thing they appeared to be quarreling, in a perfectly friendly fashion.

"It's no use," said Ted finally, "you don't leave me a leg to stand on. You can talk rings around me. It isn't fair. If," he added gloomily, suddenly aware of their lack of privacy, "if I could grab you and kiss you till you begged for mercy. . . ."

"I wouldn't."

"You wouldn't what?"

"Beg for mercy. I can take it," said Val, too demurely.

"Val!"

"Ted, for heaven's sake!"

"But," he said, after a moment, "we haven't anywhere to go. Not even the shop."

"I thought that in the shop you wouldn't mix business and pleasure."

"I've changed my mind."

"I shan't let you," she said. "Think of all the dour, strictly rational customers we would lose."

"Who cares?"

"I care. Dour, rational people are usually solvent. No, I shall hold you to that contract — during working hours."

"Even after we're married?" he inquired. She answered, a little breathless, "Even then. Or perhaps I won't have to," she added sadly, "perhaps it won't be necessary."

"Cynic!"

But they couldn't, she told him, be married for a long time . . . perhaps a year.

"Val," he said despairingly, "that isn't fair to me."

"I know." She was grave and unhappy about it too, he could see that. "But we can't do anything else, Ted. There's no use not facing facts. Mother and Father aren't going to approve. It will take them a long time to get accustomed to the idea . . . and there's Bill's mother. I have to consider her. I know it sounds silly and old-fashioned and super-sentimental, but it's so. I can't . . . I just can't." She said after a moment, "And it seems so callous somehow . . . all this happiness, founded on Bill's death."

Her voice shook. Ted said, his arm about her quite openly:

"Darling, if he had come back . . . you would have married him . . . feeling as you do about me?"

"No," she said instantly. She trembled suddenly and leaned closer to him. "No, of course, I wouldn't. I had made up my mind to tell him. I was going to tell him I couldn't marry him, his mother knows that now."

"Then, why in heaven's name . . ."

"I know what you're thinking. But, oh, Ted," she urged him, "let's be very sure . . . let's be so sure that nothing can alter us. That's why I want to wait, really. You see, we've both made mistakes. . . ."

He asked, "You think it will take a year?"

"I don't know," she told him, and smiled at him, suddenly. Then she released herself and rose. "I'm going home; after all, I have a hostess's duty to fulfill."

"What are you talking about?"

"Keturie and Junior. I left them exploring the house. Mother isn't very crazy about cats. But they're going to stay with us until the shop's in shape."

He said, alarmed, "Look here, that's not so good. I mean, it will be a couple of weeks and meantime . . ."

"You can come to the house, can't you? You'll have to stick around the shop to see that the painters do their work properly," she said, "and I'll have to stick around to see that you see that they do."

They walked back to her house and he was ridiculously careful with her at the crossings. And when they reached her steps, he asked, standing bareheaded at the foot of them, "Tonight?"

"Not tonight, darling. I've promised to go see Mrs. Rogers."

"Tomorrow night?"

"Yes. Tomorrow night. And I'll be at the shop as usual in the morning," she told him, laughing, "from force of habit."

Going to the Rogers apartment that evening she subdued herself as best she could. Yet she couldn't hide a thing, she told herself ruefully. She was utterly and completely happy and she could not conceal it. Mrs. Rogers would know at once. It would hurt her dreadfully. It didn't matter that she knew now that Val's heart wasn't in her son's keeping. She wouldn't stop to be sane about it, and practical and resigned. She would just be wounded and resentful that the girl whom Bill had loved was happy — without him.

I do miss him, Val told herself soberly, I'd give anything to have him back again.

Anything? Ted?

No, not Ted.

Almost anything, she told herself.

She rang the bell, dreading the next half hour unimaginably.

She found that she need not have dreaded it. Mrs. Rogers had no eyes for her. She was directing her maid in packing, she was dashing about her room, a determined woman with a spring in her step, and a new vitality informing her little person.

Val knew why, presently. Bill's letter,

which had reached his mother so belatedly, had given her a new hope, an added impetus. She was flying to the Coast tomorrow. She had telegraphed her agent there to charter a boat. She was going to find her son.

When they parted she held the younger woman in her embrace for a long moment. She said, "If you would go with me, Val?"

Val shook her head. After a moment Mrs. Rogers released her. She said, "Well, better not, I suppose," with a slightly hostile edge in her tone. Yet she couldn't be seriously angry at the girl. It wasn't her fault, she supposed, that she couldn't care for Bill as he did for her. Shortsighted, astonishing as it seemed. Later she'd have time to worry about that, to resent Val's alteration for her son's sake. Now nothing mattered but the possibility of finding him. The letter had given her his proposed route . . . more fully than had any previous word. She would sail on her chartered yacht, she would follow that route.

At home again Val wept a little, not for Bill but for his mother. She was so sure . . . and so doomed to disappointment and heartbreak. She found herself wishing that Bill's body and those of his companions might be recovered; that the sea would give up its young dead. Anything was better than uncertainty, than this false hope.

Mrs. Rogers left on the following day. She left a bank address which would eventually reach her. She would be on the Coast for perhaps a week until the yacht was ready to sail.

Val went with her to the airport. She stood there watching her climb into the great passenger plane, and waved to her and was pushed about by others who had come to see their friends off; and, with them, watched the great plane taxi down the runway and rise into the air. She wiped her eyes, childishly, with the back of her hand. This beginning journey of Bill's mother — so winged, so hopeful, so doomed, Val felt, to futility.

Before Mrs. Rogers actually sailed on the second, very long stage of her journey, the bookshop redecorating was completed and Val had bought herself some new smocks to celebrate. It was now July and business was not brisk. Keturie and Junior returned, unchastened by their experience, to the store and were not much at home in it until they had become accustomed to the alteration in color scheme. In another week or so Val and her mother were going away for a holiday, to friends who had a camp near Saranac. Val said hesitantly, "If Ted shut up shop over a weekend . . .?"

Her mother looked at her and replied, after a moment, "Of course . . . Alice said to have anyone you liked." She was aware, without any actual knowledge, how things stood between her daughter and Ted Morrison. She was not happy about it but she knew that Val was. That mattered most, she supposed. And she was rather fond of Ted. It amused her and in a measure saddened her to see how his small fortune, the good luck which Val had tossed into the treasury, had changed him. Oh, not completely, but perceptibly. He came quite often to dinner and talked about stability and conservatism to her amazed but approving husband. He now had a little security and he had discovered what it was worth. At least, he thought he had security.

Val had changed him too. He had been a bookish, grave young man somewhat on the sober side, the hatches battened down securely over any suspicion of a sense of humor which might be considered frivolous. Val had changed that. They were quite ridiculous together, Val's mother thought tolerantly. They didn't want anyone to know they were in love, that much was apparent, so they refrained from the slightest public demonstration. But their very arguments and absurd and lively quarreling proclaimed the fact to anyone with two eyes and common sense. Mr. Loring told her, shortly before his wife and child departed from town, "I suppose I'll have Ted on my hands."

"Do you mind?"

"No, not really. He's all right, in a way. Good company. He generously tells me he won't permit me to be lonely."

"He'll have to talk about Val to someone," said Marcia.

"I suppose so. We might do a show together or a couple of movies," acknowledged Mr. Loring. He was becoming reconciled to Ted Morrison. If Bill had lived . . . but he hadn't. Why, thought Val's father, in a species of strange impatience, should he have gone gallivanting off like that, leaving the field clear . . . poor devil?

Dining one evening with Ted in a perfectly respectable but rather Village type of restaurant which afforded the older man a childlike kick, although he wouldn't admit it, he was astonished to see a personable young woman approach their table and embrace his companion with considerable fervor. It was, he ascertained a moment afterward, the poetess, Flora Carr. When she was gone, after acknowledging the introduction graciously and inquiring affectionately for Val, he regarded Ted suspiciously.

"Does this always happen to you in public places?"

"Well, no," said Ted. He was uncomfortable, he colored a little. He was no longer accustomed to easy endearments. "I used to know her very well. I still do," he added hastily.

"So I see." Mr. Loring ruminated and searched in his memory. "Isn't that the writing girl Val wanted to have up to the house Christmas?"

"Yes."

"Your girl," said Mr. Loring deeply.

"That was a long time ago," said Ted, in the tone of a nonagenarian. "I — look here, Mr. Loring, forget about Flora. You know how I feel about Val."

"I'm afraid I do," admitted his guest lugubriously.

"I haven't much to offer her."

"Spent all the *Tamerlane*?" asked Mr. Loring, in horror.

"Well, no. And the business will be all right. I'm sure of that. We're doing pretty well, we'll do better. When the alterations are completed and we move into the upstairs place we'll have as unique a shop as you can find in town. I've acquired several collectors lately, they'll pay me pretty well. I may have to get an assistant to help Val in the autumn, as I'll take on more of this private library work . . . go to auctions for people, here and out of town."

"You and Val going to get married?" asked

Mr. Loring casually.

Ted looked up from the bread he was crumbling on the checked tablecloth.

"We want to — I'd like to, as soon as possible. She won't," he said, "she feels it's too soon after — after —"

"I understand," said Mr. Loring. He thought, She's right, too, it isn't decent rushing into things like this so soon after Bill's death. He said gently, "You'd better wait, my boy."

"You aren't opposed?" asked Ted hopefully.

"Hell, no," said Mr. Loring, and added, "What good would it do me if I were?"

But women are less sentimental than men, on the whole. Ted went up to the camp on the last week-end Val and her mother were there. There were other youngsters about and older people, but Val and Ted might as well have been completely isolated. They were very much in love. It would have taken colder hearts and older heads to withstand the combination of summer, blue water, mountains, green trees, moonlight. They went fishing and forgot to fish. They went swimming and spent their time lying on beach or raft. They went walking and walked very little. Their condition was obvious to all and sundry. And Mrs. Loring said:

"When are you two planning to be married?"

She spoke to Val. Val, who was sitting on her bed changing her frock for evening, nearly fell off. She stammered, "I didn't know you knew . . . that is, I thought —"

"My dear child, you are making a spectacle of yourselves."

"Ted wants to be married at once," said Val, resenting that remark, "but I thought we should wait."

"Because of Bill?"

"Yes."

"What would that accomplish?" inquired her mother.

She suffered Val's entire weight, flung into her arms. She suffered her strong young clasp about her, nearly strangling her, and her kiss. She asked, "You're terribly happy, aren't you?"

"Yes," said Val.

"That's all that matters," said her mother, "you have to be selfish about some things, there's so little time."

Val didn't even hear. She was back again at her duty of dressing, putting on things wrong-side out, hind-side to, swearing a little, rectifying her errors, running a comb through her dark red curls. She couldn't wait another minute to see Ted and to tell him. "I've changed my mind . . . we'll be married in the autumn."

While the alterations were under way, they'd put someone in downstairs and go off honeymooning, oh, briefly and inexpensively, and then they'd come home —

Her mother asked, sitting there watching her:

"I don't suppose you'd consider living with us?"

Val hadn't. She hadn't dared think that far. She flung down the comb. She said, "Is it fair to you?"

"You mean, is it fair to you and Ted? I don't know. But for a little while anyway, till you see how the shop goes. We can have a sort of apartment made for you on your own floor. I've been thinking of that — I thought, after you married we'd do it anyway and rent it. It would carry taxes, and we can't sell the house, you know. I thought after you left home it would be less lonely to have a young couple upstairs. You might as well be the young couple. Your father and I would try not to be in the way."

Val cried, "I'd love it. Are you sure you — ?"

Her mother interrupted:

"I have had it planned for some time. It wouldn't cost very much. And I'd charge you an exorbitant rent," she said severely, "and no nonsense about getting behindhand, just because you're relations!"

"I can see," said Val solemnly, "that you're going to be a very difficult landlady."

By the time they reached New York it had all been settled. They would be married from home in the autumn, quietly. Just the family and a few old friends. No engagement would be announced and Val would not take a ring. Not yet. She had put Bill's diamond away. Someday she would return it to his mother, someday when this could be accomplished without too much heartbreak. She wore Ted's seal ring wound with linen thread because it fitted her finger far too loosely. Keturie and Junior would come to the wedding, with large white bows about their necks. They would be, she told Ted, her only attendants. And she and Ted would go away to some quiet little place until the shop alterations and those necessary in the Loring home would be completed. And then back to town and to work.

She was in the shop one day a week or so after her holiday had ended and dusting the books. The new paint was spick and span. There were roses in the blue vases and three customers had just departed, bearing bundles. Each was sailing for Europe and each wanted "a good selection of the best new books."

Val shut the cash drawer with a little satisfied bang and Ted came up and put his arms about her. "Working hours!" she reminded him.

"Happy?" he asked her, himself besotted with happiness.

"Terribly. I'm afraid sometimes. I pinch myself. I say, It can't possibly last."

The telephone rang and she slipped away to answer it. It was the servant Frieda, rather inept over the wire, but Mrs. Loring was out and a telegram had come for Miss Valentine. What should she do?

"Read it," said Val. "Yes, open it and read it." She waited a moment. "Yes, I'm listening. What — *what's that?*"

She turned to Ted, the receiver in her hand. She said slowly, "It's from Bill . . . he's alive . . . he's coming home!"

# Chapter XVII

There was a split second of silence and then Ted said — and Val was always glad that he said it, "Gee, that's swell, Val! That's *marvelous*. What happened . . . what does he say?"

She put down the receiver. Probably Frieda was still talking at the other end. Val didn't know. She took two steps and whirled. She repeated, "Bill's *alive!*"

Ted stood watching her with his hands in his pockets. After a moment he asked quietly, anxiously, "Val — this — this couldn't make any difference to us — could it?"

Val sat down, as if her knees had given way under her. She replied, and her small glowing face was suddenly strained, "No — of course not, Ted." And then on a little, forlorn wail, "But — I'll have to tell him, Ted! I — the cable said that he and his crew had been picked up by a small cargo vessel. This was sent from the first place at which they touched. He won't get another boat, a faster boat, for some time yet. He doesn't know when he'll be back. I — I can't *not* tell him, Ted. Suppose he doesn't get back till autumn? I couldn't possibly meet him casually and say 'By the way, I'm married.' We'll have to wait until he gets back, or there's an address to which I can write." She added, as Ted stood there frowning and making no reply, "And his mother. Heavens knows where she is, or how long it will take for the news to reach her. We'll send word to the California bank, of course. . . . Or perhaps his cable to her has already been sent on."

Ted said soberly, "I'm glad he's safe. I'd like you to believe that."

"Ted, I do," she broke in.

"But," went on Ted steadily, "you have to understand this. I won't give you up. Not if you love me, Val. Are you sure? Are you sure that all this hasn't just been rebound? I mean," he went on awkwardly, "caring a lot for Rogers, believing him dead, yourself very unhappy. Does the fact that he isn't dead change things between us, Val? You've got to be honest with me!"

She said, "I am honest. It's you and I — we belong. I never cared for Bill as I do for you. But this must change the circumstances a little, you have to see that, Ted. He — loves me. The cable said so. He's saved, he's coming back — to me. He said that too. When he comes back, I'll tell him. I couldn't do otherwise. You must understand."

He did understand. But he was frightened.

He dared not show her how frightened he was. His initial reaction to the news had been spontaneous, decent, humane. Now he was more human than humane, thinking, Why couldn't he have stayed dead? Why does he have to come back and threaten us? For he believed it was a threat. Rogers — Val had known Rogers all her life, cared for him as long, he was as familiar to her as her own hands, and habit is a terribly insidious thing. When Rogers returned, a rescued hero, with the papers full of his exploits — and full, too, of his happy homecoming to his fiancée, might she not regard him in another light . . . an older light? Might she not feel that she belonged, not to Ted Morrison but to the man with the older claim?

He was white and shaking yet did not know it. Val asked, with her hand on his arm:

"What's wrong, Ted?" And then as he did not answer, she cried out miserably, "Oh, surely you believe me? Surely you realize that I can't be brutal about it, Ted, that I have to wait?"

He said, "No matter how long you wait, it will be brutal, won't it? Sometimes a surgeon's knife is the best way out, the cleaner wound. If he came back and found us married . . ."

She said, "I can't, Ted, that's all there is

to it." She was half crying with excitement and confusion. He said, after a minute, "All right, have it your own way." But he looked, as she regarded him, completely a stranger to her, the brows drawn, the mouth set.

After a while she said wearily, "I'll go home now. That's best, I think. Mother will be in presently and I'll get hold of Father at his office. There must be things we can do. Somehow we have to get word through to Mrs. Rogers. You'll come this evening?"

"All right." But he followed her into the back room where she was taking off her smock, setting her hair to rights, putting on her hat, and there he caught her and held her close in a clasp which hurt her and frightened her a little.

"I won't let you go," he warned her savagely.

"But you must," she said, trying to laugh, and to release herself. "I mean, for just a little while. Oh, don't look like that, Ted. . . . Please! It will be all right. It just means that until Bill comes back we'll have to be patient. I can't hurt him, that way, unnecessarily. I'll have to hurt him so much as it is."

Someone opened the door to the shop and a gay voice cried, "Where are you two — hiding?"

It was Flora. She came directly to the back

314

room. She said, as her amused eyes encountered Ted's inhospitable countenance and Val's disheveled confusion, "I didn't mean to interrupt. It's just that I have a customer for you, Ted."

Val said, "You weren't interrupting. I have to go home now for a while. I'll leave you to talk."

Looking back, she saw them sitting there, in the two big chairs by the fireplace she had filled with green branches, for the summer. She thought, I wish I didn't hate Flora so — now that I'm sure that she and Ted . . . Yet I was almost sure before he told me. And it can't make any difference now, it's all over and he loves me.

Flora was saying, "Terribly rich and terribly anxious to spend his money . . . If you're willing to act as agent. . . . He's apt to send you all over hell's half acre, my dear, to auctions and such, and there will be plenty in it for you."

Some of this Val heard as she left the shop. She didn't hear Ted asking more gloomily than the circumstances would seem to warrant, "What's his name and why are you so sure he'll want me? There are dozens of men in this man's town better equipped than I am."

Flora said, "He'll do it, for me." She told Ted the name and Ted whistled. He knew the man by reputation . . . a strong polo player, and between games an accomplished drinker . . . with more money than he was worth, twice divorced and once breach-of-promised.

Flora said, "I'm going to marry him."

"I thought you didn't believe in marriage!"

"I don't," admitted Flora, "and he doesn't either. Which makes it fun to try. I'd like to succeed where a leading actress and the prettiest debutante of the season once failed. Besides," she added thoughtfully, "we've no illusions about each other. I like that. It gives you an even start."

"And your work?"

"He'll permit it," she answered, and laughed a little. "It startles him, rather, and he doesn't like it — much. Too personal, he says — what he understands of it, things like that, emotions such as I've put down on paper are better kept off paper — or so he announces. Anyway, as background for a talented wife he wants one of the best libraries in the country."

Ted said uncomfortably, "Somehow — I'd rather not."

Flora looked at him a moment. She was, he noticed, rather paler than usual, more slender, very fine drawn, with a restless sparkle in her curious eyes. She asked gently, "Scruples? Oh, my poor Ted!"

"Put it that way if you like."

"But I don't like! Ted, don't be absurd. This means an income to you and Val — such as it is."

"To me and Val?"

"I'm not blind," said Flora.

Ted said, "You're right, of course. It's Val . . . and me. We — we weren't saying anything about it for a while . . . because of Bill Rogers. But now he's turned up," Ted went on, finding a certain relief in unburdening himself, "he's been picked up by some cargo ship. He'll be on his way home as soon as he reaches a port at which he can get a passenger boat."

Flora said, "If she loves you that won't matter . . . a thousand Bills could turn up. It will be a nine days' wonder in the press, I suppose."

"I suppose so, too."

Flora asked, presently, shrinking back in her chair from Junior who approached gaily to worry her shoelace, "Isn't that a new kitten?"

"It's Keturie's," explained Ted absently.

"I don't like cats," said Flora.

"So Val said."

"Val's clever. Does she know about us?"

Ted flushed painfully. Flora said rapidly, "Ted, you haven't been such a fool? I mean . . . confession may be good for the soul but

317

it is very bad for the reputation. And after all, I'm concerned too."

"I haven't told her," he said, after a moment.

"That means — you didn't have to." Flora sighed, shook her head and shrugged her slim shoulders. "But . . . just because she thinks she knows something, don't make the mistake of confirming her knowledge. It's different with Ricky and me," she said, "we aren't infants."

"Then he —" began Ted.

"Oh, Ricky hasn't demanded chapter and verse, names and addresses," said Flora.

Ted looked at her sharply. He said, astonished:

"Flora, I believe you're actually in love."

She bent her head and the pale hair fell about her face and veiled it for a moment. She said, after a minute, almost stammering, "I believe I am. I — I don't care if I never write again. Isn't that hideous? He hasn't a scrap of intellect, Ted. He's big and he's a little shopworn and he likes the fleshpots far too well. He's about as subtle as — as a boiler factory. He worried through college on his father's money and his own football. He's worried through life on the money and a sort of healthy charm. And we haven't a thing in common. I keep telling myself that he'll make me terribly unhappy and then I suppose I'll go back to writing again. But just now I don't care."

Ted said, forgetting everything but that at one time she had been extraordinarily dear to him, "But, Flora, you can't . . . I mean, with your eyes open and —"

"Oh, but I can," she told him, "just because my eyes are open. Ricky is everything I want and everything I shouldn't have. . . . Ted, please help him with this library business. It will be fun for him for a while, until he gets tired of it. It's part of my wedding present . . . the wing he's building for it and for a workroom for me at his place in Connecticut."

Ted said, "All right, Flora, but —"

"If you go on butting," she told him, "I'll believe that, after all, you do hate me."

"You know that I don't."

"Then can't you forget it all, Ted? You have Val, I have Ricky — there's no reason why we shouldn't be friends, you and I. I know that sounds very banal . . . it's what everyone says and it's generally pretty erroneous. But not in this case. We were friends for a long time, friends who believed we were lovers. Then lovers briefly, when after all we were only friends. I'll see Val sometimes. Oh, don't look so worried. I'll lie to her, Ted, and by indirection . . . because I want you to take this job; if you don't, I won't believe that you have forgiven me."

"Forgiven you!"

"It was my fault," she said, "I had a flair for ignoble experiment. I haven't any more. I won't have. So long as I'm married to Ricky I'll be stodgy and faithful and afraid it won't last and with not a thought beyond what's going to happen to him in the next chukker or shall we plant delphiniums in the border."

He said, despairingly, thinking solely of her magnificent gift, "You can't give up writing, Flora."

"I can. I shall. The fountain is sealed. I can't set a word down about what I feel for Ricky. I don't want to. I don't dare to, I'd be afraid. I have to hide it from him, Ted, and that hurts a little. But he mustn't be too sure of me. I can talk to you. Can't you see that it means something to him, the little beginning fame I've had, the rather exciting Village aura . . . it's shoddy and shabby and meretricious, but he doesn't know that. He's the sort of man so well known for himself, so self-assured, so filthy rich that he can say, 'my wife, Flora Carr,' and be pleasantly amused. If I ever so much as looked at another man he'd probably beat me. I wouldn't care," she said.

She left shortly thereafter after telling him, "It needn't come through me, Ted, not directly. I'll see to that. Someone will recommend you to Ricky and I'll be astonished. I'll say, 'Oh, how divine, darling, I used to know Ted Morrison, back in the old days.' "

She left him unable to feel any happiness for her. He was afraid for her. She was afraid too, but that didn't matter. Ted never believed it possible to see Flora Carr stripped of her poses and her artificialities again as once she had been, when first he knew her. But then she had been a hungering and restless girl. Now she was a woman, dangerously in love and adoring her danger.

He went to the telephone after she had gone and called Val. Val answered. He said, "It's Ted . . . Is everything all right?"

"Yes . . . everything's all right," she answered, "or will be when you come this evening. You'll come for dinner, won't you?"

When he reached the house he found her alone. Her mother had gone out for a little while and her father had not come in as yet. She showed him Bill's cable and winced as he winced when his eyes fell upon the endearing close, "I will be coming back to you as fast as I can darling all my love Bill," and she told him that the cable office had sent on the message to Bill's mother to the bank. Where the bank would reach her Val didn't know but she presumed at the port which would have been designated as the base of the rescue operations. She said, "Isn't it all at cross-purposes? He may get home faster than she does . . . or perhaps they'll meet. I wonder."

"What do your mother and father say?" asked Ted.

"I've only talked to Father over the telephone. Mother — Mother thinks as I do, Ted. If Bill's delayed in getting home, we must wait too. . . . It's so awfully unfair to him."

"How about me?" asked Ted.

She said, "I know," and put her head against his shoulder. She cried out after a little while, "It's all so mixed up. I'm so terribly happy about us . . . and I am so happy that Bill's alive . . . with all his life before him. And yet I'm such a coward, dreading to see him, to tell him."

Ted said, "You don't have to. I shall."

"No. I owe him that. I owe him honesty. I didn't give it to him when I said I'd marry him, Ted. It's been my fault, the whole wretched muddle. If only I hadn't . . ."

After a while she asked, "What did Flora want?"

"Flora," he told her, "is going to marry Ricky Owens."

"The polo player?" She sat up straight and her eyes were wide. "Why, Ted — he's forty if he's a day, he's been divorced a dozen times

322

and he's as rich as mud!"

Ted said, smiling, "Around forty, I think. Divorced twice. And, of course, rich as mud. By the way, is it?"

"Is what what?"

"Is mud rich?"

"I don't know," admitted Val. "It's a silly expression, isn't it? Is she happy?"

"Yes; she's very much in love with him," Ted said, "and they're building a library . . . a wing for his house. She thinks he'll want me to oversee it . . . the books, I mean, not the building."

Val said, "She thinks? She knows — that is, if she wants you to, Ted, will you do it?"

Ted said, and ruffled her hair so that it stood up like a dark red halo all about her little head, "Not if you'd rather I didn't. But I must remind you that she's in love — with Owens."

"Then," said Val complacently, "it's all right, I suppose."

He thought, astonished, So she hasn't scruples, and wondered if perhaps most women lacked them. So long as he was in love with Val and Flora was in love with someone else, Val would not give the situation another thought. Ted shook his head mentally. There was no getting to know women, after all.

The news of Bill Rogers' rescue was in the late evening editions of the papers, cabled from the port at which the little cargo boat had touched. It was not a port of call for the big boats and there would be a lapse of time — some weeks — before it would reach a harbor at which he and his crew would transfer to another ship. The press was almost hysterical over the rescue, the details of which were lacking. All anyone knew was that the little boat had come just in time and that two members of the crew were quite ill from exhaustion, hunger and exposure. They had been picked up at an uncharted island, affording scanty means of sustaining life. The reporters surmised that the men had lived on the fish and sea birds they had been able to catch, with little else. Probably there had been a spring of fresh water. The world would have to wait for detailed news of the shipwreck itself and the length of time the men had been on the island.

Bill's entire history was recounted once more, the story of the rescue yacht which even now was on the high seas with his mother as a passenger, and which one enterprising journal as well as her lawyer were trying to reach by wireless. There were pictures of Mrs. Rogers, of Bill, and, as was inevitable, of Valentine Loring. And before dinner was over reporters were camping on the front steps and Mr. Loring was irascibly dealing with them.

No, they could not see Miss Loring. Yes, they had had the news earlier in the day. Yes, of course, they were delighted beyond words. No, there was no statement Miss Loring cared to make to the press.

"It's all going to be pretty bad," prophesied Val dolefully.

The next day it was announced that Mrs. Rogers had been reached and was putting back to the west coast. It would be a useless attempt to try and make connections with her son. The probability was that he would transfer from the cargo boat at Sydney. She would wait at San Francisco for him.

Val did not go to the shop for over a week. She stayed indoors and shivered whenever the doorbell rang. She had tried going out the first morning and had fallen over two reporters on the doorstep. They had sprung up, cheerful, with broad grins and without the notebooks her motion-picture experience of reporters had led her to expect. A cameraman lurking in the areaway had snapped a picture of her which, when it appeared somewhat later, was enough to frighten little children into demanding a night-light and a kind and soothing hand. And so Val had fled into the house again, half laughing and half enraged, and slammed the door in the inquiring faces. And after that she had not ventured forth.

Nor had Ted come to the house except like a thief by dead of night, for he, too, encountered reporters, at the shop and dogging his footsteps as he turned them toward the Loring home. So he turned them away and discontented himself by telephoning her. He said, "When these damned birds of prey get through — I wish there'd be a nice juicy murder to distract them."

"They're rather sweet," said Val, "I won't have you calling them names."

"They hound me," shouted Ted, "because we're partners. I found one of them interviewing the janitor and the other, I think, was trying to induce Keturie to tell all. Look here, I've got to see you, but if I keep coming every day and they suspect something . . ."

Val said, with a chuckle that was half hysterical, "Can't you put on a long white beard, or something?"

On the third evening he did just that. Only the beard was black. A black beard, a black cape, a large black hat, he stepped out of a taxi and strode dramatically up the steps. There wasn't, as it happened, a reporter within twenty miles. Political goings-on and love nests and a sack killing had by now engaged their restless attention. The Rogers case was dead as a doornail until Bill Rogers reached Sydney and the cabled report of his experiences came over the wires.

But Ted's entrance was nonetheless stimulating. Mr. Loring laughed until he was purple and Mrs. Loring laughed until she cried. And Val, observing her young man, thoughtfully murmured, "You look rather like Bluebeard, with a dash of Cellini," which brought down the house and considerably relieved the tension of the last few days.

# Chapter XVIII

Bill Rogers and his crew landed in San Francisco in the autumn and Mrs. Rogers met them there and flew back East with them. Val had had long cables from Sydney and several wireless messages en route. But Bill would arrive home as fast as a letter could travel, for which she was devoutly grateful. These first cabled messages of love and longing were bad enough but she simply could not face a letter, she told herself. She grew thin during those weeks of waiting, and irritable and jumpy. Ted was extraordinarily patient with her at first and then came to the masculine, and possibly reasonable, conclusion that he had a grievance or two of his own. They staged several rather spectacular quarrels, both in the shop and at home.

The addition to the shop was now ready. Val wore herself out running to stores and buying material for curtains, and various gadgets. She pinched the pennies so severely that they were black and blue and she ran herself ragged. One day she came in and announced that she felt exactly as if she were lightly basted together — "all anyone has to do is pull the thread and it will snap, and I'll fall to pieces!" she announced dramatically.

The shop was full to overflowing of last-minute painters, carpenters and such important fry, or so it appeared to her tired eyes. Ted was everywhere at once. If Val was out shopping, he spent his time in the lower bookshop with an anxious ear cocked for the sound of hammering upstairs; now and then he rushed into the street to look wildly about him for certain expected shipments of equipment. When Val returned to the shop he left her in charge of the going concern and raced upstairs alternately to swear at and cajole the gentlemen who were putting on the finishing touches in, it seemed to him, a series of slow motions. Altogether everything was chaos and confusion, a couple of times confounded.

Said Mr. Loring to his wife, "I don't like it. Val looks like something the cat would scorn to drag in — if it were a self-respecting cat. She's killing herself. As for that young idiot, he graciously assists her in the process."

Marcia Loring shook her head. "I know it," she admitted. "But it's a good thing. It gives them something to think about. Val's sick with worry over the business of Bill's imminent return. She's braced herself to face him ever since the word came and it's not easy to brace yourself over a period of weeks, you know."

"Well, she should worry," said her father

unsympathetically. "Talk about on with the new love!" He snorted. "She should be ashamed of herself."

"I broke an engagement of long standing when I fell in love with you," Marcia reminded him.

Mr. Loring had the grace to look guilty. He argued feebly, "That was different . . . you'd have been miserable married to that stiffer-than-a-boiled-shirt, John Richards!"

"He was very nice," remarked Mrs. Loring, smiling. "And most eligible!"

"Then why in time did you take me and throw him over?" demanded her husband, glowering at her. He had succumbed to stewed tripe and onions at luncheon and was paying for it.

"You know why," replied his wife; "which is, of course, the explanation for Val. We can't help it, neither can she. And really, I've grown very fond of Ted."

"He's all right," said Val's father grudgingly, "but I still think that Bill Rogers —"

"You're not marrying him," Mrs. Loring reminded him with some asperity, "and this isn't a country where, as a rule, the marriages are arranged by the parents."

"Pity it isn't," said her husband, inclined to be argumentative this evening, with the memory of his luncheon seething about within him; "seems to me parents could arrange things more sensibly, after all, they've lived their lives and have had some experience."

"It would be too bad to deprive the children of the privilege of making their own mistakes," Marcia said.

"Sentimental claptrap!" decided Mr. Loring. "Humph!" Defeated, he appealed to her better nature. "Where's the bicarb?" he demanded.

The curtain material arrived and Val engaged the services of an excellent seamstress. The curtains were "run up" in the Loring spare room and then hung. Val superintended, watching Ted as he struggled manfully and finally all but fell to the floor enveloped in many colorful folds. "Here, let me," she said, "you're too impossibly clumsy."

He glared at her, his stern, flushed countenance absurdly surrounded by strange patterns of birds, beasts and flowers in chintz. "Very well, if you're so good at it then," he suggested with a dignity which ill became him at the moment.

Val retrieved the draperies and sprang blithely up the ladder. The ladder teetered. Ted, the seamstress and a handy man-by-the-hour all yelled: "Look out! You'll fall!" simultaneously, with the result that, scared to death, she did fall off, curtains and all, into

Ted's arms. She was a small person but the impact brought them both, quite uninjured except in pride, to the floor, with curtains all about them, while the seamstress giggled and the handy man coughed a couple of times behind a hand like a side of beef.

"Of all the idiotic — !" began Ted.

So it went on, yet somehow the curtains were hung and the shelves were filled with books and the prints were put upon the walls and the gift tables bore their load of gay display. The upstairs shop was bright and neat as a new pin and replete with a certain charm which wasn't in the least irritating. On the last evening, late, Ted and Val worked alone. Val's smock was filthy, her face was the same, her hands were worse and her hair straggled. She had never looked so plain and Ted had never coveted her so much. And because he was terribly sorry for her and felt himself to blame for her state, regarding her large and shadowed eyes, her white and peaked face, he shouted at her a couple of times most unnecessarily, and behaved as men usually do in the circumstances.

Val, sitting limply in a new comfortable chair, bought to coax the unwary customer to stay awhile and browse in comfort, was scribbling on a pad. She was writing an advertisement for the upstairs shop. She asked, pushing the hair from her eyes with one hand and chewing on her pencil, "Do you like 'come up and see us sometime'?"

"I certainly do not, it's cheap and over-worked, and besides — Will you stop gnawing that pencil? It's indelible and you'll die."

"I could," she said dreamily, "this very minute. I'd adore to die. It would be so peaceful."

He said, "You hadn't any business tiring yourself out like that . . . and no excuse. You know I wanted decorators in."

"Yes, and a fine thing that would have been . . . this is costing enough as it is without decorators." She actually sneered at him in her disdain. "Decorators, my eye!"

"Just the same, it would have been worth what it would have cost for the saving of wear and tear on your disposition."

"You make me sick," said Val. "Here I've been running my legs off trying to save you money and you rant around as if I'd lost you a fortune. Talk about ingratitude!"

He asked incautiously, "Who's talking about it?"

"That's right," she told him, half weeping, "pick me up on everything I say." She looked at him a moment with hatred. She added, "If you don't like the way I manage things perhaps we'd better end it all, right here and now."

For one turbulent moment he thought she was about to drink the ink or something, but she only meant the engagement. She yanked at the seal ring on her finger and as it was loose it came off with a bounce and slithered and rattled on the floor. "Take your darned old ring," said Val childishly.

"Very well." He stooped and took it, with injured dignity and then stalked downstairs. Keturie, who was wild with excitement at the doings, and had been nearly thrown out half a dozen times in empty cartons, rubbed herself ingratiatingly against Val's ankle. "Go away," commanded Val viciously, "I don't like you either; no, nor that emptyheaded son of yours."

Val wept a little, being miserable and tired. Presently Ted stalked in again, slammed a door, came over to her chair and took her unresisting hand. He jammed the ring on her finger again, nearly dislocating it. He said loudly, "You darned little fool, I think we're both nuts!"

"You're telling me?" asked Val. She put her head against his shoulder as he knelt down by the chair, and sniffled. "Lend me your handkerchief, will you, mine's just an old rag," she said. "Oh, Ted, I'm so tired I could yell, but the shop's grand and I did save us some money."

"Of course you did," he told her, "you're a marvel." He kissed her half a dozen times. "Get up and come downstairs and wash your face and we'll go out and get coffee and a sandwich somewhere. That will perk you up, won't it?"

"I could do with a tot of whisky," she said, most surprisingly, and he stared at her. Val did not go around demanding tots of whisky. Ted swallowed a couple of times and agreed. "Whisky it shall be . . . but I recommend brandy."

"Or arsenic," she said raptly.

Ted laughed He rose, dragged her to her feet. She came as limp as a rag doll and leaned against him. He shook her gently. "Snap out of it, darling," he bade her, "clean up the countenance and put on the bonnet. After a good night's sleep you'll feel like a new woman."

"I certainly feel like an old one now," she said mournfully, "about one hundred and eighty years old come next Boxing Day. All right, big boy, let's go."

All their quarrels were very much like that. The ring changed hands so rapidly that it made one dizzy to follow its progress. But none of this meant a thing, they assured each other.

And Mrs. Loring comforted them one night after the new shop was open for business. "Well, at least you know what it will be like when you're married and settling in the new flat . . . you'll merely be repeating history."

"Hysterics," corrected Ted.

The Loring house was also undergoing certain alterations. But these, her parents' wedding present to her, Val was not permitted to supervise. "Let me wear myself out," said her mother, "it will be a pleasure, we can suffer in company."

The new little upstairs flat was under way and the new upstairs bookshop was doing a thriving business when Bill Rogers landed in New York. As it happened Ted was not in town. He had finally met Ricky Owens and that young man had urged him into executing the library commissions for him. It took Ted some time to assure him that he couldn't assemble a library of several thousand volumes, including first, rare and limited editions, in a week or two. "It would be a matter of years," explained Ted judiciously. Ricky was astonished. He'd thought you just went out and bought things. He was an enormous man, wide in the shoulders and lean in the hips, with a shock of curling red hair, slightly and prematurely frosted, and very gray eyes. He had a massive jaw, stubborn and strong, and a strangely handsome mouth, obstinate and weak. He came into the shop the first time with Flora tucked under his arm as if she had been the trophy of a winning team. And Ted, prepared to dislike him, liked him almost at once, for something essentially youthful and friendly.

So Ted closeted himself with the puzzled Ricky and made preliminary lists. The moderns, the classics, that much was easy and meant a big volume of business for the shop. "Flora tells me you know your stuff . . . just as soon do it through a friend of hers as through anyone else," growled Ricky — but the rare items were harder. Flora had set her heart on having the finest collection of first editions of poets in the country. It was a good thing that she didn't want first folios of Shakespeare and a Gutenberg Bible. To be sure, Mr. Owens, when he learned that these were perhaps hard to come by, decided he'd like 'em. He went through catalogues of private sales with Ted and checked all the things which Ted told him probably would not be available at his price. "Who said anything about price?" demanded Ricky. "Flora wants this library, doesn't she?"

So when Bill landed in New York there was Ted off to Baltimore to attend a private sale.

Val had been asked by several gentlemen

of the press if she did not intend to fly to the Coast and meet her fiancé and she said she did not. This had afforded an item or two in the papers, for with Bill's actual arrival in the States the interest in the affair had been revived. Also there had been long interviews cabled from Sydney and there were a dozen others, rather garbled, wired from California. One enterprising paper had the island upon which the ship had been wrecked, after a storm had driven it out of its course, entirely peopled with magnificent South Sea maidens complete to ukeleles — made in Bridgeport — and grass skirts. It had even added a White King named Jones, an all-powerful and entirely imaginary survivor of a clan of seekers after nature who had made the island their home for many years. Another version of the shipwreck was that the crew had gone berserk and that Bill had fought them, singlehanded, stripped to the waist and with a cutlass between his teeth. While a more conservative story had had them living on terrapin and seals although what seals would be doing in that part of the world was a matter for speculation.

Mrs. Rogers telephoned Val from San Francisco. Bill had landed, they were leaving for the East after a day or two of rest. He couldn't talk to her himself, he had a terrific cold and had lost his voice. He was run down, tired out and had picked up a grippe germ somewhere. Her own small voice over the singing wires was cool and unexcited. She had believed. Her belief had been justified. When reporters asked her how she felt when she learned that her son was alive, she said merely, "I never believed that he was dead. . . ."

She said, "I'd like to keep him in bed a day or two here, Val. Lawrence Burke and Gary Mannering are staying over. They've both been in the ship's hospital on the trip back, but are better now. But I don't think I can persuade him." She added something which Val didn't entirely catch: she heard only "changed . . . worried about him." Then Mrs. Rogers said more briskly, "I'll wire when we leave. He sends his love and says you had better not plan to be at the airport when we get in . . . because of the reporters."

As his mother had feared, Bill would not stay over on the west coast. They came East as soon as was possible. And before they reached Newark he had collapsed and was taken from the plane in a private ambulance and brought directly to a hospital.

It was, his mother assured the press, nothing more than a heavy cold but they had decided that he could be better taken care of in the hospital than at home. He needed a complete rest. One of the reporters pondered that. After

339

all, the trip from Sydney had been long enough in all conscience with nothing to do but rest. He went back to his office and prepared some copy which intimated that Bill Rogers, after his hideous experience of shipwreck and an uninhabited island, had come home to die of some mysterious tropical disease which completely baffled all the better known specialists in the country.

But the tropical disease was pneumonia.

Val went to the hospital. She sat in the waiting room quite alone until Mrs. Rogers would come to her. She sat quietly in a corner trying to control her shaking hands and knees. She thought, I can't tell him — now. I can't tell him anything until he's well.

Mrs. Rogers came in presently. She was, Val saw at once, worn to a wisp of a woman. She looked much older than she had a year or so before. But her eyes were bright and her step was firm and her lips steady. She kissed Val and patted her on the back. She said, "Well, here we are."

Val said, "I came as soon as your message reached me."

"Yes, of course. He can't see you, my dear, he can't see anyone. I've the best men, the best nurses. He'll be all right, he has a splendid constitution and a lot of fight. If he hadn't, he wouldn't have survived that island, nor would the other boys. They were a pretty fine lot of youngsters," said Bill's mother; "it must have been ghastly, the waiting, day after day . . . getting on each other's nerves, wondering which would be the first to break."

She added, after a short silence:

"I've taken a room here, to be near him. I'll go back to the apartment now for an hour and get some things and do some phoning. Come with me, Val, I want to talk to you."

In the apartment, in readiness for her home-coming, with the maids scurrying about to do the packing and run errands, Mrs. Rogers took Val into her bedroom and sat down with her there. They had been silent in the car. She took off her tight little hat, lit a cigarette and offered one to Val. Val took it and found some comfort for her nervousness in handling it, in smoking. Mrs. Rogers said:

"We had a talk about Bill before I went away."

"Yes, I know."

"You haven't changed your mind?"

"No," said Val, "I haven't." She leaned forward and looked earnestly at the older woman. She went on, "I — I'm in love with Ted Morrison. I have been all along. We were going to be married, this autumn. We would have been married by now if it hadn't been — for Bill. I couldn't do that to him, of course. I had to wait, to see him, to tell him myself."

Mrs. Rogers said, "I'm grateful for that. But you can't tell him now, Val. Not right away. Not until he's over the worst of this, out of all danger. The doctors say that he mustn't be upset." She frowned and looked at the burning end of her cigarette. "I don't understand him, Val, I'm worried. He's changed, so much . . . so brown and spare and older looking. But . . . I can't explain it. It can't all be the experience. Of course he won't talk about that much, not yet. When I met him he had very little to say, and naturally all the way East he was fighting this illness. Now he's delirious, he doesn't know me." Her voice broke. She said tragically, "Val, I couldn't endure it . . . if anything were to happen now . . . I couldn't *endure* it, I tell you. Of all the monstrous injustices . . . to find him again . . . and then, to lose him."

Val was crying. She said, when she could, "Nothing will happen, we have to believe that."

"Yes, I know." She took the girl's hands and her own were like ice. "Be patient, a little longer. You and your Ted have your lives before you . . . don't jeopardize Bill's."

"I won't," said Val. Then she asked, "Has

he talked about me?"

"Continuously," replied his mother, "ever since I met him . . . everything . . . he wanted to know everything about you . . . how you looked, how you were, if you had given him up for lost. He carries your first message to him around with him in his wallet."

Val said, "I don't understand his being so ill."

"He was very run down," Mrs. Rogers reminded her, "but I don't understand it, either. The voyage should have done wonders for him; it did for the others, even for Lawrence and Gary who were taken off the island in a much worse condition."

She rose. "I've got to get back to the hospital. I'll keep you informed, I'll call you every day. Early morning and at night and whenever there is any change of course. And as soon as he's able to see people, you'll see him." Her voice was steady but her eyes pleaded. "I know it seems that you were being kind merely in order to be more cruel. But I can't have him made unhappy until he is able to bear it, Val."

Val said soberly, "Don't be afraid. I won't."

She told Ted about it in a long letter which she sent that night to the hotel in Baltimore at which he was staying. She wrote: "It only means a little longer, Ted. You understand,

343

I know. When he's well again and strong, I'll tell him . . . but not now. I can't even see him now, Ted, he's too terribly ill."

# Chapter XIX

With Ted away, Val was busy in the book-shop. Ted had engaged a young man with some experience in the ways of book consumers shortly after the opening of the new addition. He was an amiable, eager and personable soul with more intelligence than Val, after her initial look at his cherubic face, had granted him. On Ted's return she was able to report that "Cupid is working out nicely."

"Cupid!"

"Is any other name possible? All he needs is a bow and arrow."

"And a bookshop with nudist ideas."

Val laughed. It was evening, and Ted had come directly from his train to the Loring house. "How are things in Baltimore? You didn't write much about the sale."

"There were three sales, surely I told you that? The library of a retired naval officer living in Annapolis — at least he lived there recently, he's been dead for several months and they are settling his estate."

"Don't tell me that the Navy collects books!"

"This gentleman did . . . maritime subjects. He had a private income. I couldn't find anything which would interest Ricky but I did pick up a couple of good items for the shop."

"Ted!" She looked at him and sighed. "If I had known that you were shop-snooping as well, I wouldn't have let you go. I suppose you know that *Tamerlane* is down to the last thin hundred."

"Of course. But this was worth it. Then I heard of another sale in Washington so I ankled along to that. All in all Ricky should be well satisfied. I've talked to him by telephone several times. He doesn't know what it's all about but that's all right too. I'll let Flora do the explaining. By the way, they're going to be married next week."

"Ted . . . and you didn't tell me!"

"Well, I didn't know it until last night. It's going to be one of those simple quiet weddings with all the appurtenances of a literary tea and a hunting breakfast . . . polo and poets. At the Greenwich place of Ricky's aunt. Flora hasn't any people, you know. We're asked, of course."

"I'd love to go," said Val. Until she saw Flora safely married she would always be a little uneasy, although when she had met Flora and Ricky together recently she had been almost convinced that Flora, the evasive and

346

temperamental, was no longer in circulation.

"Well, Cupid can carry on for us. We'll go, all right. Ricky says he'll put a car at our disposal . . . I haven't any morning clothes," said Ted, "but I don't suppose that will matter. Ricky has a lot of strange friends, and so has Flora —"

"If that Village party we went to set any standard," said Val, "some of Flora's little playmates will turn up in pullovers and rompers. But I don't know that I can go, Ted. On account of Bill."

"He's no better?" asked Ted soberly.

"They expected that he would pass the crisis today — it's the ninth day, Ted. He's terribly sick . . . it's type three," she explained, "and not as common as the other types . . . the mortality rate is dreadfully high and the serum isn't very successful in anything but type-one pneumonia. They're afraid of his heart, of course. They've done everything, oxygen tanks and all."

"How's his mother?"

"She's marvelous. I haven't seen her much. She's at the hospital all the time. I've been down there once a day and talked to her, and she telephones me. But if anything happens to him, if he dies . . . She's found some special strength, Ted, which has brought her through all this and through the uncertainty before he was rescued . . . but she can't go on much longer."

"You can't, either," warned Ted, marking her nervousness and her pallor. "After this is over —"

"Don't put it like that, Ted."

"I mean, when he's out of danger, you must go away for a little while . . . you and your mother perhaps. To rest, to recuperate."

"I don't need anything like that," she told him. She leaned her head on his shoulder and held one of his big hands in both her own. "When Bill's better and I've told him . . . then we'll be married, Ted, and go away together. That's all I want, just to be with you, alone, if only for a week. Cupid will look after the shop."

Ted held her close. "Of course he will. The name's appropriate after all, though I don't believe he will fancy it much. By the way, what do you call him — to his face?"

"Mr. Brown," answered Val, with a faint twinkle. "It's his name, isn't it? And we aren't on more intimate terms as yet."

"It's getting on toward winter," Ted told her unnecessarily, "and it won't be any time before it will be two years. It's a far cry to that Valentine's Day, isn't it? But every day," he added with unusual sentiment, "is Valentine's Day for me. A lot has happened, hasn't it?"

She said, and laughed a little, "We've had the funniest time — both 'funny-peculiar and funny-haha' — since we've been . . ."

"Walking out together. Or would you call it sparking?" he interrupted.

"Since we met. Fights and fires, quarrels and wisecracks. It's been funny and sad and exciting and everything all mixed up. I do love you so much, Ted. I hope it will always be like it's been. I hope we'll quarrel violently about things which don't matter and never get tired of making up," she told him, and put her arms around his neck and kissed him, sweetly.

Ted said, "I wish I had a million dollars."

"What for?" asked Val.

"For you, simpleton."

"It would be swell," agreed Val instantly, "in a way. I'd adore being extravagant. Perfume at forty an ounce, hats at about the same price, imported English tweeds for daytime and the snootiest dressmaker in town for the rest, lingerie from France and stockings so fine that if you did draw 'em through a ring you couldn't even see them, a house in Florida and one in Santa Barbara and a big place on the Island with about twenty dogs and a couple of dozen horses —"

"I thought you didn't ride."

"I don't. I'm scared to death. Just for atmosphere."

"If you want atmosphere any old barn will do," said Ted reflectively. He laughed at her and then his face grew grave.

"If you'd married Bill you could have had most of those things," he said.

"I don't want them," she told him instantly. "I mean, it would be swell, but our way's better. We'll never have much money and there'll be plenty of times when we'll be so worried about the next month's rent that we'll hardly be on speaking terms. But that's firsthand living. The other's pretty secondhand. I've come to that conclusion."

The telephone rang and Val jumped up to answer it. She wondered aloud, anxiously, "Could it be from the hospital?" and ran toward the instrument. Ted rose and followed her. He was more nervous than he knew, the hands he thrust in his pockets were clenched into fists. Mrs. Loring, from upstairs, called, "Are you answering, Val?" and Ted went to the foot of the steps in the hall to reply. When he returned Val had replaced the transmitter and was sitting there beside it as if she had not the strength to move.

"Val, was it Mrs. Rogers? It isn't bad news — ?"

"No." She rose and came over to him. "He's passed the crisis," she reported, "and he's going to get well . . . with care and careful nursing and no setbacks." She began to cry. She apologized, wiping her eyes with the back of her hand. "I'm turning into a regular Elsie Dinsmore . . . I break into low sobs if anyone looks at me cross-eyed," she said, muffled. "I'm such an idiot!"

"Like this?" asked Ted, making an entirely hideous face.

Val giggled. "Do you want me to have hysterics? Ted, I'm so happy . . . about Bill. If you could have heard her voice . . ."

Ted said, "I am too." He swung her up, off the floor and dangled her like a doll. He kissed her and set her down. "And now, young woman," he informed her, "I'm going home and to bed. Tomorrow's another day and there's work to be done. Mind you're on time at the shop, or I'll dock you."

Val saw Mrs. Rogers during her lunch hour the next day. It would be some days before she would be permitted to see Bill. They sat in the waiting room and talked, the older woman's hands locked about Val's small wrists. "He's come through beautifully," said Bill's mother, "but he wasn't in good condition. It will be a long time. They have to watch his heart very carefully. There's always danger, Val. He . . . asked for you this morning."

"What did you tell him?"

"That as soon as he could see anyone, he could see you. I haven't seen him for the last few days except through the door. I was with him for about half a minute today."

She had delivered her warning again. Val accepted it, and waited until Bill could see her. He was kept as quiet as possible, would not be permitted to sit up for some time. When she did see him she was warned by the nurse that she might stay only a minute.

She went into the quiet room, with all its terrifying paraphernalia of illness and looked at him. His tan had faded, he looked white and thin, lying there, helpless. But he grinned at her in his old way and her throat ached as she grinned back. He said, "Hello, Val. You're looking pretty marvelous."

"I can't say as much for you," she told him. She stood at the foot of his bed, not touching it. She said, "They won't let me stay, you know."

"Yes, I know. I don't know that I want you to. You're a pretty dazzling sight for an old crock like me. But you'll come again?"

He was forcing himself to speak. Something

had happened to his voice. She said, "Of course, old-timer, as often as you want me," and fled, thankfully, when the nurse came to warn her that her time was up.

Later, she saw him for a little while every day and, as his convalescence progressed, for longer intervals. She sat by the bed and racked her mind to think of amusing things to tell him. She did not talk about the yacht or the shipwreck. Once when she spoke of it a look of pain flashed across his face and she said, "Don't. Never mind, Bill, there are more cheerful things to talk about."

She told him about Flora's wedding.

"You remember Flora. I've told you about her."

"Of course."

"It was the darnedest wedding," said Val earnestly, "enormous living room, fireplace piled with autumn leaves. A couple of bishops. Well, maybe only one — but he was fat enough for two. Flora looked lovely. But the strangest people came."

"Did she marry Ted Morrison?" asked Bill, turning his head on the pillow to look at her.

"Why, no," stammered Val, and flushed. "I thought you knew. I mean —"

"I've not caught up on anything yet," he told her.

"She married a man named Ricky Owens."

"Owens. Why," said Bill, "the old son of a gun. I used to know him pretty well."

Val said, "He's very good-looking . . . and crazy about her, of course. But the people who came, pink-tea people, cocktail people, stirrup-cup people and red-ink people! You'd be amazed. He's building her a wing for a studio, workroom and library in his Connecticut house. We — that is, the bookshop — are doing the library. It's meant a lot of business."

"Still gaga about your job?"

"Why, yes," she admitted. She added hurriedly, "Ricky and Flora are going around the world on their honeymoon. They sailed right after the wedding."

There was a brief silence. Val said contritely, "I've tired you," and rose to go. But he caught her hand and she sat down again at once, lest he further exert himself.

"Val — still love me?"

She said, with stiff lips, "Of course, Bill."

He released her hand, sighed, and lay back among the pillows with his eyes closed. He said, with a palpable effort, "That's all I wanted to know. Look, I can't take you honeymooning on the yacht after all."

She tried to laugh. "That doesn't matter. There are lots of boats."

"Would you mind awfully if it weren't a

boat, Val? Somehow . . . I'd like to stick to trains and earth for a while."

"No, I wouldn't mind. I've never liked boats much. It used to be a bone of contention," she reminded him.

The nurse put her head in at the door. "I'm sorry, Miss Loring —" she began.

Val rose, gratefully. She bent over Bill and touched her cool soft lips to his forehead; and went.

She tried to tell Ted about it and couldn't find the words. "It was hideous. I mean, letting him plan like that . . . but I couldn't do anything else, Ted. I promised his mother. I couldn't stand there and say, 'No, I don't love you, Bill, and I'm not going to marry you . . . I'm in love with someone else.' "

"No, I suppose not," he agreed. He took a turn about the shop. Young Mr. Brown, tying up packages for the parcel post, in a corner, looked over at them curiously. He liked his new employers very much but he couldn't make them out, or rather, he could, which worried him. If ever he saw two people in love! But Val Loring was engaged to that shipwrecked hero, what's-his-name, who was ill in the hospital at present. A mess, thought Mr. Brown, snipping string and stamping stamps, all around.

The doctors shook their heads over Bill Rogers. He was not doing as well as he should. His convalescence was even slower than they had expected. And with his constitution it shouldn't have been notwithstanding his depleted condition. Organically he was all right, his lungs had cleared, his heart was behaving as it should but there was something wrong, something upon which none of them could lay a highly trained, expensive finger.

"Is there anything on his mind?" one of them asked Mrs. Rogers, but she shook her head.

"I don't think so. It wouldn't be like Bill to brood over the loss of the yacht and his experience. After all, they all came out of it all right; he has nothing with which to reproach himself."

"Seems odd," said the doctor, "everything to live for, engaged to be married. I don't understand it, I confess that, Mrs. Rogers."

She spoke of it to Val. She asked sharply, "Val, you haven't said anything . . . you don't believe he suspects?"

Val shook her head. "I feel like a murderer. No, I haven't said a word and I don't believe he suspects anything. I go around hating myself. This whole miserable business is my fault."

"No," answered Mrs. Rogers, it's mine. I forced your hand, because I hate to see him denied anything he wants. There's nothing to do," she said finally, "but wait. I've tried, as tactfully as possible, to get him to talk. If there really is anything bothering him, why won't he tell me? He always has before."

Val said, "Perhaps it's just being so ill and all," without any conviction.

Before Thanksgiving Bill Rogers would be permitted to go home. He was to go by ambulance and be put to bed in the apartment and his nurses would go with him. His mother was no longer staying at the hospital. She was back in the apartment, putting that in order and picking up as best she could the dropped threads of her normal life. Bill had told her to. "I won't be an interesting invalid," he said, "not always. And you mustn't get so wrapped up in diets and hot-water bottles that you forget you've any life outside. For once I get strong enough to bully you, you'll be without a job. So you'd better start the charity work and the contract and the theatergoing now, to get your hand in."

Two days before he was to go home Val came to the hospital. It was dusk, she had left the shop early. They told her at the desk that Mr. Rogers had a caller. Val said, "I'll wait then," and went into the waiting room.

357

There were other people there. One was a pretty woman, with a drawn face and a little boy beside her who fidgeted and whined and demanded loudly, "When are we going to see Pop?" Another woman whom Val had seen in the waiting room before, who came every day to see a mother who was slowly dying, whispered, "It's her husband, poor soul — automobile accident." An old man waited patiently and turned, unseeingly, the pages of a magazine, while over in a corner a man and girl sat together. The girl was crying and the man held both her hands in his. "It will be all right," he was saying. And Val heard her murmur, "But I can't bear it. He's so little and they're hurting him now — *this minute.*"

Val thought, So much suffering. I wonder people endure it and don't go quietly mad. Perhaps they do, and the rest of us don't know it.

After a while she was told that Mr. Rogers was free now. She rose and went out and up in the elevator to the private medical floor. A girl waiting for the elevator to take her down stood aside to let Val pass. She was a pleasant, rather plain girl, her face blotched with weeping. Val thought, Poor dear.

She went on into Bill's room. He was sitting up, in a dressing gown, with a robe over his knees. He looked even worse sitting up than he had in bed. His face was slightly flushed. He greeted her with an effort. "Oh, hello, Val, it's you."

"Didn't you expect me?"

"Not so early. I thought it was one of the gang . . . they didn't give your name when they phoned up."

"I suppose they thought it wasn't necessary," she said, and sat down in a deep chair beside him. "Or do you have a great many female callers?" she asked him smiling. She thought, I've never seen him look so — he doesn't even know I'm here.

"Where's Miss Parsons?" she asked.

"Gone to supper," replied Bill, "they feed 'em at the most absurd times here."

The door opened and someone said, "I had to come back. . . . I forgot my bag."

In that instant Val saw the bag, a brown suede pocketbook lying at the foot of the bed.

Then the girl was in the room, the girl Val had seen at the elevator. She was tall, with a very fine figure, and she carried her head high. She was not beautiful, she was not even pretty, but there was something most attractive about her. She apologized, stopping there by the door. "Oh, I'm sorry."

She had a very pleasant voice. Bill said, "This is . . . Miss Young . . . Miss Loring."

The girl said, her heavy brows drawn, "I

didn't mean . . . but all the money I had with me was in my bag."

She was looking at Val, and not at Bill. She walked over to the bed and picked up the bag. Bill explained, "Miss Young and I were shipmates coming back from down yonder."

He spoke formally, coldly, almost as if he hated this intruder. Val said, "How nice," idiotically, and the other girl spoke abruptly. She said, "I was visiting relatives in Australia," in a preoccupied tone. She tucked the bag under her arm and nodded at Bill. "Good-bye then," she said brusquely, as a boy might have done. "I hope you get along splendidly. I won't see you again."

Val asked, "You don't live in town?"

"No, in San Francisco. Good-bye," she said to Val, "I — I've heard a lot about you."

Val cried, suddenly placing this tall girl, knowing just how she'd look if she took off her hat and displayed a head of tight brown curls, "Why, I know you. I've sold a hundred copies of your book. You're Frances Young!"

She was a shy person, the tall Miss Young. She flushed, murmured something and fled. She closed the door softly, finally. Val turned to Bill. He was lying back in the chair with his eyes closed. "Bill," she demanded, "why didn't you tell me you knew — Are you ill?

Shall I ring for someone?"

"No, I'm all right. What were you saying?"

Val went on talking about Frances Young. This was the girl who had been on two of the most successful recent scientific expeditions as historian, who had written a charming, gossipy, accurate book about one of them and had enlivened it with marginal drawings; who had raced a plane in a women pilots' meet and come off second, who had taken a turn at deep-sea diving . . . going down in helmet and equipment to see things for herself, and who was the daughter of one of America's great scholars . . . shy, never much in evidence, reputed delightful by the few who knew her well. "Why didn't you tell me you'd met her?" asked Val again.

Bill said after a while, "I didn't expect I'd ever see her again. She doesn't come East often."

Val said thoughtfully, "I liked her the minute I saw her. I saw her at the elevator as I was getting out at this floor. I didn't recognize her, of course. She had her hat on and she'd been crying."

Bill said something unintelligible. Val repeated thoughtfully, "She'd been crying."

She stared at Bill. Then she asked, leaning forward, "Bill, *why* was she crying?"

He couldn't answer. He couldn't say, "Because we love each other and because I'm pledged to you." He couldn't say anything. But Val said it for him.

"You're in love with her," she accused him, and her eyes danced and her cheeks flushed scarlet, "and she's in love with you. Oh, Bill, you sublime idiot!"

Bill sat up straight. Val said warningly, "Now don't get excited or I'll ring. This is the grandest thing that has ever happened. If you only knew how happy I am."

"Why, Val Loring!" said Bill, agape. He looked at her and she nodded. She said, "And here I've been trying to spare you. Answer me one thing honestly. You — you don't love me any more, do you?"

"I'm very —"

"Honestly," she interrupted sternly.

"No," he said, "I don't. Not that way."

"It's Frances Young."

"Yes," he said, "it is —"

"Bill, if you'd only told me!"

"How could I?" he demanded peevishly. "I'd been in love with you for years . . . you'd refused to marry me a hundred times. Then, after I left, you said you would. I was pretty triumphant about it, let me tell you. I knew you didn't care as much for me as I did for you, but I thought you would, someday. Then, on the island I had a lot of time to think. I didn't really believe we'd be rescued. I got to thinking, Perhaps, after all, this is best; perhaps Val's just sorry for me or tired of saying no. Then, on the boat I met Frances. I — I fought hard against it. She did too. She's a pretty fine person. Regular. We said good-bye on the boat, for good. But —"

"But she couldn't stand it, hearing about your illness. She tried to stay away and then she had to come and see that you were alive for herself. Bill, I've just been waiting until you were well again to tell you about Ted and me. I — I got engaged to him when — when —"

"When you thought you were a widow," supplied Bill, grinning.

"Something like that. Then, when you were saved I said I'd tell you when you came home. And when you did come home you were so ill, your mother wouldn't let me tell you, naturally. She's known all along."

"Well," said Bill, "I'll be damned."

Val slipped from her chair and to her knees. She put her arms about his waist and looked up at him. Miss Parsons, returning, opened the door softly and more softly closed it. What a pretty picture, she thought sentimentally, and tiptoed away from the door.

Val's eyes were shining and her small face had flowered into laughter. She said, "You're a darling. Next to Ted —"

"That's the way I feel about you — next to Frances," said Bill.

"Bill, you've got to get her back here, quick."

"She won't have reached her hotel yet," he said, looking at the clock on the night table.

"Call. Call now. Tell them to have her telephone you as soon as she comes in." She took from her finger the diamond which she had worn each time she came to the hospital. "There," she said, and laid it on the night table. "You're a free man and I'm a free woman. Bill, is this what's been troubling you so much, all along?"

"Yes," he said, "I suppose it is. There was just one faint hope. That you'd changed your mind, that you'd found out after all that you didn't love me. But when I asked you, you said you did. You little liar," he told her severely, and laughed as she hadn't heard him laugh since he went away.

"I was afraid you'd have a heart attack," she said meekly.

"I'm much more likely to have one now," he told her.

"Bill!"

But he was lifting the telephone from its stand and asking for a number. He was connected with the hotel switchboard. "Has Miss

Frances Young come in yet? . . . Her room doesn't answer? Ask her to call up Mr. Rogers at the hospital as soon as she comes in. Repeat that, please. It is most important. Mr. William Rogers at the hospital. Yes, she'll know!"

He hung up. "Well — that's settled. A bangup Thanksgiving. You and Ted, your mother and father, Frances, my mother, me. . . ."

"And a couple of nurses."

"I'm not going to need them long. Fran's a swell nurse. She's a swell everything."

"I think so too," said Val soberly. She rose and bent over to kiss his cheek. "The papers are going to have a lot of fun with us."

"We might make it a double wedding," suggested Bill. "I'm going to get married as soon as they let me stand on my feet. We'll go South. What about you?"

Val said, half hysterically, "I'll have to ask Ted . . . right away."

He'd be at the shop. She knew that. This was his late evening. She went as fast as she could urge her wild-eyed taxi driver. Arriving, the gentleman mopped his brow. Only by the mercy of heaven had he escaped six tickets. He looked at the tip Val gave him and scratched his head. "Someone in the family musta had a boy," he mused aloud. Val laughed. She said, "You're wrong — driver

— someone in the family has a girl!"

She galloped into the bookshop and nearly knocked down Mr. Brown. She ran, with a sharp clicking of heels to the downstairs back room, where Ted was frowning over a sheaf of bills. She cried, "Ted, it's all right, Bill's in love with someone else! Isn't that marvelous?"

Ted found himself with his hands and arms full of Val. The bills were scattered on the floor. She cried and laughed and kissed him. She said, "And we're all going to be together Thanksgiving."

"Here," said Ted, shaking her, "for gosh sake, make sense."

Val sat down. She said, "It does make sense. Bill met a girl on the boat. Frances —"

"You mean the — ?"

"Yes, of course, I mean her. They're mad about each other. He was going to marry me . . . not that he was afraid I'd sue him or anything," explained Val earnestly, "only men — men like Bill anyway, are so damned chivalrous that they'd rather spoil four lives than desert their code. Anyway it's all right now."

Ted said, "Well, I'll be something-or-other."

"You'll be a bridegroom before you know it," she warned him.

"I'd like to see Bill's mother's face when he tells her."

"You should have seen mine when I guessed it. I wish I had. Oh, gosh!"

"What's the matter?"

"Nothing," she answered in a small voice, "except when I think of all the agony I went through . . . and all the time I was being jilted, in spirit, if not in letter. That," admitted Val, "certainly wounded my pride."

"I know a specific," said Ted, and kissed her, very expertly, to the wide-eyed amazement of Mr. Brown, appearing with a volume in his hand and a question on his lips.

"Shut up the shop," Ted ordered his assistant. "Val and I are going out to dinner. To celebrate."

"Celebrate what?" asked Mr. Brown dumbly.

"Her fiancé's engagement," responded Ted solemnly.

At the table Ted said, "I wonder what he said to her."

"I don't believe he had to say anything," Val said, "just one look at him and she would have known. She's a dear. You'll like her."

In the room at the hospital Bill Rogers was holding the strong, slender hand of Miss Frances Young. And she was saying, "When I saw her — Bill, you never told me how pretty she is. How you could even look at me — I'm rather on the plain side."

"I'll show you how," said Bill. He looked at her now and she was no longer a plain and pleasant girl with a boy's head of brown curls. She was a completely happy and therefore entirely beautiful woman.

"If that girl couldn't make you happy," said Frances Young, "how on earth can I?"

"It's very simple," said Bill. "You see, Val never loved me, not really."

"Well?"

"And you, my darling, do," said Bill.

At the Rogers apartment on Thanksgiving Day Bill was allowed to come to the table. Such progress, marveled the doctors, was amazing. Miss Parsons was there too, keeping a watchful eye on him. But there were other watchful eyes. Mrs. Rogers' were a little troubled. She had her son back again and she had lost him — to a girl who loved him perhaps as much as she did. Val, slipping her hand out of Ted's brazen clasp, raised her glass. She said:

"We've all considerable for which to be thankful."

Her mouth was grave but her eyes danced. Bill rose despite Miss Parson's warning shriek. He said, "To our mutual escape," and touched her glass with his own.

"Well," said Frances and Ted simultaneously, "I like that!"

"You should," said Val.

Late that night when she was home again and saying good night to Ted, she yawned against his shoulder, "I suppose as soon as Bill is all well, after a winter in the South, they'll buy another yacht and go around exploring and digging up ruins and snooping after poor fish and generally making pests of themselves. If they have a family they'll rear 'em in diving helmets and on sights and sun shooting, or whatever it is."

"What about ours?" asked Ted grinning.

"Ours? Little bookworms," said Val rather tenderly. She yawned again. "Go home, will you? I'm thinking of getting married next week and I have a lot to plan. Oh," she added, as an afterthought, "ours will be born in an institution."

Ted, thinking she had gone mad, asked amazedly, "Institution?" He shook her. "Are you goofy? Do you mean a hospital?"

"No," said Val, "I mean marriage. Marriage is an institution, isn't it?" She gave him a slight but determined push. She said, "Go 'way . . . and don't let me set eyes on you until tomorrow!"

The employees of THORNDIKE PRESS hope you have enjoyed this Large Print book. All our Large Print titles are designed for easy reading, and all our books are made to last. Other Thorndike Large Print books are available at your library, through selected bookstores, or directly from us. For more information about current and upcoming titles, please call or mail your name and address to:

THORNDIKE PRESS
PO Box 159
Thorndike, Maine 04986
800/223-6121
207/948-2962